Assumed Dead

Eleanor Sullivan

HILLIARD HARRIS

P.O. Box 275
Boonsboro, Maryland 21713-0275

This novel is a work of fiction. Names, characters, places and incidents either are the product of the author's imagination or are used fictitiously. Any resemblance to actual persons, living or dead, events, or locales is entirely coincidental.

Assumed Dead Copyright © 2006 by Eleanor Sullivan

All rights reserved. No part of this book may be reproduced or transmitted in any form or by any means, electronic or mechanical, including photocopying, recording, or by any information storage and retrieval system, without the written permission of the Publisher, except where permitted by law.

First Edition-June 2006
ISBN 1-59133-144-7

Book Design: S. A. Reilly
Cover Illustration © S. A. Reilly
Manufactured/Printed in the United States of America
2006

For the men and women in the U. S. military who served in Vietnam,

especially the nurses,

in memory of my husband, David L. Sullivan

1938-1970

and in honor of

Dolores 'Mimi' Buehler

Acknowledgements

As always, I depended on experts who were kind enough to answer my interminable questions. These include:

Former Army Ranger Brad Sullivan and his colleagues in the U. S. Army.

U. S. Postal Inspector Scott Sullivan, who can track down anyone no matter how hard they try to disappear.

Officer Jeff Chellis and Officer Neal Kohrs of the Creve Coeur Police Department.

Sergeant Dick Buehler of the St. Louis City Police Department.

Karen Kelly, PhD, RN, an expert on the "east side" of metropolitan St. Louis.

Fran Buehler, a South St. Louis authority.

Sean Sullivan, who's scraped more old wallpaper than he cares to remember.

Gwen Tushbant, RN, BSN, who generously shared the triumphs and heartaches of serving as a nurse in Vietnam.

Elaine Level, RN, BSN, the critical care nurse I'd like to have if I needed one.

Sister Annette Moran, of the Sisters of St. Joseph of Carondelet, who described the life of a religious.

New York University students and faculty whose stories of courage told in their booklet, *Nurses Remember 9/11*, helped me understand what nurses had experienced during those terrible first days.

Sister Mary Jeremy Buckman, Archivist for the Sisters of Mercy, and Roberta Doelling, her assistant, for explaining the complicated process of archiving.

Chris Burgess, of Chris' Needle Craft Supplies, who dispenses knitting advice with her yarn.

Editor Colleen Daly, who keeps me honest.

Stephanie and Shawn Reilly at Hilliard & Harris for their tireless efforts and their committed professionalism.

And, finally, my gratitude to my "sisters and brothers" in Sisters in Crime for their friendship and support.

For all of their help, I am grateful. Any errors, though, are mine alone.

Eleanor Sullivan

When you know your name, you should hang on to it, for unless it is noted down and remembered, it will die when you do.

—Toni Morrison

Chapter 1

Wednesday, November 10, 1045 Hours

WHEN THE HUMAN head smashes through a windshield, it's not the multiple weave of lacerations criss-crossing the face that's life threatening, it's the damage you can't see. The skull stops on impact but the brain continues its trajectory and slams into the bony interior, leaving a cascade of destroyed brain tissue in its wake. Blood vessels swell, slowing and eventually cutting off the flow of oxygen to the brain. Without oxygen, the brain dies. Survival depends on the extent of the damage and how fast the swelling can be reduced. If the brain hits the skull with enough force, sooner or later—usually later—death follows.

Another person without a seatbelt, I thought, watching two burly attendants position the gurney alongside the bed in intensive care and expertly lift the supine figure onto the bed. Soon an unbelieving family would arrive, stunned, numbed, unable to believe the patient in the bed was their husband, father, son.

I'd seen the same scenario too often in my more than twenty years in nursing, all of it at St. Teresa's Hospital in South St. Louis. My recent job change, though, had me wondering if I had reached the limit of my abilities or, more likely, over-reached them. As part of our hospital's reorganization, head nurses had become "clinical managers" and, instead of managing only one area (in my case it had been the intensive care unit), our responsibilities had been doubled to manage two units. The step-down unit, an intensive convalescent ward where critically ill patients go to continue their recovery after leaving our unit, had been added to my already overworked schedule.

The man's face had begun swelling above the cervical collar that stabilized his neck and around the oxygen cannula taped to his nose. Wanda, head nurse of the emergency room, squeezed by the gurney.

Wanda had taken on managing the acute care clinic in addition to the emergency room in the recent shake-up.

"White male, approximately 30 to 35 years of age," Wanda said, checking the patient's fluids. Normal saline and lactated ringers solutions dripped into a wide-open IV taped to his arm, and a triple-lumen catheter placed in the left subclavian artery delivered blood, O-negative packed red cells, according to the label on the bag.

"Unrestrained driver, head-on into a tree, the cops said. And no air bag." She checked the chart. "Unresponsive in acute respiratory distress and shock when we got him. See the obvious chest." She pointed with the back end of her pen. "Retracts on inspiration and bulges on expiration." The reverse of normal.

"Sternum and five right adjacent ribs have multiple fractures and you can see the air cast." An inflated clear plastic tube temporarily stabilized his right arm, apparently fractured. "Mandible's fractured too, that's why the nasal intubation instead of an oral tube in his airway, although the nose might be broken as well," she said as two nurses I hadn't seen enter crowded around. Jessie and Tim, my most experienced RNs, followed behind them.

A train wreck, we called these cases.

"Alcohol?" I asked, noting the smell emanating from the patient.

"Blood alcohol .11 percent. Legally drunk. They've ordered sedation but watch for signs of withdrawal anyway." Wanda glanced at the unconscious man in the bed. "He responds to verbal stimuli, but does not follow commands." She moved to the head of the bed and pulled his eyelids up, flashing a penlight into one and then the other. "Pupils equally round, react sluggishly to light."

Wanda handed me the chart. "He's all yours."

I passed the chart off to Jessie, who stayed to finish the patient's initial assessment with help from the two newer nurses. Tim and I followed Wanda out.

"What about your other one?" I asked Wanda. "Closed head. The one you called me about."

"She's in surgery. You'll get her after that if..." She shrugged.

"What happened to her?" Serena, a nursing student who worked for us part-time, asked. "Another car accident?"

"Hardly," Wanda said, stuffing a pen and notes into the pockets of her rumpled green scrubs already stained with blood and other body fluids. "Somebody bashed the back of her head in. They've got a lot to do, get out the blood clot, skull fragments...it'll be awhile till you get her. I'd guess another several hours."

Jessie came out of our newly-admitted patient's room and stopped Wanda who had turned to leave. "There's no name on this chart. Who is he?" Jessie asked, her wandering eye giving her a deceptively distracted look.

"Sure there is," Wanda said. "John Doe," she added with a laugh as she hurried out the door.

"Check that bag of stuff they brought up with him," I told Jessie. "They probably overlooked his ID in their rush downstairs. Or maybe security has it. Someone will know who he is."

I WAS COMING back from lunch when a balding, middle-aged man ambled off the elevator and followed me into ICU, what everyone in the hospital calls the intensive care unit.

"Detective McNamara," he said, flipping open an ID badge as we reached the desk. An odor of stale cigar smoke lingered around him. "I'm here about the guy from the ER. They said you've got him up here."

"We've got a lot of guys up here from the ER," I said. "Who is it?"

"I don't know his name. The officers were in pursuit when he smashed into a tree." A toothpick bounced up and down under a shaggy gray mustache as he talked.

"We've only got John Doe on the chart," I told him.

"How about his effects?"

"His clothes and personal things?" I asked.

"My partner's down in security looking for his personal effects but so far they couldn't find them." He swiped at his mustache with his thumb and forefinger. "Do you have anything of his up here?"

"I'll check. You wait here," I added when he started to follow me into the room. I was sure he had seen plenty of accident victims, but even that might not prepare him for how bad a patient looks when hooked up to multiple lines, tubes, and monitors. Some felt comatose patients looked artificial, similar to the life-like mannequins used in nursing school labs to teach students before they use still-shaky skills on real live patients.

Jessie was finishing a neuro check on John Doe when I entered. Her black hands as sure as ever, she ran her unopened pen up his foot from heel to toe, getting no response from him. "Open your eyes," Jessie said and the man made a guttural sound. "Can you squeeze my hand? Nothing," she said to me. "They're coming up to wire his jaw and set his arm. In the meantime, I'll try to clean him up."

Large, the man's weight appeared to be more muscle than fat, and his face and shaved head were suntanned, a tan line showing at his neck and upper arms. Fragments of glass, tree bark, and fibers clung to cuts on his face and scalp along with a coating of dried blood. Bloody mucous adhered to his nose and mouth.

At that moment the man's arm flailed out, threatening to dislodge his IV, but instead it came to rest, dangling over the side of the bed, and he lay still again.

"You be careful," I admonished. "I've been hit more than once."

Although unconscious and unaware of what he was doing, his agitation could cause him to lash out, hitting whoever or whatever was nearby.

"He's still jumpy because they want to hold up on sedation to get a read on his neuro status," Jessie explained.

I picked up the clear plastic bag bundled with the man's clothes from the bedside stand and walked out. "John Doe's personal effects," I said to the detective who stroked his mustache with his thumb and forefinger. He watched me deposit the bag on the desk. All I could see through the clear plastic bag was a blood-splattered brown leather jacket.

"John Doe's his name?" Serena asked me.

"That's what we call someone when we don't know their name—John Doe for a male, Jane Doe for a female," I told her. "There must not have been any identification on him."

"How could he be driving then?" she asked.

Our ward clerk, Ruby, snorted behind me. "You don't know anyone who drives without a license? That's probably why he was running from the cops," she said, heading into the break room.

"He was?" Serena asked, her mascara-laced eyes opened wide. "You mean he's a criminal?"

"We don't know that, Serena," I said as the doors swung open and Mr. Hockstetter, the hospital's chief financial officer, strode over to us, his eyes clamped on me.

"I just heard we've admitted a John Doe," he said, ignoring the detective. "We can't keep this up, Monika, taking care of every John Doe the cops bring here."

"Redmond Hockstetter, meet Detective McNamara from the St. Louis City Police Department."

Hockstetter had the grace to blush, but he quickly recovered. "Do you know who he is?" he asked. "We can't subsidize these uninsured and still take care of the rest of you," he added with a quick smile to McNamara.

"That's what I'm here to find out," McNamara said, reaching for the bag of John Doe's property. "We'll inventory it down in security. See if we can find out who he is."

"Find out if the guy had insurance. Or any relatives," Hockstetter said to McNamara. Then he turned around and headed back out. "Somebody's got to pay for him," he added just before the doors closed.

"How are you going to find out who he is?" Serena asked the detective, motioning toward John Doe's room.

"Check with missing persons. See if anyone with his description fits the guy." He handed me his card. "Let me know if he regains consciousness or you find out anything." Then he was gone and we were left with our patients.

"What'd the cop want?" Ruby asked, placing her coffee cup on the U. S. Army coaster beside her phone.

"How'd you know he was a cop?" I asked. A ward clerk since before my time at St. Teresa's, Ruby knew everything that went on in the hospital and now I'd just given her another opportunity to lord it over me.

Ruby pulled herself up to look me in the eye and smiled that calculating smile I'd come to know. "I'd know a cop anywhere," she said.

I'D SLIPPED OUT of the unit and into my office, a tiny closet of a room stashed between ICU and a storage closet, to work on my past-due budgets when I heard the OR transporters arrive with what I guessed was our post-op patient now out of surgery. Sighing, I clicked my computer to standby and followed Tim and the gurney into the unit.

St. Teresa's intensive care unit is one large rectangle. Around three sides of the interior are ten equally-sized patient cubicles sheltered by shabby blue-and-white curtains. A hallway runs outside of these rooms with doors into each room, allowing family members access without walking through the unit and getting in the way of busy staff. Along the back wall are the medication room, linen closet, clean and dirty utility rooms, and the multipurpose room we use for meetings and breaks, which held, in addition to a rickety conference table and mismatched chairs, our lockers, a small refrigerator that stays only marginally cold, a microwave with only one setting—high—and a sink that was often plugged up.

Paint, left over from other jobs around the hospital, covers the walls in ICU. Some are cyanotic blue, others industrial yellow, depending on what color the facilities department had remaining after they'd finished sprucing up the more visible areas of the hospital. Too many scrubbings had left the paint flaking, though, and the painters were due "any day," a promise I'd been hearing for more than a month.

"Room ten," I told one of the transport attendants, directing him to the only open room at the opposite end of the unit from our other trauma patient in room one. I was glad to put a little distance between the two patients and their grieving relatives. It allowed both families some privacy—what little anyone has in ICU—and made it easier for the staff. At least the nurses wouldn't careen into each other in their hurry to get in and out of their patient's room during those first critical days when a fresh trauma required constantly-changing care.

The transporters had moved the woman, whose name was Marian Oblansky I gathered from a quick glance at the chart, onto the bed and Tim was cranking her head up to the required thirty degrees to reduce pressure in the brain when Ruby called me out.

I stepped out of the cubicle and gasped. There, with his back facing me, stood a man in an all-too-familiar military stance—ramrod posture, legs apart, and arms crossed behind him. His brown hair was cropped close, and he was just the right height, with just the right build. Then he turned around and my heart slid back down my throat. Of course it couldn't have been Rick.

"Steve Oblansky," the man said. "Marian Oblansky," he swallowed and went on, "is my wife. This is her sister, Charlotte." He nodded at the woman next to him.

He didn't resemble Rick from the front. For one thing, his eyes were brown and wider apart. And he was older.

"How is she?" Mr. Oblansky asked, his tone respectful.

"She's badly injured," I said. "She hasn't regained consciousness."

"Is she..." Charlotte faltered and looked away.

"It's too soon to know anything yet," I said, leading them toward Mrs. Oblansky's room as I passed Tim, who nodded an okay to go in.

At the sight of her sister's shaved head, the woman slumped against her brother-in-law.

"Her hair..." he said, his voice shaking.

Charlotte turned to her brother-in-law. "It's not her."

"We had to cut it off for the surgery," I said. "I'm sorry, I should have warned you." The shock of seeing a loved one's shorn head, especially that of a woman, can make a patient unrecognizable even to close family members.

"It's her, Lottie." Then to me he said, "She had such beautiful red hair."

"Long," her sister said, "down her back."

Steve took his sister-in-law's arm and led her closer to the bed. In spite of the ventilator tube protruding from her mouth, Marian looked strangely peaceful, her body unscathed. Only the swish of air pumping through the vent and the intermittent beats of the monitors beeping her vital signs signaled the internal damage.

I didn't tell them that the back of her head looked like a smashed pumpkin.

I left them and stepped outside to greet the man I'd seen talking to Ruby as I was taking the Oblansky family into Marian's room.

Detective Harding flipped open his badge as if I didn't know who he was. He'd been here on two previous occasions. "We're here about Marian Oblansky," Harding said, his voice lowered. He introduced his partner, a good-looking black man in his thirties.

"What can you tell me about her?" Harding unbuttoned a gray trench coat, shaking leftover rain around him. Droplets slid off his short, dark hair as he pulled a pen from inside his jacket pocket. "Is she awake? Can we talk to her?"

"I'm afraid not," I said, steering them away from the room so we wouldn't be overheard. "She has a serious head injury. She's unconscious. What happened to her? How'd she get hurt?"

Harding's partner spoke up. "She was attacked in the parking lot of First Federal on South Kingshighway, right after the bank opened, apparently."

Harding frowned at his partner who ducked his head. "When might she wake up?"

"Her condition is guarded."

"She might not make it?"

"We don't know yet, but the prognosis isn't good at this point."

"Is her family here?" Harding asked.

"They're in with her now."

"Would you tell them we want to see them?"

"Sure, but I have a question. Don't you think you should have someone guarding her room? What if the guy comes back to finish her off?"

Harding's partner grunted. "We don't have the manpower for that. Besides, this is probably a random assault, a robbery gone bad or something like that."

I hesitated. I didn't want to remind them about the previous attacks on our patients; on the other hand, I was afraid it would happen again.

"I wouldn't worry about it," Harding said. "I heard you've locked up the outside doors now so no one can get in, and things are pretty secure from this side, with everyone working in here."

"The fire inspectors made us unlock the outside doors," I told Harding as Steve and Charlotte came out of Mrs. Oblansky's room, Charlotte blowing her nose and Steve wiping his eyes with the back of his hands. I introduced Detective Harding and his partner to the couple and sent a part-time volunteer to take them to the family waiting room down the hall. They all walked outside together, Steve's arm around Charlotte's shoulders.

There it was again, the resemblance. Charlotte leaned her head against her brother-in-law's shoulder the same way Rick's mother had leaned into Rick after finding out her husband had been killed in an accident.

I shook off my lingering thoughts.

"We can't afford it," Dick Gerling, our chief of security said after I called to ask him to send someone up to guard Mrs. Oblansky's room.

"That's your job, not mine. You keep everyone but family out of her room."

I had my orders.

Chapter 2

Wednesday, November 10, 1215 Hours

I WAS BACK in my office again attempting to reconcile the budget when I heard the commotion from the unit. The noise increased as I slipped through the doors and into John Doe's room.

"How the hell can I set the arm with him like this?" Dr. Barkman demanded.

John Doe's unbroken arm shot out on the opposite side of the bed, hitting Jessie. She stumbled, tried to grab hold of the sink next to the bed but instead her arm hit the bedside table, knocking it over, syringes and wipes tumbling to the floor.

"I'm okay," Jessie said, waving off my offer of help. She pulled herself up and righted the table.

"Ativan, 1 milligram, IV push," Barkman said over his shoulder as he hustled out.

I grabbed the tranquilizer the orthopedic surgeon had ordered and hurried back. Jessie checked the dropped syringes to see that the needles were still safely capped while I slipped the medication into John Doe's IV and waited for it to take effect. He continued to move uncontrollably on the bed. After a few more minutes I paged Barkman and he ordered another dose of Ativan before slamming the phone down on me. When Barkman came through the doors a few minutes later, the patient was sedated. I'd already gone back to my budget but Jessie helped him set the arm and apply the cast.

UH OH, I THOUGHT, seeing Dr. Heinrich's tall figure standing at the counter. He was reading a chart when I returned from lunch. If he's here about John Doe...

"Ativan!" Heinrich cried. He slammed the chart onto the counter. It bounced onto the desk and clattered to the floor. "No wonder he's unresponsive." He turned to Sylvia, a nurse new to the staff, standing behind the desk. "How can I possibly evaluate his neuro status when he's in a drug-induced coma!" he yelled at her. "Didn't I specifically leave orders the patient was not to be sedated without my permission? Well, didn't I?" he repeated when she didn't respond.

"What's the problem?" I asked, deliberately keeping my voice steady but firm.

He sputtered. "What the hell's wrong with you nurses? Don't any of you know how to follow orders?" With that, he stomped out.

I came around the desk, picked up the chart, and set it next to the cardboard turkey Ruby had brought in earlier in the week. I spoke to the startled Sylvia as Jessie and Serena joined us. "Here's the deal: Barkman's the orthopod. He came in and couldn't set John Doe's arm because the guy was agitated, so he ordered Ativan and that worked. So now when Heinrich, the neurologist, wants to evaluate John Doe's neuro status, he can't because the patient's sedated."

"So what are we to do?" Serena asked, twisting a hank of hair, black on the ends, her natural mousy brown near the roots. "Don't doctors ever talk to each other?"

"Not when it's easier to blame us," Tim said, coming up. "Try telling Barkman he has to cast the arm of an agitated 200-pound man!"

"I just wish I weren't leaving right now," I said to Tim and Jessie later as I plopped down in a chair next to Jessie.

"Look," Jessie said as she shoved one chart back into the rack and opened the next one remaining on the stack in front of her on the desk. "You've been counting on going to this conference in DC for months. It's good for St. T's to have you on the program. Gets us some publicity, doesn't it? And we can manage," she added with a glance at Tim.

Tim had bounced back from his failure to organize a union among the nurses at St. T's. He and Jessie were the most experienced nurses on my staff. And the most loyal. It looked like they both would get out only a half hour or so after their shift ended.

With the new nurses hired by our former chief nurse, we actually had a full complement of staff. After months of working the unit short-staffed I was enjoying the luxury. It was likely that St. Teresa's had stolen them from other hospitals in the city, but I wasn't complaining.

"How's your wife?" Jessie asked Tim.

"She's been on bed rest, due any day, and I'm ready," he said, looking over the counter at Jessie.

"You're ready?" Jessie exclaimed. "I'll bet she's more than ready. I know I was."

Tim rubbed his eyes with the heels of his palms, lowered his hands and blinked several times. "You try sleeping with an eight-hundred pound elephant next to you!" he said, good-naturedly.

"You try being the elephant!" Jessie shot back.

I pushed straggly curls away from my face. *If only I'd had time for a haircut,* I thought to myself. Other than speaking at my local nursing honor society chapter meetings where I had been surrounded by colleagues and friends, my experiences as a presenter had been limited. Now I was scheduled to talk to nurse managers from around the country. In spite of my almost-obsessive preparation and hours of practice in front of a mirror, my stomach flipped every time I thought about Saturday's program.

"It's about Mrs. Oblansky," I said, deliberately shoving thoughts of the other task I planned to do in Washington out of my mind. "I can't help but worry about who attacked her and if she—and we—might still be in danger."

"Didn't that detective say it was probably a random robbery?" Jessie asked.

"Yes, but—"

"You go on, Monika, we'll be fine here." She glanced toward Mrs. Oblansky's room where a security guard sat reading. Dick Gerling had sent him up just after three o'clock, apparently relenting after my earlier call to him.

"Having him is probably more for us than anything else," Tim said. "I'd be more worried about him, he's the criminal." Tim pointed to John Doe's room.

"Who's a criminal?" Ruby asked, coming up to the counter.

"Our John Doe."

"How you know that?" Ruby grabbed her coat and purse from the top of the desk.

"He ran from the cops," Tim said.

"That don't make him a crook," she said, swinging her coat over her shoulder and turning toward the door. "Everybody I know would run from the cops."

Chapter 3

Wednesday, November 10, 1722 Hours

"I DON'T KNOW what you're so worried about," BJ said, drumming her hands on the steering wheel of her patrol car as we waited for the light to change. A grease smell permeated the car, remnants of BJ's fast food bag stuffed in the space between her onboard computer and our seats. "Flying's safe these days with all the security they've got now."

On my way to the airport, my suitcase stowed in the back seat and a plane ticket in my bag, I couldn't back out now.

"I just wish I hadn't agreed to this. I'm not a professional speaker, I'm a nurse."

"Well, can't you talk about that? It's something you know."

BJ was my best friend, beginning when we first met in kindergarten at St. Aloysius and continuing to this day. She'd entered the police academy when I enrolled in nursing school. I married Rick before he left for Vietnam, and she and Don, now a St. Louis detective, were married the following year.

"How many people? At your meeting?" She steered her cruiser onto the interstate. Although it was only five-thirty the evening was already dark. Water puddled near curbs and in low spots but the rain we'd had earlier in the day had stopped.

"I'm on a panel, a break-out session, one of four speaking."

"What do you have to talk about?" she asked as cars sped up around us. Light spray hit the windshield, and BJ clicked on her wipers. A squirt of wiper fluid cleared a curved path on the glass.

"I'm supposed to tell how we manage a small, independent hospital. Other people on the panel are talking about management in larger places like conglomerates, clinics, and home care agencies."

"That doesn't sound too bad," she said, negotiating around a slowly-moving cement truck.

"You hear anything about our John Doe?"

"Not so far. He going to make it?"

"It's hard to tell at this point. We don't know how bad the brain damage is yet."

"Is that all that's wrong with him?"

"That's enough but, no, he also has a broken arm, jaw, facial lacerations, and internal injuries we aren't sure about. Those aren't the worry; it's the brain damage that causes complications."

We came up behind a line of cars that had slowed to ogle a stalled car by the side of the road. After we had passed them and sped up again I said, "I hope they find out who he is."

"Don't hold your breath. They might get lucky, but nobody really cares about some guy stupid enough to hit a tree while running from the cops."

"Our CFO is pretty steamed trying to get someone to pay for his care."

"What about your CEO? What's his name? Hack-something?"

"Hackett. His job's external, now, they tell me. Fund-raising, government grants—not that we get very many—and courting grateful patients. He leaves management up to Hockstetter, who's in charge now until we get a new COO."

"COO? What's that?"

"Chief operating officer. According to the new organizational chart, that's who nursing will report to."

"You don't sound like you think that's a good idea."

"Who do you think knows what the patient needs? Some administrative type or a nurse?"

"Yeah, but didn't you hate your former boss? She was a nurse."

"She'd never been in the trenches, just like administrators. The only thing they care about is how much it costs."

"Every place has to think about that."

"But nursing's not an assembly line and patients aren't cogs moving along it. Sure, some things can be predicted, but it's the unexpected that requires flexibility, and few administrators factor that in."

"Same in law enforcement. We never know what to expect. Sometimes we've got enough officers on, other times—"

"Watch out!"

BJ slammed on her brakes, narrowly missing a car that swerved in front of us and sped ahead.

BJ grabbed her radio and called in the speeder.

"We're not going after him?" I asked her, more than a little excited at the thought of a chase.

"Not with you in the car, I'm not. Besides, you've got a plane to catch."

Back in the stream of traffic, I asked, "What about Mrs. Oblansky? They find out who attacked her?"

"Not that I've heard. They try to move pretty quickly in these cases."

"I'd feel a lot better if they caught whoever did it."

"The first day or so is critical. That's when most crimes are solved. Wait too long and witnesses forget, or the guy gets away."

"Listen, BJ, will you let me know? I've got my cell phone and I gave you the hotel number, didn't I?"

"Sure, Monika, but why don't you just go and enjoy yourself? Let us take care of the bad guys."

I stared out the side window. She knew what else I planned to do, but so far had avoided the subject.

"Okay?" she asked.

I nodded absently.

"Leave it behind. There are other people at St. T's to take care of your patients. Just go and have fun." She swung her car into the drop-off lane at Lambert Airport and jumped out to pull my bag from the backseat. She gave me a quick hug and waved me off.

I MADE MY way through the terminal, dragging a wheeled suitcase—bought new for the trip—and clutching my overstuffed carry-on bag, ticket in hand. The line for security snaked around a roped-off area. Sweat ran down my back as I waited. I'd worn my tan raincoat with its zip-out lining inside, and a pullover sweater over a turtleneck, prepared if the weather in DC turned out to be no warmer than that in St. Louis.

Nearing the security checkpoint, I fumbled in my bag for my driver's license and moved along behind a woman carrying a silver-metal briefcase, wondering idly what she was carrying. When we got to the conveyor belt to go through the X-ray machine, a screener asked the woman to step aside.

Shortly thereafter I stood in line to board the plane and a commotion erupted ahead of me. It was the woman in line I'd seen earlier. She was arguing with the airline agent that she'd already opened the case once and she wasn't going to do so again. The agent spoke into a walkie-talkie, and the line grew restless behind us. As I handed over my boarding pass, two police officers arrived. The woman screamed that she was being discriminated against as the officers escorted her away.

Soon I was settled into my seat, my suitcase under the seat in front of me, and my ticket back in my bag, which was stuffed beneath my seat. The flight was full, an attendant announced, and asked everyone to stow their belongings and take a seat as soon as possible as we couldn't take off until everyone was seated. From my window, I watched another plane land and taxi to the gate next to us. I observed blurry faces in the lit cabin.

Presently everyone was seated but the seat next to me remained vacant. The pilot announced that we were waiting for one more passenger.

Finally someone came down the aisle. It was the woman with the metal briefcase. She slid into the seat next to me, the case clutched tightly in her hands. The flight attendant told her it had to be stowed beneath the seat or in the overhead bin. The woman started to argue, then shrugged and put the case on the floor, propping her feet on top.

As we backed away from the gate, she sighed audibly several times. I didn't rise to the bait. I didn't want to listen to her complaints, and I wasn't altogether comfortable that her mysterious case was on this flight, especially since it was right next to me.

After takeoff, I turned my head to the window and watched the lights of St. Louis disappear below the clouds. I leaned back and closed my eyes, feeling the plane level off, starting me on a journey I'd been postponing for far too long.

I must have fallen asleep because the next thing I heard was the captain telling us to fasten our seat belts in preparation for landing. For a moment I couldn't remember where I was until I looked out the window to see the Capitol building glowing in the dark.

LATER IN MY hotel room, I went over my notes for the conference. My mind, however, wasn't on my presentation.

Chapter 4

Thursday, November 11, 0910 Hours

IN SPITE OF napping throughout my flight, I'd had no trouble falling asleep. I awoke sometime during the night to the sound of rain, and it quickly lulled me back to sleep. The ringing phone woke me, and the automated voice of my wake-up call operator explained that it was seven a.m.

I checked in at the conference and picked up my materials, making sure that my panel was still scheduled for eleven.

Outside the rain continued steadily so I turned back inside and went to the hotel gift shop to buy an umbrella at a far higher cost than I would have paid at home. Nevertheless I didn't want to wait for the rain to stop. I had planned this visit for too long to be delayed now.

Neither the umbrella nor my coat could keep the rain from blowing around my legs and soaking my feet. By the time I reached the park I was cold and wet. Shivering, I gritted my teeth. This was minor discomfort compared to what had Rick had faced in Vietnam—jungle heat, humidity, wading through infested streams, facing death.

I came up the path and turned toward the Vietnam Memorial Wall. The monument stretched ahead of me in a gentle curve. I'd seen pictures, of course, but I wasn't prepared for its beauty. I stood still, letting my emotions roll over me. I felt sad and proud all at once. At that moment the rain let up and a sliver of sun shone through, illuminating the glistening black marble. I let out the breath I didn't realize I'd been holding as people jostled by me.

I headed for the directories stationed at corners. I knew I needed to start with the year Rick had died and then look for his name alphabetically. I waited behind an elderly couple who were arguing about whether their son had died in December of 1968 or January of

1969. They must have found out because the woman slumped against her husband and they turned away.

I found 1972 easily enough, and Everhardt should have been there. But it wasn't. I flipped through the pages again. The line behind me had grown, Veteran's Day being a popular visiting time. My hands shook as I tried to hurry, turning tissue-thin pages, damp with use. *I can't do this now*, I thought, *not with all these people waiting*.

I turned toward the Wall. More than 58,000 men and women had been killed in the war, so many lives lost forever. *His name is here, I know it is.* I found the panel for 1972 and started down the names, my hands lingering on the cold marble as if I could feel the presence of Rick and his fallen comrades.

People crowded around me, umbrellas bumping as the rain began again in earnest. Rivulets of water and my threatening tears blurred the names that swam before me. A woman about my age knelt on the ground, ignoring the water running down her face and tried to rub a pencil over a piece of paper to reveal a name. But the wet paper just shredded. She sat back on her heels, then rose and walked down the path, clutching the soggy paper to her chest. I started reading over again at the top of the panel.

As the rain petered out to intermittent splatters, the mournful sound of bagpipes began. I had lost my place on the Wall again so I followed the crowd to the space set aside for an audience, moving through a phalanx of police officers, their dogs sniffing the ground as we passed. I found a seat in one the rows of folding chairs near the back. I let the sound of the wailing bagpipes take me to a quiet place within myself.

At an officer's command, I stood with the crowd to watch the honor guard walk forward in precise formation, flags protected by rifle-bearing escorts. My hand automatically went over my heart as I turned to watch the spit-polished men and women approach the stage, position the flags into stands, and come to attention at the side.

Kaboom! Kaboom! Kaboom! Rifles fired in a twenty-one gun salute. In the silence that followed a priest on the stage led a prayer, and finally we sat back down. It wasn't long before the cold had seeped through my thin coat. I stretched out my legs, trying to position them so only my heels rested on the wet ground. A young woman next to me shivered in a skimpy outfit, her bare feet shod in high-heeled clogs. Her male companion took off his jacket, draped it over her shoulders and drew her close.

My mind wandered as a speaker droned on, his speech interrupted occasionally by sporadic applause. It hadn't occurred to me that there'd be a memorial service, but I should have expected it, it being Veteran's Day. It seemed like just another recognition ceremony among many I'd attended, with too many speakers talking too long.

Military men and women peppered the audience, some in dress uniforms, others in familiar black-and-green fatigues. Patch and pin-adorned military caps identified the older veterans in the audience; frail hands held small American flags. Vietnam-era vets wore jackets covered with armed-forces patches. Some sat in wheelchairs.

As the ceremony wound down we stood for a moment of silence, "For those who gave the ultimate sacrifice," said the Army officer in charge.

Taps signaled the close of the service and my throat caught. Standing there among complete strangers, I nevertheless felt connected to them as if we were one. We shared a common bond, all touched by war and some, like me, having had our lives torn apart.

The military band began to play a slow march and people started to leave, but I remained standing, feeling the weight of all the others' grief now and in the past. In that moment I understood how military families have felt through the ages, no matter what the conflict or where they fought. In the end it all comes down to our own selves, our own family member, our own fear.

After a while park service employees began to clear the stage, loading a cart with folding chairs while two men dragged the podium off the stage and onto a wheeled platform.

Since there were so many people crowding along the Wall, I wandered over to the Vietnam Women's Memorial before heading back to the directories, which all had long lines now.

I knew the memorial dedicated to Vietnam nurses would be impressive, but I didn't expect to be so moved by it. One female soldier, her image captured forever in bronze, looked down at the wounded comrade who lay in her arms, his head tilted back, his eyes closed. Another soldier stood guard, one arm draped over the nurse and her patient. Rain dribbled down their faces almost as if they were crying. I stood silently among other women and some men, remembering their own experiences or, as I was, simply honoring those nurses who had served their fellow countrymen and women.

I turned to go back to the Wall, and bumped into a tall woman in a navy raincoat standing next to me. She looked away as I apologized and then turned back, her gray-green eyes blurred with tears.

I couldn't help but stand there, and in a quiet voice I asked, "You were there?"

She nodded and cleared her throat. "You?" she asked, sizing up my age.

"My husband was," I said as we moved along the path. "I can't seem to find his name, though."

"I'm so sorry," she said. "It is confusing, and more so when you're upset, as most everyone is. Maybe I can help. I've found a lot of people here, sad to say."

"Friends?"

She looked up toward the sky where gray, cotton-wool clouds inched their way toward us, spewing a fine mist. "Some," she said, shoving red-blond hair, frizzed, off her face. "And a few former patients. I'm Camilla Hagerty," she said, extending her hand.

"Monika Everhardt."

"Is that your husband's name? Everhardt?"

"Richard Everhardt. He was killed in 1972." I spelled our last name as we stood in the line of people waiting ahead of us at the directory, which was protected from the weather by a glass shield. As the rain increased, umbrellas went up and ponchos came out, but most people stayed in line.

"When were you there?" I asked Camilla.

"Seventy, seventy-one. July to July." She stared out into the mist, which had turned the memorial park into a blurred image, like a fuzzy photograph.

The line moved. Only three couples remained in front of us.

"I'd like to hear about it."

"Really?" She squinted at me.

"Yes, really. When Rick went over, I wished I'd been able to go, too."

We were next in line.

I checked my watch. "Darn! I'm on a panel at the nursing management conference at the Sheraton, and if I don't go right now, I'm going to be late."

"And I have to go, too," she said. "Maybe we could meet later."

"How about dinner? You could tell me about the war. That is, if you want to talk about it."

"Sure."

"It would mean a lot to me."

We settled on a Vietnamese restaurant in Georgetown, a short walk from my hotel, and planned to meet at seven.

My new friend gave me a quick handshake as we parted at the corner.

Chapter 5

Thursday, November 11, 1904 Hours

"How'd it go today?" Camilla asked when we were seated in the back of the restaurant. She slipped out of her coat and draped it over the back of the chair.

"Okay, I guess," I said, dropping my bag on the floor beside me. "I tried to be upbeat. There were lots of young managers in the audience looking to move up to administration."

Camilla pushed her menu to the side. "So they need encouragement?"

"They need more than that. Fortitude, toughness, perseverance. I tried to say that without discouraging them."

We waited while our server deposited water and Camilla ordered a pot of tea.

"That's why I'm not in management," she said. "I want to concentrate on my patients. That's enough to keep me occupied."

I asked her about her work.

"I'm a civilian nurse now at Walter Reed. I work in neuro."

"Isn't that depressing? Paralyzed patients require skills that I wouldn't be able to meet even after all my years in nursing."

"Challenging, yes, depressing, no. You notice those who've lost limbs, but we get them prostheses. Spinal cord injuries leave limbs intact but useless. They're the ones who need us the most." Our waiter reappeared and, when I asked her to, Camilla ordered for us, apparently in Vietnamese. The waiter scurried off.

"I spent twenty years as an Army nurse working neuro so this isn't too different. Except the GIs. They're different now."

"Oh?"

"Those home from Iraq weren't even born when Vietnam happened. All they want to do is get back with the guys."

"And yours didn't?"

"You kidding? All our boys wanted was to get out of that hell hole. I did, too, at first."

"You didn't volunteer?"

"Humph. When I enlisted I asked the recruiter, 'Will I have to go to Vietnam?' He promised me..." She tore paper off the ends of her chopsticks and studied them. "...that I wouldn't have to go unless I volunteered. I was in college and needed the money. Plus I wanted to travel, see the world." She grunted. "I got to see the one part I wish I hadn't."

"If they promised—"

"You've never been in the military, Monika. When I got my orders I thought there was some mistake. I told my CO that the recruiter had told me I wouldn't have to go if I didn't want to, and he just laughed."

"They lied to get you to sign up?"

"They paid for my last two years of school. It seemed like a good deal at the time."

The waiter returned with a pot of tea and two tiny cups.

"There was one plus, though," Camilla said, laying her chopsticks aside. "It kept my brother from going."

"Really? How come?"

"They wouldn't send two members of the same family into battle at the same time. I could keep him out of it for a year anyway." She opened the teapot and a lightly-scented aroma escaped.

"Did he go after you came back?"

"Nah. The war was winding down, so not as many were going over."

"That's when Rick went."

She poured us each a cup of tea. "Monika, are you sure you want to talk about this? I don't want to make you sad."

"No, Camilla, I want to hear what it was like." I warmed my hands on the handle-less cup. "Especially as a nurse. I was still in school and by the time I got out, the war was over."

Our food arrived, a platter of delicately browned pieces of chicken and julienne green onions in a thin sauce fragrant with ginger, a heaping bowl of white rice on the side. When we had filled our plates, Camilla urged me to try using chopsticks. After a few fumbles, I had the general idea but Camilla wielded them effortlessly.

As we ate, she told me about Vietnam.

"After I got my orders, they sent me for training to a mock Vietnamese village and to work on a med-surg unit—I had been working in the ER—to learn the Army's inpatient paperwork."

"So you didn't go over there right away?"

"It was a couple of months. And when I got to Vietnam and asked the nurses there about the paperwork the Army had insisted I learn, they just laughed. We had little time for charting or reports. We were too damn busy.

"After three months over there I became head nurse of a surgical unit, me, a year out of school!" She pointed her chopsticks at me. "And the stuff I'd seen at the Army hospital in Georgia was nothing like battle wounds. Frag wounds. They call them shrapnel wounds today, I don't know why, I guess frag sounds too awful—but they're just as bad. Multiple wounds from where pieces of metal enter the body. The face, legs, arms, chest. Even the eyes, sometimes. Often the metal was deeply embedded and we could only see it on X-ray. Infection is the danger, of course. But the burns—they were the worst. Especially the children," she added, her voice softening.

"Kids?"

"I remember one little Vietnamese boy. He had burns all down the side of his body." Her hand swooped down her torso. "And the side of his head. We thought he wouldn't make it, but he did. Then he got sent back to the States to be adopted. Lots of the kids who'd been orphaned were."

"So you treated Vietnamese as well?"

"No one ever said it, but we got to our guys first. Here's another thing about battlefield nursing. Triage is different. We treated the least injured first. I know," she said, shaking her head, "it doesn't make sense to you but we had limited time. All our patients came in at once, and if we spent time with some guy who wasn't likely to make it, we might lose another one who died while waiting for us. Sometimes we just doped them up and…"

I swallowed.

"I know it's hard to understand. But here's the good news. If they made it to us, almost all of them survived."

"Really?"

"Ninety-eight per cent made it if they got to the hospital. Of course, they didn't all get there."

I knew one that hadn't.

"It wasn't all good news. I worried about the quality of life ahead for some who'd lost limbs, and I worried about the ones we patched up and sent back into the field. Sometimes I'd see them again, being prepped for another surgery."

"How'd you deal with that?"

"It wasn't a problem when you were busy with no time to think about anything but the task in front of you. But the work was sporadic. We'd have a rush of casualties—after a few months there we could tell by the sound of the choppers if it was full or empty—and everyone would report in. Then we'd have slow times when a shift seemed to go on forever."

"Sounds like the police work my friend does," I told her. "She says it's either boredom or adrenaline, never in between."

Camilla pulled a pencil from her bag and spread a paper napkin on the table. "This is how we were set up. Supposedly." She drew a circle on the napkin, putting an "S" in the middle of the circle. "This is the surgical hospital, where the injured came first." She drew an arrow to another circle and put an "E" in that one. "If the surgical hospital couldn't fix them up, they got sent back to the field, or moved to the evac hospital if they needed more care, then," she put an "F" in the last circle, "to the field hospital for convalescence. Each hospital was designed to treat patients needing a specific level of care."

"You said 'supposedly.'"

"Well, there weren't any battle lines in Vietnam like there were in the world wars. The wounded came to whichever hospital was nearest and we sorted them out there. Most of the time the choppers came in with the dead mixed in with the live ones, they didn't have time to sort those out either. They had to get out of the fire zone as fast as they could."

"Even if they were dead?"

"That's an Army code, Monika. Never leave a fallen comrade behind."

I poured us both some more tea into the tiny cups and looked up at her. "Rick's body never came home."

A sound, like a mew, erupted from her throat and she stared at me, her eyes wide. She found her voice and whispered, "I'm so sorry."

"It's okay, really. I want to hear more. Weren't you afraid?"

"At first all I thought about was going home. I walked around every day thinking that if I got stuck with a needle or broke my foot, I could go home. But one day I realized that I couldn't go on that way. And then it came to me." She stared down at her hands clasping the cup. "I said, 'God has put me here.' After that, I didn't worry."

The waitress dropped our check on the table while I sat still, thinking about what she had said.

She blew her nose on a napkin. "We did have alerts, though. We'd scramble to get our patients under the beds—"

"How'd you do that? Weren't they in bad shape?"

"You don't know how macho those guys were. If they could move, they went under the bed. Others we threw a flak jacket over and then put ours on and got under the beds, too.

"Nursing was different there, too. We did everything—closures, sutures—whatever needed doing. We were colleagues with the docs. All in it together."

"You made friends?"

"That was the best part. Four of us are still friends to this day." Camilla reached for the check but I beat her to it. "Some got cynical, though. 'I'm too short to talk,' they'd say."

"Too short?"

"Their time was too short. Too near going home."

"How long were you there?"

"One year. Everyone did one year."

"Were you happy to get out of there?" I asked.

"Well, it wasn't so great, coming home."

"I remember that. People hating the war and the guys who came back."

"No one ever wanted to talk about it. Not when I came home, not later. Not my family, not my co-workers. It's as if they just want to forget it." She shrugged. "I guess they did. Finally I got a roommate who'd been there, and then my friends came back and we'd get together. We could talk about things no one else could understand."

"How did you feel about the war? Did you know about the protests? The opposition at home?"

"We didn't hear too much, although some of the guys got letters from home telling them what was going on. But we didn't talk about the war itself. The patients, they talked about what they'd been through, out of our hearing, mostly. And the language they used, whew! Let's say it was salty. I guess it helped them handle the horrific experiences they had been through. Still, we tried to teach them mouth management."

"What's that?"

"Manage their language. Gentle reminders that there were nurses present," she said, straightening up. "Of course that was back in the day."

I doubted anyone would correct such rough language today.

"It wasn't till I got home and someone spit on my uniform that I realized how angry Americans were."

"That must have been tough." I laid my money on the table for the waitress and Camilla went on.

"The big adjustment was coming back to work. I had been used to 12 hour days, six, sometimes seven, days a week. I couldn't seem to get my work done in eight-hour shifts. And I still had energy to burn at the end of the day. But it was the bureaucratic system, protocol, barriers, docs doing grand rounds without asking anything from the nurses who'd been with the patient the last twenty-four hours. Having to sneak in a few words to the docs who'll listen to try and get the orders you know the patient needs."

I knew about that.

"One good thing happened, though," she said as the waitress picked up my money. "That two-year-old boy who was burned? I was out in San Francisco, still in the Army, and I saw a picture in the paper of a Vietnamese boy who had been adopted by a local family. It looked like Tuan. And it was. I called the mother and, after meeting me, she invited me over to see him. He was doing great.

"That was the worst part of being there—never knowing what happened to your patients. We patched them up and sent them off. Especially the ones who'd lost legs, arms, sometimes both. I wish I could see how they're doing," she said, her voice wistful. "But," she said, "I'm glad I was there. It made me the nurse I am today."

"How's that?"

"I learned to manage my time, supplies, equipment. These young nurses today, they'll waste stuff. Why put a draw sheet on a patient that doesn't need it? You might need clean linens for someone else. I still save stuff—rubber bands, paper bags, foil—you never know when you'll need it. But mostly I learned there was nothing I couldn't manage. More patients coming? Bring them on. Too few staff? No problem, we'll manage. And we do. I wouldn't trade my war experience for anything in the world. Not anything."

She heaved a sigh, then gathered her coat and rummaged in her bag. "I'll tell you what," Camilla said, pulling a card out. "Why don't you try to find your husband's name tomorrow if you can." She scribbled some numbers on the back of her card and handed it to me. "Here's my home number and my cell. In the meantime, I'll go by the next time I have a day off and see if I can find it."

"You don't have to do that."

"I know I don't. I want to. It's a way for me to do something for one of our men. And for a fellow nurse," she added with a smile.

Chapter 6

Friday, November 12, 2025 Hours

"So, did you find it?" BJ asked, merging her jeep into the oncoming traffic.

I told her about my futile search to find Rick's name on the Wall. "I might have been confused, though. There were so many people there and it was raining and..."

She reached over and patted my hand.

"I met a nurse who lives there, though, and she's going to go back to look and let me know." It would have been so much better if I'd found his name, been able to trace my fingers over each letter, and let the reality of his death sink in.

"Want to know about your John Doe?" BJ asked, scrubbing her head with her knuckles. On duty she wore her hair pulled back tight in a blond French braid, but off duty she let it hang loose. Tonight she wore jeans and an old windbreaker of her husband's over a Cardinal sweatshirt. "He hit a tree in Carondelet Park."

"No! Not my park."

"The very one. I guess he thought he could lose them in there but, ha, he's the one who lost."

"You find out who he is?"

"Stolen car—no surprise—and the driver's license was for a guy in New York who's been dead several years." She slid onto the highway, staying in the slower right lane.

"So what next?"

"Not much we can do unless someone comes forward and identifies him."

"How likely is that?"

"It depends." She swerved around a line of slow-moving vehicles. "Location, location, location. One time a guy ran off the road right in front of the mayor's house. Believe me they found out who that guy was."

"How?"

"They put a picture of him in the paper and someone recognized him."

"Will they do that with our John Doe?"

BJ turned off at Loughborough, heading toward my neighborhood. "Don't know. I imagine they'll be in to get his prints."

"Why didn't they do that already?"

"Should have, I suppose," she said as we waited for a light to change. "McNamara only has another few days on the job before he retires. I think they put him on the case 'cause it's the least important one. He's probably just coasting now."

"But some family's probably missing him right this minute!"

"A bad guy? They're probably glad to be rid of him."

"BJ, you don't know that."

"The guy steals a car in Texas, has an ID from a dead man in New York, and he crashes the stolen car in St. Louis. You can bet he was up to something." BJ turned the corner and pulled up in front of my bungalow. A television screen glowed in Mrs. Warner's living room next door and a few lights burned in houses along my street.

I could hear Catastrophe, my angora, wailing before I had the door unlocked. Bits of chewed paper littered the living room rug and trailed off toward the kitchen from a decimated newspaper I'd forgotten to throw away before I left. Cat wove around my ankles, crying as if I'd left her for a month instead of two days. I dropped my suitcase and my bag and scooped her up, carrying her with me into the kitchen. Just as I thought, she still had food and water. What she hadn't had was me.

"I missed you, too," I told her, snuggling my face in her fur.

Chapter 7

Saturday, November 13, 0815 Hours

I SWUNG INTO the hospital parking garage shortly after eight the next morning. As a manager, I didn't normally work on weekends, but with several reports past due, doubled now that the step-down unit for patients convalescing after intensive care had been added to my responsibilities, and the ever-increasing paperwork required by various accrediting and certifying agencies in addition to my two days in Washington, I felt I had more than enough for a day of work without even checking on patients.

Although hospitals are open twenty-four hours a day, the work slows toward the end of the week. Fewer surgeries, especially elective ones, are scheduled on Friday to avoid stressing the lower number of staff scheduled to work weekends.

When I walked through the nearly-silent lobby, even the public address system seemed unusually quiet. I joined two lab staffers in the elevator, envying their steaming cups of foam-topped coffee from the newly-installed specialty coffee stand stationed outside the cafeteria. One woman opened her lid and a whiff of the scent almost inspired me to go back down for a cup of my own. But the doors opened on the fourth floor before I could decide.

The quiet extended to the hallway outside of ICU. I unlocked my office door and slipped inside before anyone could see me. With any luck no one would notice I was here and I could get a lot done before curiosity forced me to go see what was happening on the unit, when someone would want to ask "just one quick question."

I shoved piles of mail aside on my desk, clicked on my computer and went promptly to my "to do" list. It had taken me awhile to get used to using a computer calendar but now that I had it I couldn't do without it. I could check off items I had completed and those still waiting for action would automatically show up the next day.

Previously I had copied and recopied my list from day to day, frustrated because it felt like I never got anything done.

The list popped up. Three items, all important, all past due. First I needed to complete employee evaluations, formerly done only once a year and now due quarterly in an attempt to keep ahead of problems and encourage the best-performing nurses. Then the October budgets for both units still needed to be reconciled. Fortunately the nursing association had paid for my trip to the conference; my thin budget would never have allowed for such an unessential expense. Finally, I had three new staff who had started two weeks ago and who needed personalized orientation plans, a strategy designed to help new nurses acquire the skills they needed, especially since so many of the older nurses were retiring. Recent grads, no matter how bright or how accomplished, simply didn't have the experience of thirty-year veterans.

I flipped over to Tim's record and noted the two critical incidents I'd added to his file since his last evaluation. One credited him with mentoring a new staff member, but the other noted his refusal to work overtime. I didn't blame him. His third baby was due any day and, after his wife's two previous difficult deliveries, he didn't want her to deliver when he was too tired to help. I was debating how to handle his infraction of the rules—rules I didn't agree with—when the phone rang.

"Get out here!" Ruby demanded and hung up.

I heard the argument as soon as I opened my office door. Hurrying into the unit I found Detective McNamara, a camera slung around his neck, and Ruby, her hands on her hips. Her angry face matched his.

"What's the problem?" I asked looking from one to the other.

A crime scene unit officer stood off to the side, arms folded and a black evidence bag propped at his feet.

"He can't take a picture of a patient! No sir, no way. Even that man has a right to privacy. Tell him, Monika, tell him about the law!" Ruby added, spitting out the last word.

"I don't know about this, Ruby. It's never come up here since HIPPA's been in effect." Regulations to ensure patients' privacy had been expanded in the Health Insurance Portability and Accountability Act. "And he is the law."

"That's just who we gotta protect our patients from." She grabbed the strap and the camera smacked Detective McNamara in the chin.

Ruby lost her grip, McNamara staggered back, and the crime scene officer jumped forward to step between them.

I grabbed Ruby by the arm and pulled her back. "You keep quiet," I said, brooking no argument.

Ruby muttered and went back to her desk.

I turned to the officers. Detective McNamara rubbed his chin as the other officer showed me his identification.

"We're trying to ID your John Doe," the officer, whose badge said, "Dougherty," told me. "Get his prints and a photo. See if he's in the system or if anyone recognizes him."

"Give me a minute to check, will you?" I dialed administration and asked for Mr. Hockstetter just as he came bustling through the door. "They want to take John Doe's fingerprints and a picture," I told him quickly. "Does HIPPA allow us to let them?"

Ruby chuckled behind me but stayed seated.

Hockstetter ran a hand through his thinning gray hair. "Sure," he said, smiling at the officers. "Anything that helps us find out who he is. Go right ahead, go on," he added, shooing them toward the door as Serena came out carrying a container of urine. She stopped, the bloody-yellow liquid threatening to splash out.

"Wait," I said, "let me see what they're doing with him." Inside a ventilator pump hissed, pushing oxygen into the man's lungs through a tube inserted in his neck. "When'd he get a trach?" I asked Jessie although I wasn't surprised to see that John Doe now had a tracheostomy. His smashed-in chest made breathing difficult enough but added to his broken jaw—now wired together, I saw—and a broken nose, he wouldn't be able to get enough oxygen without artificial ventilation being forced directly into his trachea.

Jessie looked up from adjusting John Doe's various IV drips. "He had surgery to put it in on Thursday," she said, stepping back, apparently satisfied that the patient's fluids were in balance.

Trachs were a challenge, though. Comatose patients had no way to swallow so they had to be suctioned periodically to keep them from suffocating on their own secretions. In John Doe's case, swelling in the brain causes dangerously-high intracranial pressure, and suctioning increased the pressure.

I told Jessie about the police and motioned them into the room.

Detective McNamara took several photos while the crime scene officer opened his bag, extracting what looked to me like a tongue depressor. "We use this splint to immobilize the finger," he explained, placing it under John Doe's little finger. He slipped a cotton pad under the splint-wrapped finger, pulled off the adhesive covering, and rolled the now-exposed inked pad onto a card. He was continuing with the other fingers as I left.

Ruby called me over. "You gotta take Oblansky down to X-ray," she said, nodding to where two attendants stood next to an empty gurney. "She's gotta have another CT scan and those vents don't go anywhere, you know." Since ventilators aren't portable, a nurse had to accompany patients to radiology to continuously bag the patient manually and, at the same time, monitor vital signs.

"Where's Tim?"

"Off today. Nobody else to do it."

"Okay," I said to the men finally.

I helped the men transfer her onto the gurney, disconnected the ventilator, and attached an Ambu bag to her airway and the bag to a portable oxygen tank. I grabbed a code-blue box and stuck it on the shelf underneath the gurney. From past experience I'd learned that radiologists and techs are useless if the patient coded. I tossed in an extension tube and we were on our way, me squeezing air into Marian's lungs as the elevator descended to the basement.

Inside X-ray I donned lead cover-ups and attached the extension tube to Marian's airway and the other end to the Ambu bag. A tech slid Marian under the scanner while I kept squeezing the bag, a task made more difficult by the increased distance between the bag and Marian's airway.

By the time we'd finished and returned Marian to her bed, my right hand sported several blisters. Who knew how much radiation I'd absorbed.

As I passed the elevator on my way back to my office, the doors opened and Detective Harding stepped off. I pasted a smile on my face and followed him back into the unit.

Chapter 8

Saturday, November 13, 1155 Hours

"MY PARTNER'S DOWN in the ER talking to them about anything they might remember," he said as the door swung shut behind us. "I wanted to ask you what you know about Mrs. Oblansky's family, if that's all right," he said without making it a question.

Harding's black topcoat hung from well-proportioned shoulders and topped a navy sport coat, white shirt and patterned tie. Compared to Detective McNamara, who was assigned to investigate John Doe's accident, Harding's weight appropriately matched his height, his wavy brown hair was cut close to the head, and his mustache was clipped neatly above straight, thin lips.

"First, though, is she awake?" He placed a small, spiral notebook on the counter and clicked open a pen.

"I told you I'd call you if she woke up. We're keeping her sedated."

"You mean she's not in a coma?" he asked, checking his notes.

"Oh, yes, she's still comatose. The sedation is to decrease the metabolic demand of the brain, keeping the cerebral perfusion pressure optimum." At his questioning look, I translated: "The point is to keep the pressure in the brain fluid from getting too high, which would damage the brain. That's usually the cause of death in these cases," I added, lowering my voice as another patient's daughter passed us on the way to her mother's room.

"How long will that go on?"

"She was admitted when, Ruby? Wednesday," I said, answering my own question as Ruby handed me Marian's chart. "Today's Saturday. Cerebral edema usually peaks about 72 hours after the injury and subsequent intracranial surgery."

"So she should be coming out of it?" Harding asked.

"I couldn't say. These cases are difficult to predict. We just monitor her responses and wait and see."

"Has she said anything? Maybe she's mumbled something? Has any of your other staff heard her?" he asked.

Coming out of the clean utility room with freshly-delivered bed sheets, Serena stopped by the counter and balanced her load on her hip. Ruby openly stared at us, listening.

"She's in a coma, detective. And she's intubated." I clarified when he looked puzzled. "A tube is in her mouth and attached to a ventilator. Even if she were awake, she couldn't speak out loud."

He shifted to one side and flipped through his notebook. "Have you talked to the family? Have either of them said anything about who they think could have done this to her? Did they say why she was going to that bank? They live on the east side and the bank's in South St. Louis, a long way from their home. Have they noticed anything unusual lately or any problems she might be having?"

"Detective, they've just been in with her as far as I know, but why don't you ask the family these questions? Didn't you already talk to them on Wednesday?"

"Briefly. I'm just following up. I wanted to catch them so I don't have to track them down at home over in Illinois. But in situations like this I've found that family members sometimes say things to hospital staff that they might not tell us, things they don't think are important, or they're afraid of embarrassing their patient, but if we're to find whoever did this to her," he waved his pen toward Mrs. Oblansky's room, "we need every bit of information. Even some things no one thinks matters. Do you understand that?"

I nodded slowly. "I'd help you if I could, but she only came in Wednesday and I've been off for a few days. I'll alert the staff, though, and we'll let you know if anything comes up. Mostly, I've found all the family thinks about is the patient."

"Are the only two family members the husband," he flipped through a few pages of his notebook, "and the sister, Charlotte McFadden?"

"Those are the only ones I've seen. Ruby, has anyone else come in for Mrs. Oblansky?"

"They come, they go. That's all I know."

"Are either of them here now?"

"I haven't seen them yet but I'm sure they'll be in shortly."

"You have my card," he said, pulling another one from an inside pocket. "Will you tell them to call me when you see them? And you'll let me know if she wakes up?"

"What about our John Doe?" I asked him as he turned to go. "Has he been identified yet?"

"I don't think so. Not my case," he added over his shoulder as he left.

"Oh, I just told the detective you weren't here," I told Charlotte a few minutes later.

Standing by her sister's bedside, Charlotte turned pale eyes to me. "I noticed that outside door that leads into the hall, so I've been using it."

Marian's mouth stretched around the ventilator tube, her cracked lips coated with Vaseline. Her slender arms rested palms up, delicate fingers curled slightly, and her shaved head was a small oval resting in the middle of the pillow. The scent of recently-applied lotion to her face and arms lingered over her body, the hissing ventilator and beeping monitors the only sounds in the room.

"What did they do with her hair?" Charlotte asked, shoving lackluster bangs out of her eyes.

"Uh, I don't know," I said.

"Could you find out? I'd like to have it, keep it for her when she...gets well."

I knew it was unlikely that the surgical staff had saved it. The police had taken her clothing and purse, Wanda had told me.

"Her hair's one of the many things I've envied about her since we were little," she said. "It's so thick. It wouldn't break off like mine did when Mother took a hairbrush to it." With that, she seemed to fold in on herself, doubling her tall frame over the railing.

"Here, come sit down." I steered her to the visitor's chair and knelt down beside her. Her bangs fell forward over her face and after a moment she looked up at me, her eyes damp.

"Charlotte, do you have anyone to help you?" I asked her.

"Call me Lottie." She gave her sister a quick look. "We had pet names for each other. Lottie's what she calls me."

"We're taking care of her, Lottie. You need some support too, you know."

"Mom and Dad are gone and Marian's my only sister...I've always been jealous of her," she said, almost to herself.

I didn't know what it was like to have a sister. My cousin, Hannah, was also an only child, and we'd always called ourselves "sisters." Sibling rivalry, however, had never been part of our relationship. I put a hand on Charlotte's shoulder.

"All our lives, she did everything better than me. School, sports. I was taller but all arms and legs. I don't think she ever went through an awkward stage. Even after she became a widow, I was jealous. Sounds better than divorced, doesn't it?" I made a noncommittal sound and she went on. "But that all seems so petty now. I feel guilty about all of that."

"Can your husband help you through this?" I asked her.

"I'm divorced," she said, spitting out the word like she'd bitten into unripe fruit.

"What about friends? Or other family members?"

"Friends. They've called but I've either been here or at school. I'm a teacher. Middle school."

"That's a tough job."

"Oh, no, that's the best age." Her face brightened as she told me about her charges. "They're old enough to be interested and not too old to think learning isn't cool. And I have all the time off I need. But I'm going in each morning to help the sub before the kids try to snow her with some tall tales about no homework or such. I just want to do something, anything to help her," she added, her shoulders slumping inside her light-weight wool coat.

"Keep talking to her like you've been doing."

"She can hear me, you think?"

"We don't know. It might help her to hear your voice."

"I never know what to say."

"Tell her you're here, you love her, and you want her to get well. Touch helps, too. Hold her hand. Just sit and be with her."

Charlotte stood and clasped both her hands around mine. "Thank you, Monika. You and the nurses have been wonderful."

"We'll take good care of her, Lottie," I said. "I promise."

Chapter 9

Saturday, November 13, 1536 Hours

"I'M GOING," RUBY said, poking her head in my door. Her tweed coat was buttoned up to her chin and a red, white and blue scarf was wound around her head and neck.

I nodded without turning around. I'd just read a tribute to a soldier who died in Vietnam on a website for veterans and I didn't trust my voice.

She stepped toward me and placed her gloved hand on my shoulder. "What's wrong, Monika?" she asked.

This new Ruby shook me, and I turned to her, feeling the tears threatening. I took a few minutes to get my voice under control, then I told her about searching for Rick's name on the Wall.

"Why wouldn't it be there?"

"I don't know."

"I'm sorry," she said, squeezing my shoulder.

"A nurse who was in Vietnam—I met her in DC—said she'd try to find out for me."

"And in the meantime, you wait," she said, her voice heavy.

With a son newly enlisted in the Army and a nephew who'd been killed in Iraq, Ruby knew about waiting.

Chapter 10

Saturday, November 13, 1610 Hours

AFTER RUBY LEFT, I couldn't seem to get my mind back on my work so I grabbed my jacket from the back of my chair, stuffed a knit cap over my curls, and scurried out the door. I ran down the four flights of stairs instead of taking the chance of running into anyone I knew. I didn't feel like having to make polite small talk, not in my present mood.

Outside it had turned colder. Wind whipped at my jacket as I struggled to zip it, wishing I'd thought to do that inside. Finally the ends connected and I slid the zipper up to my chin and shoved my hands in my pockets, regretting that I'd left my gloves in the car. I lowered my head into the wind and headed onto a street adjacent to St. Teresa's.

When I was in nursing school at the university a few miles away, my classmates and I often walked in this neighborhood. Known for its square, brick homes and two- or four-family flats, symmetrical landscaping of evenly-trimmed shrubbery, and scrubbed front walks, this part of South St. Louis, dubbed Dutchtown, remained home to descendants of early German settlers for many years.

As recently as when I had been growing up, working-class people had lived around here and maintained scrubby-Dutch standards. But the area had become shabbier in recent years. As residents moved farther south or west, homes were sold to landlords and neither they nor their tenants had incentives to maintain the property, thereby encouraging more homeowners to move away, and so on. BJ had told me that this vicinity was a growing hot spot for drug sales and that car thefts on the surrounding streets were common.

Long shadows stretched across the sidewalk as street lights switched on. A car drove up behind me, slowing when it came abreast of me. I kept walking. The car sped up, spewing fumes in its wake. Maybe it wasn't such a good idea to be out walking on the streets after dark late on Saturday afternoon. At the next corner, I turned back toward the hospital, the wind now at my back. I stopped at the edge of the building and looked up. Light spilled from patient-room windows. "Get well," I said to the silent façade, sending a prayer upward.

I WAS STEPPING off the elevator when I spied a woman—she looked about forty—with cropped dark hair standing up in spikes streaked with gray, hurrying out of ICU, her face set in an expression I couldn't read. She passed me and pushed through the door to the stairs.

Inside, the nurses' station was empty.

I heard a sucking sound from John Doe's room. Shoving the curtain aside, I saw Poppi, a new nurse who had started last week, suctioning his trach.

"Where is everybody?" I asked, my voice betraying my fear. "And who was the woman who just left?"

"I didn't see anyone," she said without looking up. "Serena took a specimen to the lab, Sylvia's on break, and the other new nurse—I forget her name—called in sick." Her words came in quick bursts. She drew the thin plastic catheter out of John Doe's trach opening to the intermittent sucking of the pump attached to the canister on the wall. "Why don't you get some of those inline suctioning devices that attach directly to the trach? They're much more likely to keep germs out."

"You think St. T's has the budget for those? Not when we've got something that works," I said, watching her reattach the ventilator tube to the trach in his neck and switch the pump back on.

She stripped off her latex gloves, tossing them in the trash container beside the bed. "'Saturday-night fever,' we called weekend absences in New York." she said, adding, "we'll be fine."

I knew they would be. Poppi had been at Ground Zero in New York City, Serena had told me, admiration coloring her voice. In fact most of the staff were impressed not only with Poppi's experiences on 9/11 but with her skill. She was as quick as Laura, whom she'd replaced, had been slow. She noticed what needed to be done and did it, moving on to the next task without complaint. Even my favorite doctor, Jake Lord, had been impressed. "She sure brightens up the unit," he'd said a few days ago.

Unreasonably, I was jealous.

Chapter 11

Sunday, November 14, 0750 Hours

I OPENED THE Sunday paper to see a photo of our John Doe on the front page. Lacerations laced his bloated face, bruises colored his swollen-shut eyes, and a oversize ventilator tube spewed from his neck. Who would recognize that face? He looked like a dead man.

Nonetheless I braced for the onslaught of calls we'd probably get. Abandoned wives, distraught parents certain he was their missing relative. And there were sure to be the kooks that come forth in these situations, conjuring up imaginary visions of their long-lost whoever.

I opened to the inside page. Damn! Powerball was $118 million and I'd forgotten to stop and buy a ticket. If no one won tonight, the jackpot would be even larger by Wednesday. I'd double up on tickets, that way it comes out the same, I rationalized, ignoring the nagging feeling in the pit of my stomach.

I tossed the paper on the kitchen table, and turned to feed Catastrophe. She had been winding around my ankles and I had been ignoring her plaintive cries. I filled her food dish with Purina Cat Chow, rinsed out her water dish and refilled it, and bundled into outdoor clothes for a long walk in the park.

CARONDELET PARK WAS a few short blocks from my home, and its proximity was one of the reasons I'd moved to the neighborhood. The wind had died down and a thin sun peeked through gray clouds massed above the trees. Taking my usual path that wound through the park, I swung my arms determinedly in an effort to increase the circulation to my hands before they absorbed the cold.

Trees, still heavy with gold, orange, and crimson foliage contrasted with others whose bare branches latticed the pale winter sky. The pungent smell of leaves, matted into piles from the rain, reminded me of ripe fruit. My path crossed over a bridge and I stopped to tie my shoe. Below, undulating images of trees were mirrored in the water as it gurgled gently over rocks on its way downstream.

From a distance, I saw what I thought was a pile of clothes that had been abandoned under a tree, until an arm jutted out to tuck a tattered coat around the body and, nearer, I saw a battered shoe protruding from underneath the heap.

On my way back from the Wall in Washington I'd seen homeless people huddled in doorways, their layered clothing failing to protect them from the wintry rain. But I'd seldom seen anyone who was homeless in St. Louis. Aunt Octavia, who volunteered at a free health clinic in the city, had assured me that we had plenty.

Coming around a curve, I spied the accident scene ahead. Leaves fluttered across my path as a few lone birds scattered at my approach. I'd expected to see some damage to the ground and the tree John Doe had hit, but I wasn't prepared for the violence of the scene. Even from a distance I could see that the tree had a giant bite gouged out of its side. Nearer, the gash exposed chunks of raw wood as if a mammoth jaw had sunk its teeth into the tree's side, leaving bits of bark and wood slivers like so much inedible debris to be spit out. A blue jay, perched on a limb of the wounded tree, squawked at my arrival then flew off to warn of the approaching danger.

Tire tracks gouged the earth, swerved off the road, and dug parallel trenches until they stopped dead in front of the injured tree. The car had apparently jumped the curb, slid down the hill, and slammed into the tree. Had the driver tried to stop? BJ had told me that they couldn't determine skid marks in the wet ground. Had he deliberately crashed into the tree?

The ground had been wet on Wednesday. Since then the temperature had dipped below freezing, and overlapping footprints had been frozen in place around the scene. Idly, I wondered what the smashed-up car looked like until I caught myself. Things don't matter, Aunt Octavia always said. People do, she'd add.

"I suggest you start with a scarf," Aunt Octavia said, fingering some pale pink yarn. "This would go faster, though," she added, picking up a package filled with thick gray cords of yarn.

"Yuk. I want something brighter." I pulled out a package of fire-engine red yarn and held it up to my neck.

Auntie O, as we fondly called Aunt Octavia, was planning to teach me to knit. It would help lower my stress, she'd said.

"That looks great on you," said a middle-aged woman, coming up from the back.

Aunt Octavia introduced us. Claire Ann had inherited the store from her mother and lived in an apartment above the store, Auntie O explained as she placed her coat on a folding chair and pushed up the sleeves of the apple-green cardigan that she had knitted long ago. She returned to the gray yarn she'd been holding earlier.

"Each package of yarn is called a skein. You can knit directly from it like this." She pulled a strand out about a foot from the end. "Or you can wrap the yarn in a ball and knit from that." She turned to Claire Ann. "She's a beginner."

Claire Ann nodded. "You might want to try either a thick yarn or use a double strand. It will go faster."

"Is this new?" Aunt O asked, holding a package of yarn in multi-colored pastels. Aunt O showed it to me. "See how this is a thread with bits of fluff along it?"

It felt feather-soft in my fingers.

"Great for baby clothes," Claire Ann explained.

"Ooh, what about this?" I said, pulling down a package of thread with miniature feathers dangling from it.

"It's called eyelash," Claire explained.

"It tickles," I told them.

"Very expensive and not for you yet, Monika," Aunt O said.

"Actually, it's not something I'd wear but it is interesting," I said, returning the package to its slot on the rack.

While Aunt O and Claire Ann caught up with each other, I wandered down the aisles, running my hand along yarns, feeling the different textures and enjoying the new-fabric scent of the small shop. Wire shelves were stacked with neat rows of yarn, their delicious colors flowing one into the other, variegated shades of one color, strands of different colors woven together. Waves of dusty green became brighter as they melded into yellow, gave way to shades of brown that turned to red, then purple, and ending with hues of blue. Knitted scarves in varying widths, lengths, and yarns dangled from an overhead rack.

Brackets held cards of knitting needles in soft light woods and dull satin metals in lengths and widths too numerous to count along with accessories whose use I hadn't a clue about, and racks of books paraded up the wall along with instructions for afghans, ponchos, scarves, sweaters, and baby clothes. One book even had instructions for knitting clothes for dolls.

My brain on sensory overload with too many colors, textures, and choices, I couldn't seem to make up my mind. Where was that one I had liked several turns ago?

I made my way back to the front of the store and started over. Sometimes that's the only way out of a dilemma—just go back to the beginning and start over, another lesson from Aunt O. There it was—the yarn I wanted.

By the time Aunt O and Claire Ann caught up with me, my arms were full of plush yarn that gleamed in luscious shades of purple, blending lavender, orchid, violet, and deep, dark plum. Aunt O nodded her approval and added a beginner's instruction book and a small red plastic box she called a counter to my purchases.

Outside, Aunt O asked me, "Did you find his name?"

I told her about my search of the Wall, adding that Camilla was going back to look for me.

"That would help," she said, pulling on heavy gray driving gloves. "Sometimes I still think Bernie's coming home even though I saw him buried."

Aunt Octavia's husband had been killed in the Korean conflict. In addition to being my nurse mentor, Aunt Octavia was also the person I could talk to about losing Rick to a war we didn't believe in. She understood.

"I saw the Korean Veteran's Memorial," I told her as we reached our cars.

"What's it like?" she asked, turning her face away from me.

"I brought home a postcard. I'll show you."

She shook herself and we settled on next Sunday for my first lesson. In the meantime, I was to study my book.

"Yes, Sister," I responded, reminding her of the nuns who had taught us both.

Chapter 12

Monday, November 15, 0648 Hours

I OPENED THE doors to the unit to the sound of laughter.

"What's going on?" I said to Ruby, my voice louder than I'd intended.

Ruby punched the security guard on the arm and turned to me. "What you getting your underpants in a knot for? We just having fun."

The guard, a medium-sized black man, lost his smile, but Ruby just grinned.

"This is a hospital," I said, sputtering. "Not some rowdy bar."

"Oh, fer godsakes, Monika," Ruby answered, moving behind the desk. "We can't be down-in-the-dumps all the time."

The guard, who had been sitting outside Marian's room, gathered up his coffee cup and a newspaper, dribbling the coffee remains on the floor. A quick glance at my face and he blotted up the spill with the paper.

"It's serious business here, and people are trying to recover. They need quiet." I sounded like a school teacher. I took a moment to calm myself.

Ruby shrugged and plopped into her chair, the back labeled with her name on masking tape. She leaned back, crossed her arms over her considerable bosom, and waited. "Okay, Miss All Business. I'm ready for work."

The guard hurried away.

"He's just here on nights, it's our job to guard her during the day," she said.

"What could we do if someone tried to get in? Stab them with these?" I held up a pair of blunt-nosed bandage scissors.

"He don't have a gun," Ruby said.

"He doesn't?"

45

"Too dangerous. Someone get it away from them, then what happens?" She chuckled.

I had the clipboard with the day's assignments in my hand when the phone rang.

"You have my son," said a quavering, female voice.

"Your son?" I answered absently. "What's his name?" I scanned the list of assignments, automatically matching nurses' skills with patients' needs, coming up short. Two nurses had called in sick.

"Even after all this time, I knew he was still alive," the woman said, her voice faint. "Then I saw the paper."

"Oh, you mean your son is the unidentified patient here? What's his name? What's your name?"

She hung up.

"Who was that?" Ruby asked me.

"Some woman says our John Doe is her son, I think that's what she meant."

"She say who he is?"

"She hung up on me. I doubt it's anything."

"Yeah, they all be calling, wanting him."

"You've had other calls?"

"I can't remember everything," Ruby said, rattling the ice in the bottom of her big cup, a fluorescent orange one that proclaimed her name in black permanent marker.

So no one else had called.

"He's good looking, I'll give him that," Ruby continued, "but he stinks. Whew!" She waved her hand in front of her face.

"That's because we can't get his mouth clean," Jessie said as she passed by the station. "Doing AM care with his jaw wired shut is nearly impossible."

I nodded agreement as she went back to her patient.

"I wish we'd find out who he is," Ruby said. "I'm tired of hearing old Red complain about who's going to pay his bill."

"Red?" Serena asked, approaching the desk. She sported recently dyed hair, the roots recovered with black. Flame-red streaks stood out in peaks around her head.

"Ruby calls him that because he turns red whenever he gets mad—"

"Which is most of the time," Ruby interrupted.

"That and his name—Redmond Hockstetter," I said.

"His whole head turns red." Ruby laughed. "I can't help it. He's just too funny."

46

Jessie yelled from John Doe's room.

It took me only a few seconds to get out from behind the desk and into his room. His face had ballooned up to twice its size and was swelled dangerously around the ventilator tube in his neck. His fingers looked like fat sausages stuffed into tight casings dangling from his fractured arm.

Anaphylactic shock.

"BP's down to 80 over 50," Jessie said, her voice pitched higher in excitement. "Sinus tach up to 160."

"I'll call Lord," I told her, hurrying out.

He answered the page immediately. "IV epinephrine, 0.1 milligrams," he ordered as I expected he would. "In 10 milliliters saline over 10-15 minutes."

"He's a big man, over 200 pounds."

"Okay. Make it 0.5 milligrams."

I grabbed an ampule of epinephrine, drew up the dose, diluted it as ordered and dashed back in.

"BP's dropping!" Jessie said, staring at the falling numbers on the monitor. "Hurry!"

I stabbed the needle into the IV port and shoved the diluted drug into it. As we watched the solution drip into our patient's veins, I asked Jessie if the night nurse had reported anything untoward had happened during her shift.

"With his face already swollen from his injuries, I doubt she'd notice a change, not for a while at least."

I hung the lactated ringer's solution that Lord also had ordered. "Lord ordered a vasopresser if this doesn't bring his blood volume back up."

She thumbed toward his broken arm. "It was his hands I noticed first and then I saw that his feet were swollen, too." She'd pulled the blanket back to reveal his puffy legs and feet. "That's when I called you."

I glanced at the clock over his bed. Almost ten minutes had passed, but the skin still stretched tight over his bloated face, remaining an angry red. The swish of the vent as it pushed oxygen into his lungs, accompanied by the blip of the cardiac monitor, were the only sounds in the room.

Serena had come in and stood quietly watching with us. "What happened?"

"Apparently he's allergic to penicillin," Jessie answered. "Something we had no way of knowing."

Another five minutes passed.

As we watched, the color began to fade in his face and I left to check on our other patients.

Within thirty minutes our patient's swelling had gone down, his blood pressure had gone up, and his heart rate was back to normal.

Another crisis averted. For now.

LATER I PULLED a nurse from the step-down unit to help us, stopping in the unit only briefly. What trouble was brewing over there I didn't know, but it was sure to be something. Ruby had told me that her counterpart in the unit had quit and that Rosemary, who had been head nurse of the step-down unit until the reorganization, had been in twice trying to see me. If I didn't spend some time over there soon someone was sure to tell Hockstetter, and then I'd have him to deal with as well.

The doors opened and a woman, her height disguised because she was bending over a cane, peeked inside. Her head jerked around as if she didn't know where she was. Jessie was closest and asked if she could help the woman, whose eyes focused on the eye of Jessie's that looked forward.

"Uh, yes. My son. You have him." With gnarled fingers red with cold, she held tightly to the cane and leaned on it with both hands. A button was missing on her brown tweed coat, which gapped open over a graying white blouse.

"And who is that, ma'am?" Jessie asked, her voice calming, as was her way.

"Karl," she said, her voice breaking. "I saw his picture in the paper and...." Wisps of white hair peeked out of the brown knit cap that hugged her head.

"Come sit down," Jessie said, turning back toward the doors and the way to the family waiting room.

"No." The woman pulled away.

I whispered to Ruby to call security and put my hand up behind the woman to signal Jessie to stop. We didn't know who the woman was or even if she had a son. We certainly couldn't allow her to go into a patient's room even if she looked harmless.

"Where is he? Where's my baby?" she asked.

Jessie glanced toward John Doe's room and the woman noticed where she had looked. She attempted to push by Jessie, who bobbed back and forth trying to obstruct her from going into the patient's room.

"He might not look the same in here," I told her, joining Jessie in front of John Doe's cubicle. "He's pretty badly hurt."

The woman moved quicker than I would have expected, shoving Jessie aside to view the man in the bed.

"You can't go in there," I said, too late.

The woman was at his bedside. "My baby," she crooned. "My baby." She swayed back and forth as if rocking a child. "I knew you were alive, I just knew it!" She turned to Jessie and me. "They told me he was dead but I didn't believe them. I knew my baby would come home to me." She turned back to the man in the bed. The woman stroked the man's hand as she continued to rock back and forth. "I knew it, I knew it, I knew it," she continued to repeat. "I knew you'd come home."

I heard a security guard asking Ruby what the problem was.

"Ma'am, would you come with me for a moment?" I asked the woman. "So we can get some information."

"Oh, I can't leave him—not now after I found him. Don't make me leave!" She pulled away from my hand on her arm. The woman swayed as if she might faint, and I grabbed a chair, sliding it under her just as she collapsed into it, her cane clanking to the floor.

I hooked the cane over the chair arm and motioned for the guard to wait a moment. I kneeled at her side and asked her name.

"Wilma," she said, "and that's my son Karl, Karl with a K," she added, nodding toward the bed. She pulled off her knit cap, exposing a thinning pink scalp beneath white, straggly hair. She smelled like moth balls. "They told me he died, but I never believed it."

"Mother, what are you doing here?"

A woman, close to six feet in height and with a slight facial resemblance to the older woman in the chair, entered the crowded cubicle and glanced fleetingly at the man in the bed, her postal delivery uniform giving her an air of authority. "The neighbors told me where you'd gone," the woman said.

"I told you," Wilma said, her eyes tearing as she smiled up at the woman, "I told you he'd come home. Your brother's come home."

The postal worker squinted at the man in the bed and shook her head. "That's not Karl! What in God's name made you think it was him?" she said with a snort.

"It's him, it's my baby."

"Ma'am, are you really sure?" I asked the woman. "People look different when they've been injured."

"It's him. It's his hands. I'd know them anywhere," Wilma said.

The man's hands lay immobile atop the sheet, one finger clipped with a pulse oximeter, looking deceptively undamaged, his lacerated palms obscured.

I stood awkwardly, my knees creaking after crouching too long. "Let's go out where we can talk," I said to both women.

"You go on out, Roberta. I can't leave now that I've found him." To the injured man, she said, "Where's your curls, baby boy? Did they cut them off?"

Nodding for Jessie to stay with Wilma, I led the younger woman out to the desk.

"Mother's never accepted Karl's death," she said, shaking her head.

"You're sure it's not your brother?"

"He's been dead since '01."

"Oh."

"And that guy's too skinny. My brother was heavy, and he never would have shaved his head. He was too damn proud of his hair," she said, struggling to button her too-small jacket. A clip, heavy with keys, jangled on her waistband.

"What makes her think it's him?"

Jacket fastened, she tugged it down at the waist. "They never found his body so she's kept up this fantasy that he's really not dead."

"The war?"

"Nah, he wouldn't do anything that heroic," she said as a security guard, new on the job according to Wanda, hesitated inside the door.

"Git over here," Ruby ordered. The young man scurried to obey.

"Don't worry," Roberta said to all of us. "You won't be bothered any more." With that, she marched into John Doe's room, said something to her mother who rose awkwardly and hobbled out behind her daughter. At the door, Wilma turned back to me. "My boy," she mouthed silently.

The guard hurried out behind them.

"You know his name?" Ruby asked, joining me at the desk.

"Karl, she said. The mother's Wilma, the daughter, Roberta, I think. They didn't tell us his last name."

Ruby chuckled. "Some detective you'd make. Don't worry, though, they'll get them down in security."

"HAVE YOU HEARD anything about the search for a new COO?" I asked Wanda as she tore open an alcohol wipe.

50

As head nurse of the clinic giving the staff their flu shots, she'd whisked me to the front of the line, getting frowns from others waiting. I'd relieved my guilt by thinking about all I had to do.

"Not yet." She grabbed my upper arm, stretching the skin taut. "How's things in your world?" Wanda asked. "Those guys in the step-down unit giving you trouble yet?"

"What? Do you know something?" I asked as she said swabbed my arm with alcohol.

"I heard a few things," she said, sticking the needle cap in her mouth and expertly pulling out the unsheathed needle and syringe.

"So tell me, will you?"

She wiggled the needle cap in her teeth.

"That's great, Wanda, whet my appetite for gossip and then you can't talk."

She jabbed the needle into my middle deltoid, withdrawing the syringe to check for blood, then plunged the fluid into my arm. "Bull's eye," she said. I felt only a tiny sting. She tossed the needle cap into the red plastic safety disposal box and dropped the used syringe in after it. "I was just playing with you. Those nurses are no better or no worse than any others. They're overworked and tired and management's the target when they're mad." She tore open a Band-Aid and slapped it on my arm. "With the clinic on my plate now I can pretty well imagine how overscheduled you are. At least the clinic here is only open ten hours a day and I can monitor what goes on. Both of your units are staffed around the clock. You can't be there all the time."

She waved to the next person in line to come forward. To me she said, "I'll keep my ears open and let you know if I hear anything."

I was sure she would. Between Wanda and Ruby I could learn all the latest news crawling along the hospital grapevine.

"YEAH, I WAS there," Poppi said, studying the list of meds for her patient. "I wish I hadn't been," she added, her usual staccato speech slowed with remembering.

"What was it like? What'd you do?" Serena asked, her voice animated.

"The worst day of my life," Poppi said, turning around to face us, her upturned nose belying her seriousness.

Storing supplies in the cabinet, Sylvia turned to listen.

"Come on, Poppi, tell us about it." Serena looked at the other nurses who had come in.

"We'd like to hear," said a new nurse to murmurs from her coworkers.

Ruby had told me a phone call was holding but I, too, stayed to hear Poppi's story.

Poppi let out a sigh and leaned back against the counter, her hands splayed on its edges. Her voice picked up speed. "When we first heard that a plane had hit the Towers, we went into disaster mode. All off-duty staff was called to come to the hospital immediately. ER set up a special triage area and any patients that could be moved out of ER and ICU were relocated to step-down units or regular floors. Fortunately, we'd had a disaster drill just a month before and it had gone smoothly.

"We prepared for the worst which, of course, never came. Well, yes, it came but not what we thought." She stopped and gathered her breath. "You sure you want to hear this?"

"Yes, yes," Serena answered for all of us.

"I was working in ICU but they called me down to the ER where we all stood outside waiting." She stopped again and clasped her hands in front of her. She twisted her wedding ring around for a moment and told us about her husband. "Barry was a cop there."

The sound of breaths drawn in filled the space.

"We lived in Jersey where he worked but he was supposed to attend a class in the city and I couldn't remember where. I kept trying his cell and the station but all the lines were tied up. I tried to keep calm, but the waiting didn't help.

"Time passed—that was not a good sign. Sirens wailed continuously. I remember standing there watching the sun shining through the dust that had already begun to choke us and knowing that something was terribly wrong. The injured should have arrived by then.

"There we were—too many doctors and nurses and not enough patients—something I thought I'd never see.

"Finally a doctor who'd been in Desert Storm said we should go find people on the street that needed care. He said they wouldn't be coming to us. Two other nurses and an EMT who'd just delivered a patient to the ER before the first plane hit joined me and Dr. Williams. We'd bagged up supplies and headed out.

"We went to the firehouse nearest to Ground Zero. It was nothing like you saw in the news." She shook her head as if to clear the memory and went on. "The front door and wall were blown out, layers of dust, ash, and debris covered every surface. The power was off. It felt like going into a cave in the desert.

"We set up right there. A coat rack became an IV pole and the firefighters and rescue workers, our patients. I worked triage. We did what we could, patched up some, and flagged down any vehicle we could to take them to the hospital. Everyone got a tetanus shot. We'd brought along suture kits but we couldn't use them."

"Why not?" Serena asked.

"The scene was too contaminated. We taped them up and got them out. We used the normal saline in IV bags to clean out eyes that had seen the most horrific...some of them told us but others kept the images to themselves.

"The next day I was back at the firehouse along with all my coworkers when it began to rain."

Ruby stuck her head in the door. "You going to stay in here all day?" she asked me. "You think everbody just has to wait for you, don't you?"

"I'll be right there," I told Ruby.

Serena spoke again. "Didn't that make things worse?"

"Not really. It washed down some of the dust and it felt like, like it was cleansing in some way."

Serena spoke into the hush that followed. "I wish I could have been there."

I didn't hear Poppi's reply as I went out to take the call.

"Agatha," I said when I answered the phone. "How are you? Still a nun?" I asked, smiling to myself. Agatha had started nursing school with my class but, after a year, dropped out to join the convent.

"Monika," she said, her voice serious. "It's my mother. I think you met her."

"Huh?"

"My mother was in there this morning. And my sister. Mother thinks your patient is my brother."

"Wilma's your mother?"

"Yes," she said with an audible sigh.

"And your brother's Karl?" I jotted down "Niedringhaus," on a scrap of paper I pulled out of my pocket.

"I don't think it's him, Monika. They never found his body so Mother's never been able to accept that he's dead." She stopped. "He was her favorite," she said, under her breath.

"I'm so sorry. Maybe you should come in to make sure."

"I can't. I saw the picture in the paper and it doesn't look like him."

"That's what your sister, Roberta, said, too."

"Nonetheless, Mother thinks it is. Could you come here so we could talk about it?"

"I suppose I could come by after work if you think it would help."

"Four o'clock."

I started to say I might be late if I got held up at work, but she'd hung up. Just like a nun to issue orders and for all good Catholic girls to obey.

"Mrs. Oblansky's still unconscious," I told Detective Harding who called immediately after I'd hung up the phone.

"Is any of the family there this morning?" Harding asked as Steve Oblansky came through the doors.

"Mr. Oblansky just arrived," I told Harding.

"Tell him to wait. I'll be right over to talk to him."

I stopped Steve Oblansky and told him Detective Harding was on his way to talk to him. Steve stood at the desk, tapping the fingers of one hand on the counter, his eyes toward his wife's room. He turned to me. "They think I did it."

"Oh, surely not." I stood up and came around the desk to face him.

"I was home by myself that morning and I have no way to prove it. Of course I'm the most likely suspect. My dad was a detective. I know how they think."

"They said it was a robbery, didn't they? That wouldn't involve you."

"That reminds me. My wife had a ring with her. She was on her way to the bank when she was...." He choked, then seemed to gather himself together. "Did you find it with her things?" he asked in a rush.

"I don't think so, but I'll check on it," I told him.

"I'd appreciate it. It was her grandmother's. It means a lot to her."

He'd been in with his wife for about ten minutes when Detective Harding arrived.

"Is there a room where I can talk to Mr. Oblansky?" Harding asked me.

"You can use my office," I offered.

While we waited for Serena to send Steve out of his wife's room, I told Harding about our visitor for John Doe. "A woman came in this morning saying John Doe is her son."

"You get a name?"

"I know the sister. He might be Karl Niedringhaus."

"I'll pass the info on," he said, copying down the name.

Steve came out of Marian's room and headed straight for Harding. "What is it you want to know?" he asked, his eyes narrowed.

"Mr. Oblansky," Harding said evenly. "I need your help to—"

"You need to find out who did this to her," he said, stumbling over the words.

"I just want to get some details about your wife," Harding said, moving closer. "You want us to catch this guy, don't you?" He waited while Steve looked everywhere but at Harding.

Finally Steve mumbled agreement and I led them out of the unit, unlocked my office door, and scooped up a stack of files, newsletters, and nursing journals and placed them on my desk on top of more such stuff.

As I shut the door, I heard Steve ask if he needed a lawyer. I didn't hear Harding's answer.

"Where'd you take them?" Ruby asked, hanging up the phone.

"I let them use my office."

"Uh oh."

"What do you mean, Ruby?"

"You know what they thinking? They thinking he done it."

"Harding just wants to some information about his wife."

"What's wrong with you, girl? Don't you know people hurt loved ones all the time?"

"Ruby," I said, picking up a file. "It's obvious he's crazy about her."

"Don't you watch TV? The cops on those stories always look at the family first."

"I just don't see him hurting her. And not like that. Why hit her on the back of the head in broad daylight? If he wanted to, he could do it any time."

"Maybe he's smart that way. Figures they wouldn't suspect him." She headed into the break room with her cup. "You gotta watch way more TV if you want to know what really goes on," she said over her shoulder.

Chapter 13

Monday, November 15, 1650 Hours

I'D ONLY BEEN to the motherhouse once and that had been when I was a child of about nine or ten. Aunt Octavia had taken me along with her to visit a friend. I'd escaped from the parlor where they were talking and had wandered the halls, my patent leather shoes tapping on the polished parquet floors. When I'd turned a corner into a long hall, I'd seen my opportunity. I'd skipped as fast as I could to the end, sliding into a sculptured wall—I later learned it was called a relief—that depicted nuns in full habit climbing a hill. A jangle of beads and a glimpse of black fabric had caught my eye and, before I could turn around, my arm had been caught in a steely grip.

"What are you doing here?" That nun's voice had held the authority I recognized from my grade school teachers.

I'd felt like I would shrink in shame. It was Catholic guilt, the kind that comes unbidden if you've broken even a small infraction.

I stood up from my chair when Sister Agatha walked into the reception area. She looked thinner than I remembered, and gray was beginning to touch her strawberry-blond hair. She wore a nondescript navy skirt that fell to just below her knees, and a tailored blouse under a beige cardigan. She smiled at me through outdated, plastic-framed glasses and clasped my hands in hers.

"Thank you for coming," she said.

"This must be tough on your family," I said with a glance at the receptionist who didn't try to hide her attention to our conversation.

"Let me show you around," Agatha said. "Then we can talk," she whispered as we moved away.

The motherhouse had recently been restored, Agatha told me, from inside out. I could remember it filled with nuns busy with their work in spite of their cumbersome clothing. Even the postulants had looked overdressed in their black skirts and white blouses, but it was their heavy orange hose that had intrigued me. Thick brown seams, decorated with lumpy scars from too-frequent darnings, wiggled up the back of their legs. No wonder they kept their eyes down as they hurried by.

Now the halls were quiet and the rooms empty. Immaculate, the gleaming wood floors shone with attention, and the airless scent reminded me of a museum.

Agatha introduced me to several people working in an office but, since they were all dressed in street clothes I couldn't tell who were nuns and who were laypeople. I asked Agatha how to tell the difference.

"You can't," she said with a smile. "When our order was founded in the seventeenth century in Europe, all widows wore black," she explained, "and we dressed similarly because it was safer for a woman alone. The clothing said the woman wasn't available."

"I've always wanted to ask—weren't the habits uncomfortable?"

Agatha's laugh tinkled. "You bet they were. Twenty-six pieces and each piece had to be pinned in place. Some people kept them looking perfect, but on me something was always askew."

"So everyone's glad that ended."

"Not everyone. Some people thought the clothing taught us obedience and that there was nothing wrong about looking different from the people."

"You didn't agree."

"I thought it was pride talking."

"So exactly what is it you do?" On the phone, she'd told me she was the convent archivist.

"Come see the archives. I'll show you." She led me down the hall and turned toward the stairs.

"Are archives always in the basement?" I asked as we made our way down concrete steps below ground.

"Often they are. Besides, we like it that way. Keeps people from bothering us."

"So are you a librarian?"

"Sort of. An archivist preserves the records and artifacts important to the organization's history, including the things people used every day."

"But you're not a historian?"

"Again, sort of. I learn more and more of our history as I collect and work with records and materials. Also we manage displays similar to those in museums. You passed one in the glass case in the entry. That one is about our founding in the 1600s. Photos, books, clothing, mementos of any kind can be used to illustrate the purpose of the exhibit. Displays are rotated periodically so, in that way, archivists also serve as museum curators."

As we walked down the hall, I asked, "So does every religious order have an archivist?"

"Usually," she said, motioning for us to turn left at the corner. "Some, though, just assign a retired sister without giving her any training. That's a problem because they don't know how to catalog, what to keep or not, or how to preserve materials." She pointed toward a door on the right. "There's an art class going on in there or I'd show you. We have quite a few sisters who are talented artists and they teach some neighborhood children after school."

"So do you have a degree in archiving?"

"Hardly," she said with a smile. "I went to Catholic University for a short course for archivists. You probably don't know," she said, pulling a key out of her pocket when we reached the next door, "that in addition to religious congregations, educational institutions, associations, and even corporations have archivists." At my surprised look, she continued. "Yes, every organization, even those in business, needs to keep records not only of what happened but about the process, how decisions were made and who made them." She unlocked the door in front of us and ushered me in.

I jumped back at the sight of a nun in full regalia.

"Oh, that's Sister Unique," she explained, laughing.

"I thought she was real."

"Someone gave us the mannequin and my old habit fit her." Turning to the door on our right, she said, "Here is repository number one—we have three."

Inside the room four dark gray metal bookcases stood back to back in rows, reaching to the ceiling. Their shelves were filled with vertical boxes of lighter gray with labels attached to the front.

"The boxes and file folders inside are acid-free cardboard," she said, pulling a box off the shelf and opening it to show me. Papers stood upright in the box. "Unfortunately the paper isn't acid-free so we do our best to preserve it."

She turned a spoked wheel on the end of one row of shelves and the entire bookcase rolled to the side. "These shelves are too heavy to move, and if we had to leave space between each row we wouldn't have enough room for all the files we need to keep. This way we can fit them up next to each other and move the one we want."

"Ingenious," I said.

"All archivists learn to conserve space. It's always at a premium.

"That's our fire extinguisher," she said, pointing to a red tank in the corner. It was the size of a small person. "It's part of our fire suppression system. If sensors detect fire or smoke, it releases halon, a foam that absorbs the oxygen in the room."

"And with no oxygen…"

"The fire goes out. We can't use sprinklers, water would ruin the archives."

"What would happen if someone was in here with no oxygen?"

"They would have time to get out."

"Could they get locked in?"

"Heavens no, Monika. The lock's on the inside of the door in any case."

Outside, she motioned me back up to the main floor.

"This is my favorite place," Agatha said when we'd reached the double doors at the end of the hall.

The chapel was sunshine-bright in spite of the dark November evening. The room glowed with light from numerous bulbs dangling from long-corded chandeliers that hung from the ceiling where soaring buttresses met in the center. Warm hues of green, cream, and rose covered the walls and wood trim. The main altar stood at one end, light spilling onto the tabernacle.

Agatha pointed toward chairs along the wall, and we seated ourselves, settling into the quiet. After a few moments, Agatha began her story. "He was in New York," she said, stopping. "On 9/11."

I sucked in my breath.

"They never found him. That's why mother believes he's alive."

"You've never heard from him?"

"I thought he was trying to get away but it turns out he was staying with some woman and apparently she lived near the Twin Towers. She said he went out that morning and never came back. That's what the police told us. They never recovered a body."

"How can you be sure if they never found…anything?"

Agatha looked at me. "There were lots of people whose remains they didn't find."

"But you're sure?"

The door opened and an elderly nun motioned to Agatha.

"I'll be right back," she said.

I sat still and let the peace surround me.

A sound like a cough or a bark interrupted my contemplation. It came from the front, near the main alter. I stretched to see but a pillar stood in my way. I waited for the sound to come again but the room remained silent, only the faint hum of heating came from somewhere in the building. I stayed where I was, letting the beauty of the room soak in until Agatha returned.

"What can I do to help you?" I asked her, thinking about Cat at home pacing the floor, impatient for her dinner.

Agatha straightened up in her seat. "I want you to find out who the man is, the man my mother thinks is Karl."

"Why? You said you don't think he's your brother."

"I think it's unlikely. But mother does. I talked to her this afternoon and she's beside herself." Agatha looked toward the altar. "I just don't want her suffering any more. Once we know for sure who the man is, then maybe she can get on with grieving."

"Closure," I said, although I hated the word. It was too much of a cliché and it implied one had recovered from the loss. You never totally get over such a loss. I knew that only too well.

"Will you help me, Monika? Please."

"I don't know what I can do."

Her glasses had slipped down. She leaned her head back and studied me over the top. "Don't you want to know who he is?"

"Administration sure does," I admitted. "They want someone to pay."

"Can't you ask around? See what they've found? Don't you have some police officer friends? Maybe you could ask them." She shoved her glasses back up on her nose. "I've learned you have to dig through lots of materials to find out what has happened."

"Sounds like you should be doing the investigating."

"I tried when it first happened, but all I found was confusion. And I don't know anyone in law enforcement."

"Why don't you just come in and see for yourself if the man's your brother?"

She wrapped her arms around herself and pulled her sweater closer. "It's hard for me, Monika, to go into a hospital. That's why I had to drop out of nursing school."

"Why?"

She waved off my question. "Besides, I leave tomorrow for our annual meeting of convent archivists and I'm still preparing my presentation."

"You probably wouldn't recognize him anyway. In fact, that's why I doubted your mother. The man is pretty badly injured. His face—" I stopped, noticing that the blood had drained from Agatha's face, her freckles standing out in sharp relief. "Look, I'll do what I can. Try to find out if the hospital's learned who he is or see if my police friends know anything."

She clasped my hands in her long, thin fingers. "I can't tell you how much this means to me. No mother should have to go through this, not knowing."

Driving home I thought about what Agatha had told me. If the man was her brother, why had he been missing since 9/11? Wouldn't he have contacted his mother at least? She seemed so devoted I couldn't imagine any son being so cruel as to let his mother think he was dead. Or, had he been in touch with her and she hadn't told anyone? The man could only be Karl Niedringhaus if, for some reason, he'd wanted to keep his survival a secret.

Chapter 14

Tuesday, November 16, 1150 Hours

"You've got to be over here more often," Rosemary said, as she caught me waiting for the elevator. She tugged on her lab coat, attempting to fasten it over her faded blue scrub suit, but a button was missing. "No one's in charge since they took me out as manager. If I try to suggest anything, they all say I'm not the boss anymore." She tucked a strand of washed-out brown hair behind her ear.

"All?"

"Well, no, just a couple but they're the most vocal and they're getting everyone else upset. To the others, I've become their 'unofficial leader,'" she said, making quotation marks in the air. "Instead of handling conflict themselves, they want me to go into babysitter mode."

"Babysitter?"

"You know, settle their squabbles. 'She said this, she did that,'" Rosemary added, changing her voice to a child-like chirp. "Much like my kids."

"Can't you just tell them to handle it themselves?" Secretly, I thought that Rosemary enjoyed the role of mediator. Seven children under twelve at home kept her in practice. The problem was that the staff wasn't children, hers or anyone else's.

Jiggling coins in her lab coat pocket, Rosemary continued. "The office is piling up with mail, vacation requests, the schedule for next week isn't even started, and I can't imagine what emails have collected."

"Can't you check those?"

"Listen, Monika, I'd help you out if I could. I'm full time on patient care now. Besides, they changed the password. I can't get into the management system and that includes emails."

"I'll give you my password."

"No, no. I don't want it. I can't get my work done now as it is."

62

"Okay, I'll get over there later today and see what I can do."

"And then there's Missy," Rosemary said, grimacing. "She's been begging for a chance to work in ICU."

"I pulled someone out of your unit yesterday to work for me in ICU."

"She was off then and besides, I don't think she has the skills."

"I've got one nurse going on vacation tomorrow, I could try her."

"Suit yourself," she said with a shrug. "But don't say I didn't warn you."

TIM AND SERENA were in with Marian when she had her first seizure, at least the first one anyone noticed.

Serena leaned out of Marian's cubicle to report. "Hurry! Tim needs you! She's convulsing!" The curtain dropped back into place.

"I didn't know it was a seizure," Serena said when I joined them.

Marian's leg twitched and her head gave a jerk to the side.

"We need blankets," Tim said to me. "And get some Valium. It's ordered PRN." Turning to Serena he said, "Protect her central line," as he steadied the intracranial pressure line inserted in Marian's skull.

Back with Valium and blankets, I handed Tim the medication and began rolling the blankets into fat cylinders that I placed along side Marian's body. Marian's shoulder spasmed and an arm jerked out to hit the blanket tucked next to her.

Tim cleaned the IV port and deftly inserted the 0.2 milligram dose of Valium into Marian's central line inserted in her jugular vein.

"Is that why she's been on Dilantin IV?" Serena asked. "They thought she might seizure?"

"Always a possibility in the presence of depressed skull fractures," Tim explained. "That's why the prophylaxis anticonvulsant, but breakthrough seizures can, as you can see, still occur."

Serena kept her eye on Marian's central line as Tim had directed. "But why now?"

"You might not have noticed them because she's on the anticonvulsant and unresponsive besides," I told her. "She's probably had some seizures before this." I tucked the last blanket around Marian's head. "Any activity or movement can stimulate them."

"We had just turned her," Serena explained.

"It's been almost ten minutes," Tim said with a glance to the clock above Marian's bed.

"I'll call Lord," I told her.

As I expected, Lord increased Marian's dose of Dilantin to 150 milligrams IV. Later Tim reported that Marian's seizures appeared to be under control.

"NO AMOUNT OF money makes up for it," Poppi said, her words tumbling over each other.

"Makes up for what?" I asked, joining Poppi and Serena in the rest room.

"The money 9/11 families got," Poppi answered, soaping her hands.

"How much did they get?" I asked from inside the stall.

"Anything over a thousand dollars probably sounds like a fortune to you, Serena," Poppi said. "I remember when I was in school and counting every cent.

"It depended on the person's age, income, and family situation," Poppi said, running her words together so that following her train of thought felt like you were always a few words behind. "A single guy working maintenance and living with his parents wouldn't get as much as a married stock broker with a wife and four kids. They tried to calculate what the person would have made over a lifetime. It varied." I neared the sink as Poppi fluffed her chin-length hair, shiny with highlights, while Serena examined the possibility of a pimple on her nose in the mirror.

"And paid the families for all that time?" I asked, trying to rinse my hands under the trickle of water offered up by the ancient plumbing. "What if the wife worked or they didn't have kids? How about if she remarried? Did that change it?"

Poppi studied my reflection in the mirror. "You don't know what it was like. This was the biggest tragedy for our city, our country. Everyone felt like we had to do something. More than something. A lot."

I turned and faced her.

"And it helped us," she added.

"Still," Serena said, giving up on her pimple, "A million dollars?"

"A million! That right?" I asked Poppi.

"I know it sounds like a lot—"

"It is a lot!" Serena said. "Some got millions and millions."

"Some got much less, Serena," Poppi told her, "a few hundred thousand."

"That's still a lot of dough," Serena said as we headed out the door.

I DIDN'T KNOW what I'd do when it was time to evaluate Poppi. That she was a top-notch nurse I had no doubt. But could I put aside my feelings about her to be fair? I'd always prided myself (well, not too much because pride is a sin) on being absolutely fair with my evaluations of staff, and this was the first time I'd wavered. Taller, younger, and prettier than me, Poppi had released a giant green monster in my head, and I wasn't proud of that.

At least I'd been doing critical incidents, reports of daily events where the staff member does something noteworthy, on her. Most managers meticulously reported negative incidents, but I had made it a practice to collect positive actions on my staff as well.

I clicked onto Poppi's file. Her latest incident was typical. "9/1, 0950 hours, voluntarily stepped in to help student with complicated dressing change procedures in spite of heavy workload."

Nothing but positive incidents in Poppi's record.

Darn.

THEY ALL TRIED to talk at once. My first meeting with the step-down unit staff and already I felt as if I'd lost control.

I raised my hand. "Hold it! Let's start around the room and tell me your concerns." I studied the list of staff members on the legal pad I'd passed around so they could put their name in the corresponding place on the paper to approximate where they were sitting. I nodded to Anna on my left.

"Supplies are our biggest problem," she began, eliciting nods around the table. "Just this morning I needed IV tubing and went to get it off the cart and it wasn't there."

"You didn't have any tubing?" I asked her.

"Not what I needed for a nipride pump. I had to go down to central services and get it myself because now we don't have a ward clerk to keep supplies ordered. What kind of use of a registered nurse is that? I took me almost a half hour because no one was there. They were off delivering supplies to other units and I had to track down security to get in and then he gave me trouble. Watched me the whole time I was in there. As if they had anything worth stealing!" she added with a grunt.

"At least you got some," a young man at the end of the table volunteered. "When I came on this morning, my patient's tubing hadn't been changed at all."

"That's 'cause central supply doesn't work nights," Anna said. "Tubing's supposed to be changed on nights because they're not as busy. Then we come in and it's not done and—"

"I'll check with human resources about where they are on getting you a replacement clerk," I said, interrupting her. I made a note on the yellow pad in front of me.

Next in line was Marie, an older nurse with the heavy air of one who has seen it all.

"What are you going to do about our overload? We each carry four, five patients, sometimes six. Over in your unit, they get one or two at the most." She looked around for confirmation and received nods of agreement from several coworkers.

Her complaint was a long-standing dispute between the two units that I could ignore no longer. Because the patients aren't as critical in the step-down unit, the patient-to-nurse ratio is higher than in ICU where each nurse cares for one or two patients, depending on their needs and, admittedly, on how many staff we have available.

"If you look at patients on the two units, you'll see the difference," I said. "ICU patients are much sicker."

"Humph. You been over here?" Marie asked, her hands coming down on the table. "You ever seen how sick they are? Let's go out right now and I'll show you a sick patient, in fact, I'll show you all of them. It isn't fair." She sat back, getting affirmative murmurs around the table.

"Fair? Patients are assigned based on their acuity, not body count," I said to blank looks.

The meeting went downhill from there. As I expected, the schedule was a major problem. Several nurses were trying to do their own scheduling and getting grousing complaints from their colleagues, one nurse had gone on maternity leave with no plan to fill her shifts, and Hockstetter apparently had ordered outside agency nurses to fill in.

"They're more trouble than they're worth," another staff member said about the temporary replacement nurses. "They don't know where anything is, have never worked in ICU, or step-down for that matter, so they don't have the skills. We have to run in to do most of the care ourselves."

I called a halt to the meeting, saying I had to take a phone call. A young woman followed me out, introducing herself as Missy.

"Rose said you told her I could transfer to ICU," she said, twisting her hands in front of the teddy-bear scrub jacket she wore. Her face scrubbed bare of makeup and her light-brown hair tied up in a pony tail, she looked more like a nursing student than a nurse.

"Rose?" I asked. I didn't know who she was talking about.

"Rose," she answered. "Rose Marie." She saw my confused look and smiled. "Rosemary. We call her Rose, sometimes Rose Marie. She doesn't mind. She even had a name tag made up with that name on it when she was head of the step-down unit. So when can I transfer to ICU? I heard the money's better, too."

"Not transfer. You can come over for a few shifts until I see how you do in that environment. It's pretty fast-paced. You know that, don't you? You better have your skills down pat."

"I do, I do, oh, thank you, Monika. Can I start right now?" she asked, her pony tail bouncing with her words.

"Tomorrow morning will be soon enough," I said.

She hurried away, her white clogs stomping on the floor.

At least she's enthusiastic. That's something anyway. And more upbeat than most of her coworkers.

Back in my office, I wondered how I would ever be able to manage their problems and handle my own at the same time. And on top of that, I'd promised to help Agatha.

THE REST OF the day went by in a blur of anxious family members' faces, irritated physicians, harried co-workers, and missing reports, time running like a tape on fast forward. One code followed another. One patient arrested three times before he finally expired, the pharmacy mixed up the medication orders, two nurses and one assistant called in sick for evening shift, and Mr. Hockstetter's office called twice about my budget. I filled in on patient care and zipped through my budget reconciliation, checking it with only a cursory glance, and dropped it off to Hockstetter's secretary before I left, long past the time when the rest of the day shift had gone home.

This was another night that Cat's dinner would be late, but I wanted to get some answers first. Now that Agatha had asked me, my curiosity was aroused. I wouldn't be satisfied until I'd done everything I could think of to discover the identity of our mystery man.

AGATHA'S MOTHER LIVED in a cracker-box house, one of the many that had sprung up after the Second World War in the outskirts of the city to meet the demands of returning GIs and their burgeoning families. Built from identical floor plans, a living room, kitchen, two bedrooms, and one bath were crammed into a thousand-square-foot structure. After interstate highways had bisected the area, most original residents had moved away south into the county to roomier homes with larger yards. Escaping from urban decay, newer homeowners, including recent immigrants, had taken their places. But Agatha had told me her parents had stayed in their home even after her father's death. Her mother and sister lived here still.

I stepped over cracks in the sidewalk with dead grass caught in the gaps, and avoided the crumbling concrete on the side of the steps leading to the stoop abutting the front door. I knocked on the screen door and scraps of peeling paint fluttered to the ground.

By comparison, the house next door had been freshly painted and the roof looked new, a fact I'd been noticing lately since mine was due to be replaced. A carved jack-o-lantern sat on the porch, listing to the side where it had begun to rot.

Wilma answered the door dressed in the same blouse she'd had on at the hospital. Dried perspiration had left stains on the under arms. "Yes?" she said, her expression puzzled.

"Monika Everhardt. From the hospital. You said our patient was your son," I added when she didn't seem to recognize me.

"Yes, yes. Is he better?"

"About the same, but I'd like to ask you some questions about him. To help us identify him."

"You don't have to do that, I already told you who he is."

"We need some more information. Can I come in?"

She held open the door, her cane hooked on her arm.

Once we were settled on the worn sofa, I told Wilma about Agatha asking me to see if I could help.

"You know, every Catholic mother wants to give a child to God." She rubbed at a flower on the sofa's faded fabric.

The back door slammed open and Wilma looked puzzled as if she couldn't imagine who'd be coming in.

"Where are you?" yelled Roberta.

"It's my daughter," Wilma said, a shake in her voice.

"What are you doing here?" Dressed in postal blue, Roberta dropped a canvas mail bag on the floor. A can of mace stuck out from a side pocket of the empty bag. Roberta remained standing by the door frame that separated the living room from the hall.

"Your sister asked me to look into the man your mother thinks is your brother," I said, my voice as forceful as I could make it.

Roberta crossed her massive arms over her chest. "My sister?"

"Agatha, dear," Wilma interjected.

"Humph! She's not my sister!" With that, Roberta turned and disappeared down the hall. The door to a back bedroom slammed.

"She has a hard job," Wilma said, smiling apologetically. "Delivering the mail." She held a corner of her food-splattered apron in her hands, rubbing the edges together between her fingers. "It makes her nervous."

"About your son," I began again. "If he was in New York..." I hesitated. I didn't want to encourage her fantasy if the man was not her son. On the other hand, I was here to learn all I could. "Where's he been all this time?"

"Amnesia," she said without hesitation. "It was so awful, he just blocked it out. Poor thing, he's been wandering around who knows where since then. But he knew to come home."

"You know he was speeding, don't you? His car hit a tree."

"I know that. It's from the amnesia. He couldn't help it."

I decided to try a different tack. "What's he look like?"

"Handsome. My boy was always beautiful. From the time he was born." She looked out the window. "One time at school Sister asked him if he thought he could get by on his good looks all his life and he'd told her 'yes.'"

Roberta came back in dressed in jeans that squeezed in her ample bottom and a stretched T-shirt that didn't quite reach her waist. "And he did, too," Roberta said, looking like she might say more. But instead she shrugged and turned into the kitchen.

"Do you have a picture of your son?"

Wilma stood, balancing herself on her cane. "In the bedroom. I'll go get it."

Her mother tottered out of the room as Roberta returned. She leaned against the door frame and popped the tab on a can of beer, keeping an eye on me as she downed a quick swallow. "She's confused, you can tell that, can't you?"

"Um," I said, noncommittally.

"She's kept up this dream since 9/11 about his having amnesia and coming home sometime." She gulped another swallow of beer.

"It must be tough on you, living together."

"Evenings she's worse. They call it the 'sundown syndrome.' They get more confused and it makes them nervous. She calls me Agatha or thinks I'm her sister, long dead. Sometimes she thinks he's coming home from work and she sets a place for him at the table," she said with no effort to lower her voice. "How bizarre is that?" she added, not expecting an answer.

I glanced toward the bedroom.

"Don't worry, she's hard of hearing, too. It's enough to drive me batty," she said.

"But she said she recognized his hands. Wouldn't she know?"

Roberta snorted. "I saw his hands. They weren't my brother's." She hit her chest as she burped and her T-shirt popped up, revealing her navel. She stretched the shirt down with one hand. "His hands were full of calluses. He worked construction all his life. He's always been in trouble, but she thought he could do no wrong. Not even die," she added as her mother returned.

Wilma wiped the glass of a frame with her apron and handed me a black-and-white photo in a brass frame.

He was good-looking in that cocky sort of way men have when they know how charming they are. The diminutive woman next to him was squinting into the sun.

"Who's this with him? His wife?" The woman didn't look like Agatha or Roberta.

Wilma plucked at her apron, her head jerking from side to side.

Roberta had gone into the kitchen and came back out, minus the beer can.

Wilma looked at her daughter. "She wants to know about Mary Ann."

"Your sister-in-law?" I asked Roberta.

"She's not my sister-in-law. Not any more," Roberta added.

Wilma twisted the rings on her finger. "She thought he was dead just like—"

"Do you know where she is?" I asked as Roberta started to turn away.

"Nope," she said, "and I don't care."

Wilma spoke up. "Well, she helped me."

Roberta snorted. "Not enough."

"A hundred thousand dollars is enough for me," Wilma said, her eyes suddenly focused.

"A hundred thousand? She gave you a hundred thousand dollars?"

"Yeah, but she got three hundred thousand," Roberta said. "You shoulda' had half. At least. After the way you babied him."

"She's leaving it to me," Wilma said, now seemingly in command of her faculties.

"As if she'll die first." Roberta left, banging down the basement stairs.

"Do you have her address? Or phone number?" I asked.

The sound of a power saw whirled from the basement.

"Somewhere, maybe, I don't know. I better go. I have to get Roberta's dinner. She works so hard, you know."

With that, I was ushered out, barely grabbing my bag as her hands flapped, waving me toward the door.

Outside, I spied the smashed pumpkin first, its scattered pieces littered the yard and sidewalk. Then I saw the three teenage boys lounging against my car. One, sitting on the hood, jumped down when he saw me and tossed a lit cigarette onto the street. A taller boy leaned against the door, feet crossed in front of him. He slapped the door behind him with his palm. "Nice ride," he side with a flip of his head.

Black Beauty, I called my '69 Cadillac DeVille convertible that had been my dad's.

I glanced back at the house. Wilma was surely in the kitchen at the back of the house and from the noise I'd heard, Roberta was sawing away in the basement.

"Thanks," I said without expression. Keeping my eyes on them, I pulled my keys out of my pocket and walked purposely around to the driver's side. A younger boy had gone but the other two had turned to watch me approach. In a flash I had the door unlocked and was inside and relocked. Black Beauty started right up and I put her in gear. The taller boy had moved in front to stand directly ahead of me. He stood with his feet wide and his arms crossed, a slow smile spread across his face.

So he wanted to play chicken, I thought, remembering how BJ had faced down a bully in grade school. She'd said, "Never give an inch because they'll take it." At the moment, I had the bigger weapon. Ignoring the boy's stare, I inched forward and, at the last moment, he jumped out of the way, giving Black Beauty's hood one last slap.

I MADE A quick stop at home. Cat couldn't be put off any longer without doing some serious damage to my plants, my shoes, or anything else I'd left lying around. She dug into her Purina Cat Chow as if I'd had her on a starvation diet for weeks, and I snuck out before she realized I'd left her yet another night.

I called Agatha on my way, who'd told me she had a few minutes before she had to leave for the airport.

BUNDLED IN A snug brown coat and her hair awry in the wind, Agatha opened the front gate for me. Sadly, the neighborhood, like many others in the city, drew car thieves, whether they were out for a joy ride or the more serious business of stripping a car and selling its parts, apparently a lucrative business. When the gates swung shut, Agatha climbed into Black Beauty, joining me for the ride up to the convent parking lot.

After we parked, Agatha led me through the halls, quiet now. And dark. She switched on the lights to the basement and led me down the stairs.

"So what's your meeting?" I asked her.

"The Society of American Archivists is meeting in Washington, and we have our annual meeting in conjunction with that." She said, draping her coat over a chair in her office. "Archivists for Congregations of Women Religious is our organization. I'm speaking to the larger meeting as well as being president of ACWR."

"What do archivists talk about anyway?" I said, sitting in the only other chair in her office.

"We have a new challenge now. It's the Patriot Act."

"That affects you? What do religious women have that the government wants to see?"

"It's not what we have, it's who might access them."

"I don't understand. Who sees your files?"

"That's the issue. With the Patriot Act—passed within a month of 9/11, by the way—the government can retrieve your library records, what books you buy, and find out what files you may have examined."

"But, still, what does that have to do with you?"

"It hasn't so far, but it could. What if a religious order had records about a priest who was being investigated?"

"You're saying the government could get those."

"They could have subpoenaed those records before with good enough cause. The new law, however, allows them to find out who had looked at those records. They could discover if a bishop, for example, had examined records about the abuse but hadn't intervened."

"That sounds pretty far fetched."

"Whoever thought we'd be torturing prisoners? Or holding people without charging them?" Agatha asked me. "Everything's changed in our world, Monika."

"If you knew what they went through in New York that day, what it was like. I have a nurse who was there, she took care of people on the street...maybe there are good reasons for tightening security."

She checked her watch. "We can argue this some other time. I don't want to rush you, but—"

"You've got a plane to catch, I know. I just wanted to ask you a few questions about your brother."

"Mother said you'd come by. I really appreciate this, Monika. Don't think I don't just because I'm in a hurry." She ran her hands through her hair. "These days it seems as if I'm leading more of a scanned life now than an examined one."

"I'll make it quick. First, why did Roberta say you two weren't related? Or did I mistake what she said?"

Agatha shook her head slowly. "She's like that. Mother and Dad had me and, after Dad died, she married Kenneth and they had Karl and Roberta."

"Kenneth?"

She cocked her head to the side. "Ken Magnason was mother's second husband, Karl and Roberta's father."

"Magnason? Your brother's name's not Niedringhaus?"

"Sorry. I thought Mother had told you their last name."

"Gosh, that changes everything. I told the police his name was Karl Niedringhaus."

"Roberta's my half sister," Agatha continued, "but you'd think she was the only child the way she goes on, but I can't say I blame her. Ever since he was born, Mother's doted on Karl. It's Karl this and Karl did that. Never Roberta. He didn't get his way, he'd throw a temper tantrum and, of course, Mother would give in.

"I was in high school when he was born, but Roberta was only two. I think Mother dumped Roberta off her lap and replaced her with Karl. Roberta's been trying ever since to get her share of attention."

"She has it now."

At Agatha's puzzled look, I told her how Wilma had acted in Roberta's presence.

"Mother can be annoying when she gets confused, and Roberta's never had much patience." Agatha tapped her fingers on the desk.

"Okay, now what can you tell me about your brother? How tall was he? How much did he weigh? Any scars? Moles that you know of?"

"He's about six feet I think. No scars that I can remember. I can't judge weight very well but he tended toward chubby." She smiled. "Mom's good cooking."

"They didn't seem to know where his wife is now."

She chose her words carefully. "I didn't know Mary Ann very well, and I lost touch with her after the funeral, but I thought Mother kept in touch with her."

"How about her family? Do they live around here?"

"No. Her parents died long ago and she had a sister in California. But they were from the east side. Maybe she moved back there. She was a school teacher, as I recall."

"You know where on the east side?"

"Sorry. And I didn't see him very often. I was so much older and in the convent by the time he started school. I didn't even know he was in New York until the bombing."

"What are you not telling me? Yesterday you said you thought he was trying to get away. What'd you mean by that?"

She studied her hands on the desk before returning to look at me. "He wasn't what you'd call 'reliable.' He drank, for one thing, a lot."

"An alcoholic?"

"I wouldn't know, but I'd suspect he was or was becoming one. He never could settle into a job. Always getting fired or quitting, each time saying the bosses had it in for him. Mother said he'd started his own business, doing work on people's houses in the neighborhood.

"Too bad he never had time to work on Mother's house," she said. "And he might have cheated some people. Maybe on repairs or something he didn't do and should have. He may have thought the police were after him or someone was suing him. I don't know. I just got that impression from what Roberta said. Also, I didn't want to say this, but I think he had a girlfriend."

"I thought he was married."

Agatha looked at me.

"Oh. So he was unfaithful."

"I don't know if he broke his marriage vows, but I met her at the funeral."

"You had a funeral? Even though they never found a body?"

"We had a Mass, yes. Mother didn't want to, but Mary Ann insisted. She wanted to say goodbye even without a body."

"This woman you met. She said she was Karl's girlfriend?"

"She didn't realize I was his sister. She couldn't even tell I was a religious since we don't wear habits anymore. And I think she wanted to brag."

"Why would she do that?"

"I guess because of 9/11. He was the only one from St. Louis who was killed there."

I nodded my head. "Except for your family, few people in St. Louis were affected directly but we wanted to say how we were connected. I told people about my cousin's friend's husband, who watched the second plane hit from a hotel room window."

"It made us all part of our nation's tragedy."

"Shared experience, even though we were thousands of miles away. Aunt Octavia talks about Kennedy's death in the same way, remembering exactly what she was doing when she heard."

"We'll always remember where we were when we learned about 9/11, won't we?" Agatha stood, gathering up her coat and briefcase. "I'll walk out with you," she said, "and tell you where you can find Val."

"Val?" I asked as Agatha locked the door.

"Karl's girlfriend."

"Hey, Val, you got flu shots?" a man asked the bartender, motioning toward the sign propped up in the window.

I joined him at the bar, leaving an empty stool between us.

"Yeah, we got them, Syd," she said, waving toward the bottles behind her. "Guaranteed to cure the flu and anything else that ails you."

"Then I'll have one a them." He flashed her a smile.

I pulled a five out of my jacket and dropped it on the bar while the bartender mixed a drink on the shelf below. She handed it off to her customer and turned to me. "You want a flu shot, too?" She reached across the bar to clear the soggy napkins bunched under an empty glass.

I rubbed my arm absently. "Just a Busch Light."

The man looked at me in the mirror. "Hey, Val, tell her how you got your name."

I waved away the glass Val offered me. "Short for Valentine," she said, sounding as if she'd told the story often.

"Because..." the man said. "Do what Karl taught you."

Val's smile slipped but she shrugged and turned to him, forming her cupid-shaped mouth into a fake pout.

"Ain't that cute?" he asked into the mirror. Two men playing video poker at the end of the bar glanced our way.

"Karl?" I said.

"Her old boyfriend," the man said. "I'm Syd," he said, saluting my image in the mirror with his drink.

"He's not around any more?" Coming in, I'd had no idea how to begin but, thanks to Syd, I had an opening.

"Killed in WTC," Syd said as Val stowed the dirty glass under the bar. "And she's still mad she didn't get any money."

Val picked up a damp cloth, wiping a spot on the bar as if she could scrub it clean.

"Can I talk to you?" I asked Val.

Syd looked interested.

I leaned forward and lowered my voice. "It's about Karl."

She hesitated, but my diminutive size must have reassured her.

"You guys all okay?" she asked the bar patrons. When no one answered, she motioned me toward the back and led me into a cramped room stacked with cases of beer and soda, bottles of liquor and boxes of snacks. She pulled open a potato chip bag and offered me some.

"Maybe you saw the picture in the paper Sunday," I said, declining the snack. "A man who'd been hurt that we can't identify at St. T's. I'm a nurse there. Karl's mother came to the hospital and says it's him. I'm trying to find out if anyone had heard from him since...they think he died," I added.

"He called me," Val said.

"He did? When?"

She heaved a sigh and a roll of flesh escaped from her waistband and spilled over onto her jeans. "That day. He was there. He saw people jumping out of windows. He couldn't believe what he was seeing. That's when I turned on the TV and saw what was happening."

"The worst thing we've ever seen," I said, encouraging her.

"He said not to worry. He was all right. He was going to go down to see what was going on." She swiped at some crumbs on her jeans.

"You in here, Val?" asked a man who'd been working the other end of the bar when I'd first come in.

"Be right there, Benny. That's all I know," she said, shoving the empty chip bag into an overflowing trash can.

"She tell you about Karl?" Syd asked when we came back out. "That guy was a charmer. Even when you knew he was scamming you, you liked him. I heard he—"

"Shut up, will ya, Syd?" Val said. "Have a little respect for the dead." Val turned on her heel and walked out.

The other bartender, Benny, joined us. "She's still mad because his wife got all the money," he explained in a lowered voice to me.

"His wife should have, shouldn't she?" I tapped my beer bottle, signaling I wanted another.

"She says they were getting a divorce and Karl and she were getting married. She says that phone call from him that day added to her grief. I think she read somewhere that families who got calls like that had more 'pain and suffering' or something like that. Anyway, she was pissed." He headed back toward his station at the bar as Val returned.

"Can you tell me something about him?" I asked her, catching her before she followed her coworker down the bar.

"What?" she asked with an obvious sigh.

"Did he have any marks on him that might identify him?"

She smiled to herself. "Not so you'd see."

"Believe me when you're in intensive care, someone's seen every part of your anatomy. Nothing's a secret. Is there anything you can tell me?"

"No, not really. He said he'd been injured in the Army but I never saw any scars."

"He say what it was?"

"Nah, he didn't want to talk about it, he said."

The man who'd been sitting down the bar from me came back and straddled the stool. Val picked up a bin of dirty glasses and turned. "I got me a new boyfriend now. I don't care about Karl any more. 'Sides, he's dead."

She sashayed away, the bin of glasses clanking on her hip.

Chapter 15

Tuesday, November 16, 2215 Hours

RESTLESS, I DROVE around after leaving the bar. I swung down BJ's street in Dogtown where she and Don had recently bought a two-family flat that they were rehabbing. Light filtered through the window of their top-floor living room and the porch light was on. In spite of working the day shift this week, BJ must still be up.

Dressed in paint-splattered jeans and dirty-gray sweatshirt, BJ motioned for me to follow her up the narrow stairs. I started to say something but BJ hushed me. "New baby," she whispered, thumbing toward the wall separating the stairway from their lower-level tenant. Renting out one unit of a two-family flat was a way for new homeowners to make their mortgage payments. Hard-working and reliable, South St. Louisans usually made good tenants.

A life-size, cardboard cutout of the Blues Brothers in their familiar dress—dark suits, white shirts, and opaque sunglasses—guarded BJ's living room. The movie was her favorite, which had always puzzled me. In the movie the police were caricatures of themselves, bumbling from one false move to another. BJ said that's why she liked it; it made people think cops weren't very smart. An advantage, she'd said.

She motioned me toward a sofa, pulled a tattered sheet aside, and kicked dried pieces of wallpaper into a pile. Sheets covered the other furniture in the room, and a step-ladder stood poised in front of the radiator, a bucket balanced on its shelf.

"Keep your coat on, Monika. I've got the heat off to keep the radiator cold." She joined me on the sofa. "Hey, you look beat, kid."

"I can't even keep up with my own work, now I've got step-down, too."

"Step-down? What's that? Some kind of physical therapy?"

"I told you they gave me another unit to manage, but it has twenty-four beds to our ten. It's just what it sounds like. The unit where patients step down from intensive care. Everything ends up there: post-op, trauma, cardiac, neuro, surgery, burn, whatever put someone in ICU, step-down is where they go before going onto the floor or directly home, which seldom happens. I met with their staff today.

"My biggest challenge, I knew up front, would be to get a feel for how the staff works, their rhythm, if they're in sync. Now I've learned that they can stick together, at least to fight a common enemy, which at this moment is me. What is it that makes people think fair and equal are the same thing?"

"It'll be there tomorrow. That's my motto." BJ pointed to the ladder stationed in front of the radiator. "Here, hold this, will you?"

Steadying her on the ladder, I said, "And I haven't even dealt with the docs. They're used to going to Rosemary so I'm sure they're having a hard time adjusting."

BJ put her sneaker-clad feet one by one on the radiator rails, wiggling a bit to get her balance. "Sounds like they aren't the only ones." She pulled a dripping sponge out of the bucket and squeezed out some of the liquid. She studied the corner where the last strip of wallpaper was still intact, the rest of the wall stripped clean except for dried patches of wallpaper paste and the chips in the plaster where it had been nicked by her scraper. "Just do what you can, then let it go." She stroked the dampened sponge over the top patch of maroon floral wallpaper near the ceiling. "Work your eight hours like I do and go home."

"I can't do that. I'm salaried, supposed to get the work done no matter how long it takes. Even if I am doing two jobs."

"Didn't you get a raise with that?"

"Yeah, two thousand."

BJ whistled. "That'd make me work harder."

"You know how much that is once they take federal and state taxes out, social security, retirement—"

"All right, I get it. Just listen to me." She turned to see if I was paying attention. "You've only got twenty-four hours in the day, same as everyone else. You can't let it get to you, the job. God knows I can't."

"I suppose," I said, unconvinced. "But that's not why I came by. John Doe might be someone I know. Or know his sister."

She studied the water-soaked paper, beginning to peel away at the edges. "Hand me that scraper, will you?"

A foot-long tool shaped in a T lay in the midst of wallpaper scraps.

"Be careful. There's a razor on the end."

I handed it to her handle first, keeping my fingers away from the sharp edge.

One hand on the wall for balance, BJ slid the scraper under the edge of the dampened paper, stopping when she met resistance. She leaned back to survey her work.

She'd loosened the layer of flower-patterned paper to reveal a green-and-white striped pattern underneath. She handed the scraper back down to me and sponged the layer beneath. "Not again, Monika, you're not getting into something like that again, are you?"

When I ignored her reference to my efforts a few months ago to solve a murder, she went on. "I thought you were too busy. Isn't that what you've just been complaining about?"

"I have to tell you what I know," I began and, when she didn't stop me I told her the story of Wilma's visit, Roberta's denials that our patient was her brother, and Agatha's request that I help them. And about the confusion over Karl's last name.

"Mrs. Magnason insists he's her son, but the one sister and the girlfriend are sure he's dead."

"Mothers are like that," BJ said, waving off Mrs. Magnason's beliefs with the sponge, leaving a dribble of water on the paint-splattered drop cloth at her feet. "I've seen it plenty of times. Fathers, too."

"I know, I know. Denial. But it doesn't go on for years. After a while people begin to live their lives, making new memories without the person—" BJ interrupted me with a look. "And," I said with emphasis, "they realize the death is final."

"Some do," she said, noncommittally and dipped her sponge in the water.

"But not this woman," I said, "and not now after she's seen him."

BJ tackled the green-striped wallpaper with a heavier hand than she had before and a vertical strip came free. She leaned over to follow the pulled paper down as far as she could reach. "Okay, let's say it's him. Why didn't he get in touch with his mother before this? Or the girlfriend?" BJ asked, jumping down off the radiator. "Just answer me that."

"He was married. Maybe his wife knew where he was."

"And didn't tell his mother? What's the wife say?" She used her foot to shove loosened paper into the pile with the others.

"No one knows where she is. His family's apparently lost track of her."

BJ wiped her hands on a paint-stained rag. "Maybe he and the wife are in it together."

"No, his mother told me Karl's widow got money from the World Trade Center fund and gave some of it to her."

"Ahhh."

"What do you mean by that?"

"A scam. He wasn't dead, the wife collected the money, and they're off somewhere spending it."

"Gosh, BJ, you think everyone's a crook."

"They wouldn't be the first ones to try it. You know how much some families got from that fund?" She tossed her rag on the pile of discarded scraps of paper.

"As a matter of fact, I do. It was a lot." I told her what Poppi had said about the 9/11 compensation to families.

"Most of us would consider even the lowest amount to be a fortune," she said. South St. Louisans were frugal, but seldom wealthy. "People have killed for less, much less," she went on, plopping down on the lowest rung of the ladder and stretching her feet out in front of her. "And this only required that they hide out, and there's lots of places in the world you can get lost, places that won't extradite even if you get caught."

"Well then, how did he end up here being chased by the cops?"

"Look, Monika, we don't go after every case. We got murderers, rapists, drug dealers all roaming the streets causing trouble. Those are the ones we want to catch."

"What about accident reconstruction? You've said that's what the cops do after a crash."

"Nah, wouldn't bother. This guy, they figure he's going to die, no one else got hurt. Besides, McNamara's about to retire. They gave him this case 'cause it's easy."

"I went there, to where he hit the tree." She didn't say anything so I went on. "It didn't look like he even tried to stop. Do you think maybe he was trying to kill himself?"

"A variation on 'suicide by cop,'" she said.

"Huh?"

"That's when a perp tries to get a cop to kill him. He doesn't have the nerve to do it himself so he puts himself where a cop has no choice but to shoot him."

"So he headed toward the tree, thinking it would kill him?"

"Does he sound like someone who'd want to kill himself?"

"No, he doesn't, not from what his sister said. So when McNamara retires, that's it?"

BJ shrugged.

"Then I'll have to try," I murmured under my breath.

She picked at an edge of wallpaper near the baseboard, revealing a third layer of paper underneath. "You go poking around you never know what you'll uncover."

"One of the sisters—she doesn't think John Doe is her brother—is a friend of mine. And a nun. I promised her I'd find out who this guy is. You know what a promise to a nun means."

"Don't pull that religious stuff on me. Didn't you get in enough trouble last time? Wasn't that enough to scare you?"

"Must I remind you, I did find the murderer?"

"Yeah, and almost got yourself killed."

"I'm not going to do anything dangerous, just check on a few things. Aren't there some directories or online sources I could use? Maybe I can rule out this Karl Magnason and that's all I'd have to do."

She cleared drop cloths off the radiator, wadded them into a bunch, and tossed them in the corner.

"Help me, please, BJ. Give me some pointers," I said as she turned the heat back on.

"Try information. You'd be surprised how many times people are listed. You can get the address, too."

"Didn't Detective McNamara already do that?"

"Probably."

"You just trying to give me something to do to keep me busy?"

Knocking in the radiators signaled the return of heat.

"Aren't there cross-reference directories?" I asked when she didn't answer.

"Sure, some only for law enforcement. But try the library. They might have something. Get their old address, try the phone number. She might have had her phone forwarded. Go on the Internet and search around."

"What if the wife remarried? Wouldn't McNamara have checked that, too?"

"You mean marriage licenses? I doubt it. But that's stretching it. She could be anywhere by now. Maybe dead even. Give it up, Monika. Doesn't sound like he's the guy anyway."

"I just want to find out if he's Karl Magnason or not."

"Tell your friend to call the detective. Let him worry about it."

With one last look at her handiwork, she motioned me into their newly-remodeled kitchen. "Coffee? Decaf?" BJ asked with a glance at the black-and-white cartoon-face clock on the wall. "Don likes some when he gets home. Something to help him unwind."

We both knew what it was like to come home after working the late shift. No matter how tired you were, there was no way you could jump into bed. You had to shut down the adrenaline pump first.

"So how much more do you have to do here?" I asked her, pulling out a white wrought-iron chair at the ice cream table. The wall was newly-decorated with wallpaper in a black-and-white ticking-stripe pattern.

"The living room and dining room are it, but there's six or seven layers of paper under there. We get that off, then finish off the plaster and start on the woodwork. It has to be stripped and revarnished. Then we paint the walls and ceiling, refinish the hardwood floors and—"

"Okay, okay, you're wearing me out just talking about it. Hey, look around. Your kitchen's finished and it looks great."

A gleaming black granite slab topped snowy-white cabinets that coordinated with a ceramic tile floor in black-and-white squares. "Right now it feels like we'll never get done," she sighed.

"What'd you say your motto was? Something about, it'll still be here tomorrow?"

"I get it." She ran water into the glass coffee carafe. "Say, how's your roof coming?"

"They're still supposed to have it finished before winter."

"They better hurry up. Thanksgiving's next week."

"I'm just glad to have a roof, even one with a leak." I told BJ about seeing a homeless man in the park and several in Washington.

"They just need to get their lazy asses up and go to work."

"BJ, you can't believe that! Most of them are mentally ill, my friend who works in psych told me. Since the government, in its wisdom, stopped funding community mental health clinics adequately—her words," I said, raising my hand to stop BJ from interrupting.

She measured coffee into the basket, turned the switch to on, and when she turned around, I said, "Aunt Octavia volunteers at the free health clinic. Lots of people barely make enough to live on and then one catastrophe puts them on the street. Haven't you seen some families with little kids? Some people are just one paycheck away from homelessness."

"You're too good-hearted, Monika. If you saw what I face every day, you wouldn't be so sympathetic."

I changed the subject. "You know anything about what they've found about Marian Oblansky's attacker?"

"Harding's on that case so you don't have to worry about her. He's like a bulldog; he'll find out who did it. At least you're not involved in that one," she said as coffee gurgled in the pot. "I tell you she was hit with a tire iron? The perp tossed it back in the trunk with her blood still on it."

"So they can get fingerprints?"

"The guy used gloves, but we got a specialist who can get prints off most anything."

The aroma of brewing coffee filled the compact kitchen.

"Harding interviewed the husband today. Poor guy."

"Humph."

"What's that mean?"

"Nothing, nothing." She pulled two white diner mugs out of the cabinet. "Get the milk out of the fridge, will you?"

"Harding badgered him," I told her, putting the half gallon of skim milk on the table.

"How'd you know that?"

I stirred sugar and milk into my coffee and took cautious sip. "After they came out of my office, Steve looked pretty upset."

"That's routine. Try to ruffle the suspect, make him mad, maybe he'll say something he shouldn't, SOP."

"Huh?"

"Standard operating procedure. Don't you watch the cop shows?" She chuckled. "They're not always accurate, but they get that right. Anyhow, I'm sure they're checking on the husband." She reached for a decorated tin behind her on the counter and opened it. A sugar and vanilla aroma rose from the array of cookies displayed in the canister. "Mother's already started her holiday baking."

I took a butter cookie topped with red sprinkles. "Why him? He's such a nice guy. And he's crazy about his wife."

"Or just crazy." BJ sorted through the box and brought out a Mexican wedding cake, her mother's specialty.

"BJ, I've been a nurse a long time. I've seen crazy, and this guy isn't it."

"You've been fooled before," she said, letting the words hang in the air.

I couldn't argue with her. A few months ago, a killer had been able to disguise his intentions from me and many others.

"Okay, but this is different. When you see someone under this kind of stress, they can't cover up their feelings. Besides, why would he hurt her?"

She wiped powdered-sugar crumbs from her mouth and passed me the napkins. "Always suspect the spouse. First rule in a homicide."

"But if he wanted to kill her, he had lots of opportunities. Why would he attack her in public, in the bank parking lot, in the middle of the day? Wouldn't he pick a more secluded place and time?"

"Some of them are so smart—or think they are—that's exactly what they want us to think so we ask that very question. And let them go. At least they need to rule him out. Hey, why do you care about this one?"

I bit back a response. No way was I going to tell her how much Steve resembled Rick.

"I'm worried if someone tried to kill her, they might try again. And why don't the cops have a guard on her room?"

"You know what kind of budget we have for that sort of thing?" BJ made her thumb and forefinger into a circle. "Zero. Nada. Zilch. Besides, what would happen when the guy had to pee? Or get something to eat? They'd have to send another officer over to relieve him. That, I know, we can't afford. Not with all the drug dealers, pimps, and murderers running around. 'Sides, you've got those wannabe cops, they can handle it something like this."

"You mean our security people?"

"Most of them wanted to be cops but couldn't get in or couldn't cut it so they take security jobs so they can strut around in uniforms and issue orders."

"I'd think the police would take this more seriously. Remember, someone did get in and kill a patient."

"Don't ask me, I can't make sense of what the bosses decide."

Chapter 16

Wednesday, November 17, 0915 Hours

CASSANDRA WIGGINS BUSTLED through the door full of self-importance, clipboard at the ready.

"Oh, Lordy," Ruby said, pushing up from her chair. "I'm outta here." She grabbed her sweater and headed out the door.

Cassandra had been a nurse in psych until she'd been appointed patient advocate by Hockstetter a month ago, replacing an army of eager volunteers, elderly neighborhood women mostly. She'd taken to the job with gusto.

"Any visitors in here?" Cassandra asked, looking pointedly at Serena who stopped laughing at something Poppi had said. Mousy brown hair, tightly permed, framed Cassandra's round face, squashed into a persistent frown.

"Not yet," I told her.

Cassandra paged through the papers on her clipboard until she found what she wanted. She tucked the sheets behind the board and turned to us. Jessie and Tim stood beside me, all of us bracing to hear her latest complaints.

"Mr. Dieterman." She looked up over half-glasses, their cord dangling around her neck. "His wife says..." Her finger traced down the page. "His call button isn't being answered numerous times. That she's been left waiting at the nurses' station...a lot."

"Doesn't that tell you something?" Tim asked. "About her, that she's complaining all the time?"

"It tells me she wants good care for her husband," Cassandra said, her mouth pinched.

"Or she's a chronic complainer," Tim said.

She slapped the sheets on her clipboard. "I don't have to read anymore. We're here to serve our customers, not make excuses." Cassandra rocked back on her heels, her glasses flopped down on her chest, clanking against her name tag clipped to the lapel of her lab coat.

Tim and I both tried to speak at once. I motioned for Tim, who'd cared for Mr. Dieterman until Marian Oblansky had arrived, to explain.

"He's lucky to be alive," Tim said, his tone dismissive. "He came in with a massive stroke, we didn't think he'd make it and—"

"It's only because of his excellent nursing care that he's here," I said, interrupting when I saw Tim's face turning red.

"But she, she's a pain in the you-know-where—" Tim tried again, his voice raised.

"Nevertheless, we have to keep the family happy," Cassandra said. "You fix this. All of you."

"Tim, go see to your patient," I told him. "I'll handle this."

Tim looked like he was going to say something more before he turned away toward Marian Oblansky's room.

A man and woman had come through the door with Ruby, and she directed them to a patient's room.

"Why don't we go in the conference room?" I asked Cassandra.

"No time," she said, tapping her watch. "Here's the list of complaints. I don't have time to go through all of them." She jerked out several pages from those on her clipboard and shoved them toward me. "See that you take care of them." She left without waiting for my response.

"Now we got the nurses fighting us," Serena said. "On top of administration."

"She is administration, Serena," Tim explained, returning.

"And they pay more attention to complaining patients than they do to the staff," I added.

"If we have complaints," Tim said on his way to the med room, "just forget it." He tossed an empty IV bag on the counter and came back through. "According to her, whatever patients or their families complain about is a problem that must be solved. If the staff have concerns, we're expected to just suck it up. Who advocates for us? That's what I'd like to know."

"You'd think she never worked as a nurse," Jessie said, shaking her head.

"If she had, she'd understand," Serena added.

"Only in psych, never in ICU," Tim said over his shoulder. A lab tech held the curtain to a patient's room open, waiting for Tim.

Missy came through the swinging doors, smiling as if she owned the place.

"Where've you been?" I asked her, my irritation showing.

"Uh, I had to go downstairs."

"She was getting a new ID," Ruby said, "to work here."

"What? I told you this isn't permanent."

"I'm sorry, I thought—"

"You didn't think," I shot back.

"She can work with me," Jessie said before my temper got the better of me and I sent Missy back to the step-down unit.

"I'll help orient her," Jessie added, motioning for Missy to follow her into John Doe's room.

As if Cassandra hadn't been enough, less than twenty minutes later Mr. Hockstetter came through the door demanding to see me. Dr. Lord and I were making rounds so I asked Jessie to join Lord while I attended to whatever Hockstetter wanted.

Hockstetter tapped manicured fingers on the counter. "We've got to get him out of here," he said.

"Get him out? Just where do you think he can go?"

Hockstetter's face reddened and Ruby chuckled behind him. Hockstetter flipped his hand in the air dismissively.

"What's his prognosis?" Hockstetter asked Lord, who joined us at the desk.

Lord's face creased with concern. "Not good," he said. "But you never know."

Hockstetter's eyes narrowed. "What's his code?"

"He's a full code for now since we don't have any family to decide," I said, knowing where Hockstetter was going with this. "That's the law."

Hockstetter grimaced, then left.

I stood at the counter thinking. Surely Hockstetter didn't expect us to ignore a code. Or discontinue life support.

"You don't think Hockstetter's going to do anything, do you?" Tim asked, giving voice to my thoughts.

"Like what? Try to transfer him somewhere?"

"A nursing home maybe?" Serena asked.

"They couldn't handle him," Tim said. "Not with the care he needs."

"I think administration's stuck with this one," Lord said to all of us. "Hockstetter's going to have to eat this bill," he added, leaving.

"Aren't you trying to find out who he is, Monika?" Serena asked. "You've found out other stuff before."

"Yeah, like who's a killer," Ruby said with a giggle.

"Hush, Ruby. That's not for public announcement," I said.

"You are smart, Monika, I think you should try," Serena said.

"Actually I am trying to find out. I may know his name."

"What?" Ruby asked. "You sticking your nose into this?"

I looked at Serena who was trying to keep a straight face.

"This from the nosiest of them all," I told her, nodding toward Ruby.

Serena giggled.

I opened my mouth to tell them about Sister Agatha wanting to find out if John Doe was her brother for her mother's sake, but it seemed too complicated to explain. "I'm just checking a few things," I said.

Detective McNamara didn't say anything right away when I reached him on the phone and told him that if John Doe was Karl, his last name was Magnason, not Niedringhaus.

"Sorry," McNamara said finally. "Someone was talking to me. What was it?"

Ruby waggled pudgy fingers in my face. I waved her off and turned my back to repeat my report to the detective.

"They want you," Ruby said loudly enough that McNamara surely could hear her. "Something bad going on over in step-down. If you don't care, it's not my fault."

"Yeah, yeah, we already know the name," McNamara said, hanging up.

I headed over to the step-down unit to see what trouble was brewing there.

It didn't take long to find out.

"There you are," Cassandra said, clipboard hugged to her chest. "Come here and see what's not been done." From a jangle of keys, she unlocked the cubicle tucked in next to the linen closet that served as the manager's office. I had yet to set foot inside the place, but Cassandra was about to change that.

"After you," she said with a flourish, and then followed me inside. She wiggled around me to the desk and tapped a pen on the overflowing pile of letters, large brown envelopes, newsletters, flyers, and advertisements that cluttered the top. "And this computer..." she jiggled the mouse, "hasn't been turned on in two weeks." She turned around to face me. "Not since you became manager of this unit," she added with a click of her tongue.

I pulled out the desk chair and started to sit down, then turned back to her instead. Irritation swelled up inside me like a bolus of stomach acid pushing into my throat. I pulled myself up to my full four feet eleven inches and said, "Wait a minute, Cassandra. You're not administration. What business is it of yours what I do or how I manage?"

"Well!" she sputtered. "I'm just trying to help."

"Help who? Yourself?" There was a name for people who tried to curry favor with the bosses but I kept that to myself. "Since this office is assigned to me and you've had your say, you may leave." With that I sat down at "my" desk, picked up the phone and resorted to one of Ruby's tricks that she used to appear busy. I dialed a familiar number and listened to the recorded message. By the time I had learned the correct time and that the temperature was expected to drop below freezing tonight, Cassandra was gone.

ASPIRATION PNEUMONIA IS such a common complication with severe brain injuries that I wasn't surprised to hear Jessie report that Lord had ordered chest films for JD, as Ruby had taken to calling John Doe. An X-ray tech had arrived with a portable machine and was positioning it over JD's bed when I joined her and Missy.

I'd made some headway on the accumulation of mail in the step-down manager's office, trashing most of it, and filling a folder to take home to read tonight.

"Why does he need an X-ray?" Missy asked Jessie as the technician ushered us out of the door.

"Lord wants to rule out pneumonia," Jessie told her. The technician joined us outside the room and punched the remote to trigger the picture.

"You heard his lungs? What about his secretions?" Jessie asked her as we waited for the technician to finish.

Missy screwed up her face, thinking. "His lungs sounded okay to me, but his temp's up."

"Listen to his lungs again," Jessie instructed. "Then tell me what you hear."

Uh oh. Missy should have heard wet, decreased lung sounds. A skilled nurse also would have noted the decreases in O2 saturation despite no change in the vent setting as further evidence of pneumonia.

"Because of the increase in secretions, he needs frequent suctioning," Jessie explained, "but that's a problem because it increases his pressure, so we have to watch how he tolerates that."

"How serious is it? I mean, I know he's pretty bad but..." she bit the inside of her lip.

"Keeping him on mechanical ventilation makes the lungs even less flexible," Jessie said. "But what can we do? He can't breathe on his own. It's not unusual to get pneumonia in these cases, but he can survive it. There's plenty of options for drugs besides the penicillin he's allergic to."

Looking toward JD's room, Missy clicked a pen open and shut. "He seems to have so many things wrong with him. What else could happen?"

"We can't know that, Missy. That's why we keep such a close eye on him." Even Jessie's patience seemed to be wearing thin.

Missy's pen clicked again. "I guess," she said, following Jessie back into the room as the technician wheeled his machine out the door.

While we waited to hear the results of JD's X-ray, I dialed the convent. Sister Agatha would be back from her meeting on Friday, the receptionist informed me. I tried Agatha's mother, Wilma, who answered on the first ring.

"How is he? How's my son? Is he awake yet? Can I talk to him?" she asked, sounding lucid.

"There's no change, Mrs. Magnason. I'm still trying to find your son's wife. Do you have her phone number or address or know any of her friends or family? Somebody who might know where she is?"

"They weren't married very long, and with her being from Illinois..."

"Who's this?" Roberta's husky voice bellowed over the phone.

I told her.

She slammed the receiver down.

Boy, those sisters were nothing alike.

I SPIED PEGGY at a table by the window in the cafeteria and made my way through a group of students to join her. She pushed her tray to the side and wiped up some water spills with a napkin, tucking it under her empty plate.

An excellent clinical nurse, Peggy had worked for me in ICU until her drug problem had forced her into treatment. She'd opted to work in psych after that, saying she didn't want the temptation of working with so many accessible narcotics.

"What's up with you?" she asked me as I moved my soup bowl, crackers, and a water glass from my tray to the table.

I must have let out a sigh as I sat down because she said, "That bad, eh?"

"Two patients," I began, stirring my chicken noodle soup to cool it. "Both traumatic head injuries—one woman bashed on the head during a robbery and the other's a guy being chased by the cops till he ran his face into a tree."

"Yikes. How are they doing now?"

"I don't think either one will make it." I tucked dollar bills and change into the pocket of my lab coat.

"That's one of the reasons I left, Monika. Too many sad cases."

Her move to the psychiatric unit had been good for Peggy. She'd let her auburn hair, which she had kept pulled back in a tight bun when she worked in ICU, grow out to shoulder length, and her deep-green eyes were clear. She smiled more these days, looking more at peace than I'd ever seen her.

"And you don't have that in psych?" I lifted a spoonful of soup to my mouth and tested it, burning my tongue. I put my spoon aside and took a drink of water. "It seems much sadder to me to see people who don't know reality or are so depressed they can't do anything,"

"Not really," Peggy said. "Not to me anyway. I like talking with them." She played with her empty water glass. "And we see more of them go home."

"Don't they come back, though?"

"Sure, some of them."

"When their insurance kicks in again?"

Peggy bristled. "And when it's medically necessary."

"Okay, okay." I tried another sip of soup, cooler now. I concentrated on enjoying the chicken chunks, thick noodles, rich broth.

"You're right, Monika, we do have to listen to the payers."

"As we all do. That's one of the problems," I said and told Peggy about John Doe's mounting bill.

"Boy, I wouldn't want to face Hockstetter with that problem, especially with what it's costing. How much is it now?"

"I don't know, but he's been in for a week. More than fifty thousand at least. Probably more with the surgery costs." I tore the cellophane of a package of crackers and nibbled on one.

"Who's that?" Peggy asked, looking toward Cassandra and Poppi settling in for lunch at a table near the wall.

"Didn't she work for you?"

"Cassandra, yes, but who's the other nurse?"

"Poppi. She came here from New York. Her husband's in the accelerated nursing program for college grads at SLU," I said, naming my alma mater, the Jesuit school's name shortened from St. Louis University. "She told us he was a cop in New York, actually New Jersey, on 9/11. That's what made him decide to come back to his hometown and become a nurse."

"9/11 did that?"

"I think she talked him into it. She said he'd been thinking about nursing for a while."

"Another helping profession. I've known a few police officers who became nurses, as you probably do."

Poppi's laugh rose over the conversational murmur.

"Cassandra came after us today like she'd never faced a patient. What's with her? And why'd she leave psych?"

"Frankly," Peggy said, leaning forward, her hair brushing her labcoat collar. "I was glad to see her go." She shoved her hair back in a brisk sweep. "In fact, I recommended her for the job."

"Why, if you wanted to get rid of her? This job carries a lot of clout. We don't need someone like that representing us."

"She's not representing us, Monika, she's representing the patients. Her clinical skills weren't very good, but she's meticulous with details. I thought it'd be a place to use her talents."

"This doesn't sound like you, Peggy, foisting your cast-offs on the rest of us."

"We all do things we wouldn't have in the past," she said. "Better to use her than a clinician we can't spare."

"Well, it's gone to her head. She's acting like the queen bee around here. And just after we got rid of Judyth," I said, referring to our chief nurse who had been fired a few months before.

"Maybe she'll settle down after a while," Peggy said, piling her lunch trash on her tray.

"Did she ever settle down with her clinical skills?"

"No," Peggy said with a grimace. "In fact, she wouldn't hear of it. Said she was doing just fine, that I was always picking on her."

I hesitated, not knowing if I should tell Peggy about my efforts to discover John Doe's name. In the end I let it go.

"It's the other head trauma I'm more worried about," I said. "The woman attacked at First Federal."

"I heard about that."

"The police think her husband did it."

"Did he?"

"I'm sure he didn't. He's in every day, hovering over her. He's distraught."

"And cute, I suppose." I couldn't tell what was in Peggy's voice.

"What do you mean?"

Peggy looked out the window, her eyes envisioning something I couldn't see. "We had a patient one time when I was working in Kansas City. Nicest guy you'd ever meet. He kept saying there'd been a mix-up. He shouldn't be in psych. He even helped with the other patients, talking with them, assisting some who had trouble walking—those meds will do that—there wasn't a sign that he had a mental problem."

"So how'd he get in there?"

"He murdered his mother."

I sucked in my breath and choked on a noodle.

Peggy asked if I was okay as I sputtered. I shook my head when I finally could take a drink of water. I wiped my mouth with my napkin and asked, "What happened?"

"Apparently he wanted her money. Cool as can be. He came home one day and strangled her as she watched the news on television. Then he called the police and said he found her like that."

"Why was he in the psych unit instead of jail?"

"His lawyer had him hospitalized while the police were still investigating. They arrested him while he was in the unit."

"I thought you got off if you were officially mentally ill."

"Diagnosing someone and proving it in a court of law are two different things. Psychopaths have no feelings, for themselves or for anyone else. They just go after what they want. They never feel revenge or regret. Or grief, for that matter."

Moral imagination. That's what my philosophy professor had said they lacked. He'd suggested that people who couldn't imagine the feelings of others couldn't feel empathy for them.

"I don't suppose the courts would have much sympathy for someone like that."

She shook her head.

"Is there any hope for him? If he ever gets out of prison, that is?"

94

"Nothing can be done with them. Psychopaths are born that way—sociopaths the same thing—and they die that way."

"So you're wondering if this woman's husband might be a psychopath."

"I wouldn't know, Monika," she said as she gathered her tray. "That case just stuck with me. Probably your guy really is what he seems."

Wanda waved to me as she wiggled through a throng of students all trying to push toward the exit at once. She settled into the chair Peggy had left. "I heard you got a John Doe. Why didn't you tell me about that?" she asked, depositing French fries, sandwich, and giant soft-drink container on the table.

"You mean JD?" I asked with a laugh. "That's Ruby's name for him. She gives everyone a nickname, you know. Hockstetter's 'Red,' I'll bet Cassandra's got a good one."

"What's she call you? Or doesn't she say it to your face?" Wanda tore open a ketchup square and squirted some on her plate.

"It depends on the moment."

"Well? Come on, spill!" she said, dipping French fries, three at a time, in the ketchup.

"Boss Lady, Smarty-Pants. She called me 'Miss All Business' the other morning."

Wanda grabbed a napkin to wipe her hands. "And worse behind your back, I suppose."

"I doubt it. That's one thing about Ruby, she tells you straight out. You always know where you stand with her," I told her, putting my dishes on the tray.

"Hey, you haven't told me about your JD. Sit, sit," she demanded. "You can't leave yet." She spread mustard on her bun and topped it onto a deep-fried pork tenderloin slab that spread beyond the roll, smashing meat, lettuce, and tomato together.

"His wife might be from Illinois," I told her. "Like you."

"You don't know much about the east side do you, Monika?" Wanda asked me, not expecting an answer. She clutched her outsized sandwich and stretched her mouth around a bite.

"It's just been the 'east side' to me," I said while she chewed.

"You and everyone else in St. Louis," she said after swallowing.

Although the Illinois' cities were directly across the Mississippi River and were included in the metropolitan St. Louis area, St. Louisans considered residents who lived on the Illinois side of the river outsiders, foreigners in their own community. East side cities seemed as far away as Chicago.

"Can you name the cities east of the river? No? Of course not." She ticked them off on her fingers. "Collinsville, Edwardsville, Alton, Belleville, Cahokia, O'Fallon, Granite City—"

"Okay, okay, I get it. There's lots of people there."

"More than half a million."

"You're kidding. I thought there were just a bunch of sleepy little towns. At least that's what I see signs for from the highway."

"You gotta get out more, Monika. There's a whole different life over there. I'll bet you didn't know that we Germans have been in Belleville as long as you've been on the Southside."

"I didn't," I admitted.

"Belleville's a beautiful city. We have lots of churches like St. Louis, and historic old homes, too, but we're not so scrubby Dutch as you are. Also, when we meet someone new, we ask 'what parish do you belong to' instead of what St. Louisans ask."

"What school did you go to," I supplied.

"Right. We have something of a reputation, too. I'm sure you know what that is."

"Oh?"

"Come on, Monika, guess."

"Uh, I don't know."

"Surely you've heard of the lawsuit capital of the world, jackpot jurisdiction or judicial hellhole, depending on which side you're on. So...what else do we have?"

"Lots of lawyers!"

"Right you are. Personal injury lawyers come from all over to file their suits where they can get big settlements. We believe in taking care of the little guy."

"That's nice but isn't that what's made insurance costs jump, sending docs away? And isn't that why they're changing the law to cap settlements?"

"That's what the insurance companies would like you to think."

"It makes sense."

"Really? You see any of the insurance companies going out of business? Of course not," she went on. "They're using trial lawyers and the settlements—remember these guys lost in court because someone got hurt—as an excuse to try to get legislators to cap settlements, which in turn—"

"Benefits the insurance companies," I finished for her.

"I'll have to admit, there's some truth to it, though. When I worked in a hospital on the east side, we used to have an attorney who sat outside the ER, just waiting for potential clients."

"Why do you come all this way to work, then?"

"How far do you think it is?"

"I don't know, thirty, forty miles."

"It takes me about twenty minutes to get here. But I'm one of the few. Most of my nurse friends wouldn't 'cross the river' to work, even for more money. We are very provincial."

"Not unlike South St. Louisans."

We were walking out when Wanda said, "Cassandra and that other nurse look like they're in a huddle over there."

I told her Poppi had come to work for me a month ago.

"She any good?"

"Good? Better than good. She's quick at everything. Talks fast, works fast, a human dynamo."

"Oh, is someone a teensy bit jealous? No longer BWOC?"

"BWOC? What the H is that?"

"Big woman on campus."

"Of course not, I'm just glad to have someone so good working for me."

"If you say so. Maybe they know something," Wanda said, with a look in their direction.

"So what are you going to do? Go over there and ask them?" I said, laughing.

"I'd like to. That Cassandra gets around."

"Don't I know it."

"Watch out for her, Monika. I wouldn't trust her."

"I DON'T MEAN to complain," Jessie said, catching me before I went into the unit.

"What's wrong?"

"It's Missy." Her brown face creased in concern and she tucked a strand of gray hair into the bun at her neck. "I hate to tell on people but…when it involves patient safety…"

"What's happened? Did she hurt someone? Damn, Rosemary warned me!"

Jessie grabbed my arm to hold me back. "Wait. Everything's okay now. I caught her starting to suction John Doe."

"And? Come on, Jessie, tell me!"

"I heard the vent alarm go off and hurried in there. As his O2 dropped, that alarm went off as well. She just stood there as if she didn't know what was wrong."

"Is he still breathing?" I asked.

"I reached him in time and showed her what to do."

"What had happened?"

"She had unhooked his trach before she had everything ready and I don't think she had preoxigenated him either. She already had sterile gloves on when I came in. She had yet to hook up the catheter to suction."

"Where is she now?"

"She disappeared into the restroom, crying, I think."

"She should be, risking a patient's life like that. If he had died—"

"But he didn't, and I'll help her. She really wants to work here. That should motivate her."

"All right. But I'm going to talk to her first and lay out the consequences. She goes back to step-down if she can't cut it here. You let me know if she pulls anything else, okay?"

"Try to keep your temper, Monika. She's sort of fragile."

I didn't answer.

I found her in a stall, sobbing. I ordered her out.

"Do you know what you did? Do you know he could have died?"

She squeezed a wadded tissue in her hand and sniffed.

"Do you?" I demanded.

She nodded, tears filling her eyes again.

"You compromised your patient in several ways. First, you didn't have everything ready before you disconnected his trach from the oxygen pump. How did you think he'd breathe?"

"I saw Jessie do it that way." She dabbed at her eyes.

"No, you didn't. Jessie would have had her equipment and supplies all laid out first and she would have preoxygenated him."

"Huh?"

"You don't know what that is?"

"Extra oxygen?" she asked as if she wasn't sure of the answer.

"Finally you put on gloves before you did everything else. How did you intend to keep them sterile while you got ready?"

Her chin shot up. "You can't keep both hands sterile while you suction. One hand's clean, the other's dirty."

I slapped my hands together in front of her face and she jumped back as if I'd hit her. "Listen to me," I said, enunciating every word.

"You have one more chance. You screw up again, you're outta here!"

At that moment, I'd have fired her from St. T's if I'd had the authority. She was lucky I didn't.

Chapter 17

Wednesday, November 17, 1610 Hours

As I was walking out, glad that for once I was getting out of work on time, Steve Oblansky was crossing the street to the main entrance of the hospital. Again, the way he walked in a precise, military style reminded me of Rick. Although I hadn't seen Steve smile since his wife was so ill, I was sure that if he did he wouldn't squint like Rick had, with crinkling tiny laugh lines around his eyes.

I'd forgotten about their age differences, too. Rick had been twenty-two when I'd seen him last. Steve must be in his early thirties although his boyish face made him look younger. If he had lived, though, Rick would have been much older than Steve was now.

Steve spied me as the sliding doors to the exit swished open.

"Is she..." Steve began, his shoulders drooping forward. His face cleared when I shook my head.

"She's the same, Mr. Oblansky."

We moved aside to stand next to the life-sized poster promoting our upcoming gala. Smiling babies, happy elders, and a young boy on crutches were flanked by two physicians while a nurse hovered in the background.

"I thought yesterday that she looked better," he said, staring at me hard as if he could convince me that his wife was improving. "She looked just like she did at home and when I'd...wake up early and look over and see her sleeping. She doesn't have a mark on her, does she?"

A family of four, toting a plant and a basket of fruit, passed us.

"She'd be glad to know that she looks good. Not that she is vain. In fact, she's never realized how beautiful she is." He chewed on his lip and his eyes followed the family as they walked through the lobby toward the bank of elevators in back.

"I keep thinking about who did this. And why? She doesn't carry large amounts of money around with her, she works in a school, for godsakes, and I'm still struggling to make a go of my flight school." He ran a hand through dark hair, left mussed by the action.

"I keep going back to the bank. I even went inside and asked the tellers if they'd seen anything. The way they looked at me, I think I scared them. And they're probably shaky enough after they heard about Marian's attack. The police found the ring, by the way. It was still in her bag," he said, taking a breath, his nervousness making him run on. "They asked me if she had any problems." He stopped, worry lines creasing a hastily-shaved face. "Something had been bothering her. I just wish she'd told me what it was. If I got my hands on the guy who did this," Steve said and punched his fist into his palm. "Sorry, Monika, it's just that I can't think about what he did without feeling like I'll explode." He ran his hand through dark-brown hair, rumpling it.

"I can't imagine how hard this must be for you."

"I'm so lucky to have found her, finally."

"Finally?"

"We were high school sweethearts but lost track of each other. Then Marian showed up at our tenth reunion not long after her husband died. I was in the midst of a, let's say, acrimonious, divorce. And when I saw Marian again, well, that was that. When will you know something? Anything?"

"It's difficult to tell. She took a hard blow to the head."

"I thought they fixed everything in surgery. Tim told me about it. How they got the blood clot out, put the pieces of her skull back...I'm sorry," he said, his voice breaking. He took a moment to compose himself and then said, "Thanks, Monika. You and the other nurses have been wonderful."

"That's why we're here," I told him as we parted.

Bundled up against the wind in my parka, I hurried up the ramp in the parking garage. As I turned the corner, a car zoomed by me, its tires squealing on the pavement.

"Damn!" I muttered, jumping back.

For a brief second, the driver's face appeared framed in the windshield. It was Agatha's half-sister, Roberta. Her eyes intent ahead, she didn't seem to see me as she continued her mad dash down the ramp.

My hand shook as I unlocked Black Beauty. I slid onto the seat, sucking in her old-leather scent until my heart rate came back to something near normal. Black Beauty fired up without a sputter. She didn't like cold and sometimes was reluctant to start her engine, especially after she'd been sitting all day in the open garage. I drove slowly around the curves in the garage, thinking about what I'd just seen.

Why was Roberta in such a hurry? And what was she doing here anyway? Maybe she'd come back to see our John Doe again. But why? Had my call to her mother prompted her to visit him?

Fighting a traffic jam on Interstate 44 kept my mind off Roberta and, by the time I made it to my favorite convenience store, I was thinking about something else.

"You want random numbers?" a bored clerk with stringy hair flopping across a pimpled forehead asked me, already punching out my tickets.

"No."

He pulled the few tickets he'd already printed, laid them aside, and started over.

I told him the numbers I wanted. In order.

He gave me a look and an audible sigh before punching in each number with deliberate slowness.

I pulled my wallet out of my bag. It yielded seventeen dollars and some change. I hunted through my jacket pockets, coming up with quarters and two wadded ones. I counted out twenty dollars. The clerk scooped it up and put it in his drawer, handing me my tickets, which I quickly stuffed in my pocket.

Chapter 18

Wednesday, November 17, 2045 Hours

"WHAT ARE YOU looking at?" BJ asked, dipping her onion ring into a smear of ketchup. "You're coat's okay," she said. She waved toward the chair between us where I had piled my down jacket, scarf, and gloves under BJ's black leather uniform jacket. Her cop hat rested on top. She bit off a crunchy morsel and spoke around the food. "You're with a cop, remember?"

BJ had left me a message, asking me to meet her at O'Donnells, home of the best hamburger in St. Louis, possibly the world. Working the evening shift, she'd scheduled her dinner stop for six, barring any emergency calls. Two male cops had been sitting with her in a booth along the wall, but when I approached they had moved away to join a colleague at a nearby table.

"Don's working tonight?" I asked as the waitress returned with a refill on our drinks, beer for me, Diet Coke for BJ.

"He's teaching a class at the academy, and they've got me on desk duty." She grimaced.

I smeared spicy brown mustard on my bun and concentrated on lining up the onion slice with my hamburger. If BJ knew what was in that coat...I didn't need her yelling at me to know I should have restrained myself.

"Has Don heard any more about Mrs. Oblansky's attack? What about the glove prints on the tire iron?" I wrapped my hands around the generous bun, preparing for my first bite. "Anything on that?"

"Not yet. The guy who does them is on vacation."

"On vacation? Don't you have anyone else doing fingerprints?"

"He's the specialist. And a civilian, not a cop. Civil service, you know?"

"No, I don't. What's that got to do with it?"

BJ spread ketchup on her burger and mashed the top down. Beef juice squeezed out on the oval plate. "Civil service is for life," she said, biting into her sandwich. More juice dripped onto the tiny shamrocks that marched around the plate's edge.

"Oh, come on, surely if someone's not doing their job, they can be fired."

"They have to die before we can fire them." She wiped her hands on a napkin. "This guy is so slow; it'll probably be Christmas before they get anything back from him."

"So I suppose they're still thinking her husband did it?"

She rolled her soda bottle around on the tabletop and replaced it on the coaster decorated with an Irish coat of arms. "I haven't heard."

"But he's such a nice guy," I said, tossing an onion ring onto my plate.

"I'll introduce you to a nice guy," BJ said with a grin. "Come on, Monika, let me fix you up."

I waved her off. "No thanks."

"He's my new partner, divorced, no kids. I think you'd like him."

"It's just that Rick's been the only one and—"

"Don't tell me you were a..." she lowered her voice, "a virgin when you got married?"

"That's why we married."

"Where've you been, girl?" she whispered. "You don't have to have a license to have sex." She chuckled.

"It didn't take us long to figure it out. And it wasn't as if we hadn't...you know, fooled around." I kept my voice low but it wouldn't have mattered over the noise of the crowd around us.

"So how'd you put it off with all those hormones bouncing around your two bodies?" BJ asked.

"It wasn't that hard, um, difficult."

"So you're telling me you've only had sex with one man in your whole life?"

I nodded.

"Monika, you're too good for your own good."

I stared down at my plate. Congealed fat surrounded a stream of ketchup.

"You heard anything yet from your nurse in DC?"

"She said she'd go back on her next day off." I pushed my plate aside. "You know any more about our John Doe, if he's Karl Magnason or not?"

"Nope."

"I'm going to try Sister Agatha again Friday when she gets back. If I could find the wife, maybe she could come in and see him."

"What about Sister? She'd know her brother, wouldn't she?"

"For some reason she doesn't want to come to the hospital. And, besides, she's at a conference in DC. The girlfriend doesn't want to try to ID him at the hospital, either. She doesn't want anything to do with him." I drained my beer. "Someone's going to have to make a decision about keeping him on life support."

"What about the mother?"

"Mrs. Magnason was always making excuses for him, Agatha told me. Spoiled him, is what Aunt Octavia would say. I'm certain she wouldn't agree to discontinue life support. And if he has a wife and if we could find her, she'd have first right of decision."

"Unless the courts get involved. Remember that case in Florida? We had Congress and even the President intervening in that. So what happens next? The hospital decides to pull the plug?"

"Eee-gads, no. Not in a Catholic hospital."

"So you just keep him hooked up and hope he dies?"

"I really don't know. I suppose legal will get involved, maybe get a court order or something, the ethics committee may be on it, for all I know. For sure, they'll do something. It's costing them thousands a day."

"Might he just die?"

"He could but, BJ, we can keep almost anyone alive—if you call it living—indefinitely."

"Somebody better find out something before next week. That's when McNamara retires." She stood up. "Be back in a minute," she said, leaving.

Someone had turned the sound up on the news as the restroom door swung shut.

I grabbed my jacket, spilling BJ's cap on the floor. I snatched it up before pulling the tickets out of my jacket pocket. With a quick glance toward the hallway, I scrambled to put my jacket back under BJ's belongings. A burly man in the kitchen threw a ball of raw ground beef on the counter and smashed it with a spatula, scooping it onto a sizzling grill. The restroom door remained closed.

I spread my tickets out on the table. The TV screen filled with the tumbling balls and the first number popped up.

I sucked in my breath. The first number was a seven.

Two more numbers dropped.

"Yikes!"

My squeal caught the attention of two men at the bar.

"I've got two of them!"

"A hundred thirty million's a lot of juice," one man said, nodding approvingly.

"Not touching," I told them. Even though the seven and four weren't in order, I could still win a hundred thousand if I got two more.

We turned to the screen as the next ball scuttled down the ramp and settled into the tray. I slumped in my seat when the fourth number didn't match.

The fifth white ball fell into the tray.

"Oh, my god! I've got a forty-two!" I screamed, the ticket wobbling in my hand. I dropped it onto the table, smoothing the paper with my fingers. That's all I'd need—to destroy it and lose my winning chance.

I couldn't win the jackpot, but the four balls were worth $100. If I held the winning Powerball number, $5000.

The room was quiet as everyone turned to the television and several people crowded around my table. The guys at the bar joined them. "I think I'm in love," one of them said to the audience's laughter.

"Yeah, don't let your wife hear that," said his buddy, punching him on the arm.

I shushed them, waving toward the screen.

My breath came in spurts. Damn, I felt good!

"What's going on?" BJ demanded, her cop voice sending my audience scrambling to give her room.

"Here comes the Powerball!" someone said, and everyone in the room turned to the television, including BJ.

The Powerball rolled into place. "Eighteen," several people roared, turning to me.

I tossed the ticket onto the pile on the table.

"Well, you'll get something for three of them, won't you?" someone asked.

I stared at my winning ticket. Sure, I'd collect the hundred dollars but nothing like $130 million. I stuffed the paper in my pocket and wadded up the remainders. "It's just the lottery. That's not gambling," I told BJ, who was glowering at me with her hands on her hips.

"Yeah, and I'm not a cop."

Chapter 19

Thursday, November 18, 1005 Hours

"You try to get on that committee?" Wanda asked as we walked toward the elevator. We'd just come from the first meeting of the nursing management council, formed recently to give us an opportunity to help each other since most of us had found our administrative duties doubled. "I got a bad feeling about it."

"Huh?"

"The search committee for the new COO. A big corporation's trying to get their guy in is what I heard."

"What corporation? What are you talking about?"

"Don't you read the paper? A for-profit health care chain is looking for small hospitals to buy up and they've got their eye on St. Louis."

At my skeptical look, she raised her chin. "They're trying to get a foothold in the city and the first step is to get their guy into administration in a targeted hospital. Then when they make an offer, they've got a high-up honcho on their side." She nodded to a physician who passed us. "You should be on the search committee now that you're chair of the management council."

"I didn't need that, either." I gave her a glare. "I intended to nominate you for the job but you were too quick for me." She'd rallied the vote before I'd had time to respond. "So now you've got to help me."

"I got you into this. I'll do whatever you need."

"You better." I grinned. "My first action is to name you co-chair."

"Hey, wait—"

"I'll announce it next week. That way if I can't be there, you can substitute. It makes sense since we're meeting every week. Another of your bright ideas."

Cassandra came out of the restroom in front of us. "Oh good, I wanted to talk to both of you."

"Caught now," Wanda said under her breath.

"You have to make your staffs get their money in for the gala next month," she said. "We haven't seen many nurses sign up yet. I'm liaisoning with the auxiliary."

I groaned inwardly. Ordering my nurses to buy tickets to our annual fund-raising banquet and silent auction sponsored by the hospital auxiliary was the last hassle I wanted to give them even though the hospital would be the beneficiary of the proceeds.

"How come we don't get a discount like before?" Wanda asked. "Fifty dollars I could do even if I don't go, but a hundred? For a measly chicken dinner? No thanks."

Cassandra pulled her lab coat tight across her chest. "That was my recommendation. Nurses are well-paid these days and, after all, the hospital benefits from the proceeds."

"We're supposed to take money the hospital pays us and give it back?" Wanda asked. "That doesn't make any sense."

"I'll be there," I said as animated as I could to distract Cassandra before she followed Wanda's thinking to its logical conclusion: that instead of asking us to buy banquet tickets, the hospital should just cut our salaries. "With my family. We always come."

Wanda frowned at me. Encouraging the enemy, her look said.

Cassandra gave us a quick grimace that served as a smile and said, "Talk to your people. We need one hundred percent from the staff. And that means everybody, Wanda."

"Count me out," Wanda replied.

"I don't think she heard you," I said as Cassandra stopped a physician going by.

"It doesn't matter. I don't report to her. Besides, you ever hear of the word 'liaisoning?'"

As Cassandra turned away, a trail of something white fluttered behind her.

Wanda snorted and I tried to keep myself from laughing, turning around so I couldn't see her. "Do you think we should tell her?" I asked when I could get the words out between snickers.

"Nah, let's just enjoy it. Think about all the people who will see Her Highness before she notices." Wanda turned me back around to watch.

A long strand of toilet paper, originating from the waistband of Cassandra's pants, followed her like a waving tail.

"CONGRATULATIONS," JAKE LORD said when I told him about my election when we ran into each other a few minutes later. "That puts you on the ethics committee, and we have a meeting tomorrow."

"What time?"

"Seven a.m. in the CEO's conference room." Before he turned down the hallway to our right, I stopped him.

"What's on the agenda? Anything I should know about?"

"Oh, yeah. What to do about patients without insurance. And Hockstetter's going to be there." He gave me a backwards wave as he hurried off.

Coming off the elevator, I saw an argument in progress. A woman shook her finger at Tim as he stood, his arm barring her way into ICU. Nearly Tim's height, the woman's head bobbed as she gestured in jerky motions. With her back to me, I couldn't hear what she was saying, but every few words were interrupted with quick coughs. Before I could reach them, the woman turned and stomped by me, slamming through the stairway door. The door banged against the wall as the woman dashed down the stairs.

Tim's foot propped the door open and he waited for me.

"What was that about?"

"She wanted to see Marian Oblansky."

"Who was she?"

"A friend, she said. When I told her only family, she started arguing with me so I told her to come outside and—"

"She got inside the unit?"

"She was almost in the room when I caught her."

"And us with no guard on the room."

"Then she wanted to know how Mrs. Oblansky was and, when I couldn't say, she really blew her top." He pushed the door wider and motioned me inside. "Some friend. I told her to talk to the family if she wanted to know how Mrs. Oblansky was. You saw what she did then."

She was the same woman I'd seen coming out of ICU last Saturday.

CHARLOTTE WAS WAITING at the desk when I came back from the step-down unit with their budget. I had forgotten to reconcile it.

"I just heard about Nadine," she said, grabbing my arm. "Don't let her in, whatever you do!"

"Nadine?"

"Steve's ex. I can't believe she came here." Charlotte sank heavily against the counter.

I pulled Charlotte into the conference room and motioned toward a chair. "Lottie, sit down and tell me what you're talking about," I said when she continued to pace. "I can't help if I don't know what's going on."

Finally, she sat and I joined her.

"She stalked them. For months, even after she and Steve were divorced and he and Marian were married. She blamed Marian for the marriage breaking up, but it was on the skids long before they got together. She sat in her car across from Marian's school, just watching her. It creeped her out."

My mind skittered to the woman I'd just seen trying to get in. "What's she look like?"

"Tall, about my height. Spiky, grayish hair." She twisted her hands in her lap.

"Are you sure it was her? Did you see her?"

"I didn't need to. When Tim told me she had a nervous cough, I knew. Steve said they hadn't heard from her since they got the restraining order, so I thought she'd stopped. It was only good for thirty days, and I think that time's up." She fumbled in her bag and came up with a tissue. "And the phone calls. She kept calling and then hanging up if Steve or I answered. Please, Monika, do something! Keep her out!"

"You don't have to worry. Our policy only allows close family members in to see patients." That much was true. I didn't tell her we'd already failed to keep the woman out of the unit on two occasions that I knew about. "You told the police about his ex?"

"They think I'm just trying to cover up for Steve. They're only after him," she said, blowing her nose.

Tim stood in the doorway of the conference room and motioned for Charlotte to follow him.

"Keep her away!" she said, turning back to me, her hand on the door frame. "Whatever you have to do."

"THERE'S NO WAY to keep her out," the officer in security told me a few minutes later. "With all the entrances here, we can't screen people coming and going. You should know that, Monika."

I did know it was impossible to protect the hospital from intruders. Not if we wanted to encourage community goodwill.

I called Detective Harding. He was out but the woman who answered the phone asked if she could help me. I explained about the restraining order against Steve's ex-wife and her attempt to see Marian.

She put me on hold.

It was probably futile to try to get them to send an officer to guard her room again, but it was worth one more try.

I learned I was right when the woman returned to the phone.

"We don't have anyone right now, but I'll tell Detective Harding you called," she said, hanging up.

"A lot of good that will do," I said out loud.

"I'll take care of it," Ruby said, grinning.

"How? How are you going to protect Mrs. Oblansky? With your bare hands?"

She jiggled ring-bedecked fingers at me. "No, no, missy. I know how to lock them out."

"You're going to lock the outside doors?" I asked her. "The ones to patient rooms? Against Hockstetter's orders?"

"Never you mind. I'll handle it."

"You can't do that," I said, shaking my head. "It's a fire code violation."

"I think she called here." Ruby tapped a red-painted finger on the desk.

"Who?"

"His ex."

"You know about that?"

She tilted her head to the side, black topknot bouncing. "She tried to disguise her voice but she called a bunch of times and each time she sounded a little different but she had that," Ruby barked a couple of coughs, "every time. I passed her coming in," Ruby explained. She leaned back on her heels and smacked her lips. "Ain't I one fine de-tective?"

"You think it was the woman who called?"

"Who else?"

In the end I ignored what Ruby was doing to protect access to Marian. What was more likely? A fire in ICU or Nadine trying to get in?

I HADN'T EXPECTED Detective Harding to come to the hospital in response to my call so when he and his partner came through the door, my first thought was that they were here to arrest Steve. My second thought was that I was glad Steve had left.

"Detective Harding, you got my message?" I motioned for him to follow toward the back wall and out of Ruby's hearing.

"What message? You called me?"

"About Mr. Oblansky's ex-wife stalking them."

"We're looking for Mr. Oblansky," Harding said as Ruby pushed by us into the so-called clean utility room. Not exactly clean, nonetheless it held unsoiled equipment as compared to the dirty utility room next door where nothing in it was sanitary. Ruby stuck her cup under the spout of the ice machine and stood there, apparently waiting to hear what we would say next.

"Do you consider the ex a threat?" I asked.

Ice clanked into Ruby's cup.

"What's that smell?" Harding's partner asked. "Whew! It smells like—"

"Shit, it smells like shit," Ruby said, coming out. "'Cause that's what it is."

I moved them away and asked again, "Is the ex-Mrs. Oblansky a suspect?"

His partner blew his nose and spoke up. "We know about her."

"Mrs. Everhardt," Harding said. "We don't discuss our cases with civilians. "Have either of them said anything to you or your staff?"

"About what?"

"Any problems Mrs. Oblansky had, trouble at work or at home."

"Just that they had to get a restraining order against his former wife, but you know about that."

"Nothing else that you've heard?"

When I shook my head, he asked, "Is Mr. Oblansky here now?"

"Only the sister is in with her now," I said.

"The husband's not around here?" he asked. "Maybe went downstairs? Getting a cup of coffee? Anywhere in the hospital?"

"No. He's a flight instructor and he had a student pilot, he said so before he left."

"Has the husband been in his wife's room by himself? Without a nurse or her sister?"

"There are times when he's alone with her. Tim's her nurse, but he's not in there every second." I squinted at him. "Didn't you say you thought it was a random attack? That whoever did it was robbing her?"

"We've revised our theory," Harding's partner said, earning a frown from Harding.

Ruby came out with Charlotte, who blinked in the bright light, her sister's room dim by comparison.

As his partner asked Charlotte to step outside with them, Harding turned to me. "You need to make sure he's never visiting his wife's room by himself."

"What? How can we do that?"

"Just don't let him be alone with her," he said, following Charlotte and his partner out the door.

"Humph," Ruby said. "What's he think we do all day? Sit and watch her husband when he's here? Well, to think of it, maybe I'll volunteer to keep an eye on Mr. Handsome myself." She was still chuckling when I walked away.

"Do you know what budget variance is?" Hockstetter asked me, catching me on my way out.

What hadn't I done on the budget? I had turned it in, but it had been a rushed job.

"Negative variance, in particular?" he asked, his tone sarcastic. "You're using too many nurse hours per patient, way more than any other unit, and more than we budgeted."

"I don't remember a discrepancy like that. Are you using the ICU ratio of nurses to patients?"

"I'm sending it back to you. This time," he poked a finger in my face, "use the right figures."

"Do you know the street address?" the librarian asked me, leading me toward a shelf. "These are the Haines Directories." She flipped one open expertly and ran her finger down an inside page. "You can find the address, phone numbers, and total number of residences on the street. X marks the intersecting street, there's even a wealth code."

"Wealth code?"

"Average income."

How did they know that?

A slender, middle-aged woman with blond, graying hair cut becomingly around her narrow face, she pointed to a stack of directories piled haphazardly on top of a cabinet. She pulled several directories down and placed them on a nearby table. "You can start on these and then there's the telephone directories," she said, pointing to a shelf along the wall crammed with yellow and white-page directories.

"All these are for cities by the river?"

"It's a growing area. And, I might add, the best-kept secret in the metropolitan St. Louis area. I live on the east side myself," she added. "And I've heard all the jokes. 'You pack a lunch to get here?' they ask me." She nodded toward the library proper.

I thanked her and began with Alton, then Belleville where Wanda lived, Cahokia, Collinsville, Edwardsville, and Fairview Heights. No one named Magnason lived in any of the cities or at least they weren't listed in the directories. My stomach began to grumble as I stared at the three remaining directories for Glen Carbon, Granite City, and O'Fallon. I scribbled the three city names on the back of a check I tore out of my checkbook and hurried out.

As I pulled out of the library parking lot, I dialed information for the remaining Illinois cities and in a few minutes I had the answer. Unless she'd changed her name, Mary Ann Magnason didn't live on the east side of St. Louis.

Chapter 20

Thursday, November 18, 1755 Hours

I NOTICED THE blinking light on my answering machine midway into my ham salad sandwich. I'd fed Cat, cleaned her box, and read part of the paper before I'd taken my food into the living room to watch the news while I ate. The phone and answering machine sat on the table beside the sofa.

I wiped mayo off my hands and pushed the button.

"Monika, it's Camilla," her message began.

I muted the TV.

"I'm sorry it's taken me so long. I've had to work overtime, and it's been raining so I haven't gotten back to the Wall yet, but I've tracked down a veteran who was in your husband's unit." Her voice was calmly reassuring, like I remembered. "His name is Comstock, Rory Comstock, and he lives in Missouri. I don't know how far Fenton is from you, but I have his phone number." She repeated the number as I scrambled for a pencil. Cat had batted it onto the floor and was chasing it away.

"Give me that," I told her, grabbing the pencil.

Cat hung on by her teeth, but I jerked it out of her mouth and wiped her saliva off on my jeans. I pushed the replay button again and stopped in time to write down the name and number on the margin of the newspaper, tearing the strip away.

I stared at the words.

Did I really want to know what happened?

I pushed the button again and Camilla's voice went on. "I didn't ask you, but have you tried the Web? I think all the Vietnam vets, including those missing in action, are listed on the DOD website. Department of Defense," she added. "Anyway, good luck. I should be able to get out to the Wall this weekend. I'll call you then. Take care." She stopped. "I guess that's all." She hung up.

I finished my sandwich and blotted crumbs of barbeque potato chips up with a spit-moistened finger. Cat pushed my paper plate aside to climb on my lap. We sat that way, me stroking her, she purring until the phone rang.

A wrong number.

I dumped Cat on the floor and retrieved the knitting book Aunt Octavia had instructed me to buy. My first lesson was coming up on Sunday and I had yet to even open the book. Now I settled in, the book on my lap and two knitting needles and a skein of yarn in multicolored shades of purple on the table beside me. I pulled out a strand and rubbed it between my fingers. Then I held the package of velvet-soft yarn up to my neck, imagining the plush scarf I'd soon have.

Casting on. "First, make a slip knot," I read out loud. I pulled out a strand of yarn. "I can do that." Next, put one needle into the knot, cross over the needle with yarn and pull the second needle back out. Huh? I stared at the drawing and then at my efforts. I yanked the yarn off and started again.

I had just about mastered the casting on and was reading how to knit my first row when the phone rang again.

"Is this Mrs. Everhardt? Rick Everhardt's wife?"

"Uh, yes. Who's this?"

"My name is Rory Comstock, ma'am. A buddy of mine called me. He said a nurse friend of his told him you were looking for someone who knew your husband." When I didn't say anything, he continued, his voice soft and controlled, "Are you there? I don't want to bother you, ma'am, if you'd rather not talk about it."

"You knew him?"

"In 'Nam, yes. We were in the same unit."

Neither one of us said anything.

"You know what happened to him?" I asked, finally.

"I was there," he said, his voice muted. "I live just outside of Fenton. I'd be glad to tell you if you want to meet me."

"Will you be home on Saturday?"

"All day. Let me give you my address and directions."

We agreed I'd be there at eleven. Unless I changed my mind.

Chapter 21

Friday, November 19, 0920 Hours

I WASN'T SURPRISED to find myself the only nurse among four physicians; that wasn't unusual. What did take me back, though, were the number of administrators on hand. Redmond Hockstetter had been joined by three of his accounting staff, as well as Gary, his administrative assistant, and the facilities manager, Willard, who planned to retire as soon as we hired the new COO.

I soon found out the reason for their attendance.

Hockstetter asked one of the accountants to bring us up to date on uncompensated care costs, preempting Lord, who was this year's committee chair.

"Hey, this is the ethics committee, not finance," he said to Hockstetter, who smiled without mirth.

"You'll see in a minute," Hockstetter said as Gary passed out stapled reports.

The accountant pointed out the previous years' figures and then went over the first quarter of the fiscal year, which began 1 July.

"I'm no accounting genius," one MD said, "but even I can see we're eating a lot more for those who don't pay."

"Or won't," Hockstetter said, his lips set.

Lord stepped in. "What do you want this committee to do?"

"Glad you asked, Lord," Hockstetter said, pushing himself up on his seat. "You have one in ICU. No one seems to know who he is." He looked around at the group. "Tell them, Gary, how much his care is costing us," he said to his assistant.

"About ten thousand, give or take, depending on what meds and treatments."

"A day," Hockstetter added.

"I still don't know what we can do," Lord said, shuffling his notes for the meeting. "You don't expect us to get rid of him, do you?"

"That's exactly what I do want!"

"Where do you suggest?" Lord asked, his voice rising.

"There's St. Benedict's," offered a surgeon. "They take terminal cases with multiple conditions."

Hockstetter's assistant, Gary, shook his head. "They won't take anyone without insurance."

"Especially if we don't know his name," another doctor said, laughing.

"You aren't suggesting," Lord began, his voice close to seething. "You want us to...to..."

"Of course not, Jake." Hockstetter said. "But if he's terminal...think about extraordinary means."

A resident spoke up. "We've got to stop trying to keep them all alive forever."

"This is a Catholic hospital," Lord said. "We do everything we can. It's not our decision."

"Where's Father Gooden?" I said into the silence. "What would he tell us?"

One physician looked toward the door, another shoved papers into a folder, and a flush spread up Hockstetter's neck.

Lord answered me. "He's out of town at a meeting," he said, moving his large body in the small chair. "And Monika's right to remind us. He's on this committee. Would we even be having this discussion if Father was here?"

"You do what you think is right." Hockstetter stood and motioned for his staff to join him. "Remember, the survival of St. T's depends on all of us."

"And what if we get slapped with a wrongful death suit?" Dr. Heinrich, the neurologist consulting on John Doe's case, said as the door closed on Hockstetter.

"If not worse," Jake said. "Manslaughter."

Heinrich waved him off. "We're not going to do anything like that," he said to murmured approval.

The resident in attendance brought the coffee pot to the table and refilled cups all around. After that we got back to the agenda. Two research projects submitted by medical staff members were quickly approved.

The next item was to review the code system. Previously we'd used a method of A, B, and C codes to indicate decreasing levels of intervention to resuscitate patients after a cardiac or respiratory arrest. Confusion over which code had been ordered had led to a patient not receiving the appropriate intervention and he'd died, although his survival was unlikely regardless of anything the team could have done. Subsequently, we'd gone back to our original procedure of code or no code. Now, it seems, that was being disputed by a newer member of our medical staff.

"I've worked in bigger hospitals," she said, shifting in her chair to accommodate her belly distended by an advanced pregnancy. "Most of them are using some form of categorization."

"We tried that, it doesn't work here," said Dr. Heinrich, drumming his fingers on the desk. He studied his diamond pinkie ring glittering in the light.

"Harry, you always say that about everything," Dr. Norris said. "You don't want anything to change."

"If it's good enough—"

"Yeah, yeah, there's the right way, the wrong way, and St. T's way," Dr. Norris said to laughter.

"Let's table the code issue to next meeting and all give it some thought." Lord collected his papers, readying to leave.

Heinrich wasn't finished with me. "I've been hearing some things about ICU. Complaints. Lots of them." A tiny vein throbbed on his cheek.

The group quieted down.

"From Cassandra Wiggins, I suppose. What's she said?"

"You better shape up there," Heinrich said, standing. "Before you get a new boss."

Did he know something about the search for a COO?

"What was that about?" Jake asked as he followed me out. The others had gone ahead.

"Cassandra's just showing off to make herself feel important." I told him what Peggy had said about her skills. "For Hockstetter, maybe. In front of patients' families. I don't know. She's taking every complaint from a family member as gospel, but anything we say, she assumes we're trying to cover up our mistakes."

"She's the nurse liaison to the medical staff now," Lord told me.

"Is she liaison to everyone around here?"

To his puzzled expression, I explained her role with the auxiliary.

"The women in the auxiliary do a lot for St. T's," he said. "Most of the older doctors' wives are members, including retired docs' wives. And some of them stay active even after their husbands are gone."

"I appreciate what the auxiliary does. They donate a lot of money from their bake sales and such."

"Don't forget the gala next month. They get most of their money from that, and the silent auction."

"It's only Cassandra that's causing trouble, not any of those women in the auxiliary."

"Hockstetter seems to think Cassandra's doing a good job. I'd watch out, Monika. Hockstetter's holding all the cards now. I need you in your position."

I smiled as I watched him go. Why didn't we have more doctors like him? Or administrators, for that matter?

"Why didn't you just demand it?" Serena asked me. She stood with her arms crossed and a determined look on her face. She'd done something to her eyebrows. Dyed them black, apparently.

Jessie rolled her eyes and walked off.

I had told them about trying to get on the search committee for the COO. Gary had been firm when I'd spoken to him before the meeting. Hockstetter had put Cassandra on the committee, Gary had said, making it very clear that one nurse was all he'd allow to be on it.

"That's not how administration works," I told Serena.

"But they need you. They'd do it if they thought you'd leave. And she's not even a real nurse any more."

"You don't know administration," Tim said, joining the conversation. "They let everyone blackmail them like that, they'd have no control. There's only one thing Hockstetter really likes," he added, noting Jessie's signal that she needed his help to turn her patient. "And that's control."

"But you'd be so much better than that crabby Cassandra."

"Let it go, Serena, and get back to work."

I'd been distracted by what I wanted to do, and before anyone could catch me for anything else I made it into my office and locked the door. I'd had something important to do this morning. What was it?

In the meantime, I clicked onto the Web and Googled the U. S. Department of Defense. The official website popped up. Current news, recruiting information, veterans. That was it. No services for veterans, nothing about Vietnam veterans. I tried "v" on the menu but only got voting and victims. I put "Vietnam" into the search box.

Nothing.

Okay, so start over. I Googled "Vietnam veterans" and waited as it searched. With so many public records available online these days, surely the list was somewhere on the web.

Someone tried the door and, when I didn't answer, began pounding. "What you doing with your door locked?" Ruby yelled through the closed door. "Don't you have a meeting?"

Alert the staff about Nadine! That's what I'd planned to do. Before I'd left last night I'd told Ruby to call an emergency staff meeting for this morning. How could I have forgotten that? Too much on my mind and too much to do was no excuse for jeopardizing a patient and possibly my staff.

I reached around the phone cord to open the door.

"About time," Ruby said. "What you doing in here? Daydreaming?"

EVERYONE EXCEPT POPPI and one new nurse, who had stayed behind to watch the patients, were seated in the conference room when I entered. I'd scheduled the meeting for ten to give the staff time to complete AM care and finish rounds with the doctors before eleven when lunch hours started, lunch half-hours, to be correct.

"We know why we're here," Tim said, refilling his coffee.

"Ruby told us," Serena said.

Tim returned to the table and explained. "I described Oblansky's ex-wife to the rest here. They know about the doors."

"Will you get in trouble for that?" Serena wanted to know. "Isn't it against the law?"

"The fire code," Tim said. "I vote we ignore the code to protect our patient."

I nodded agreement and, after they had gone, I lingered at the table, marveling at my luck in having such a supportive staff. That they would keep the ex-Mrs. Oblansky out, I had no doubt. And that would keep all of us safe.

"You got a visitor," Ruby said, coming in.

Steve Oblansky waited outside, standing at attention, the skin stretched tight along his chin and over his cheekbones as if someone had pulled it up behind his head. "Lottie said you wanted to talk to me about Nadine," he said with effort.

I motioned him into the conference room and motioned him toward a chair. He hesitated a moment and then lowered himself into the seat and turned to me. "You can't let her in here! She hates Marian. If she saw her lying there helpless, I don't what she'd do."

He rubbed a hand down over his face as if to wash away his thoughts.

"Don't worry, I told Lottie we only allow family members and, now that we know about her, we know she's not a legitimate visitor."

"You don't know her. She's clever that way, the bitch! Pardon me, Monika. She might pretend to be some other patient's family. Or come late at night when no one's watching. You just don't know her," he added to himself.

"We're here around the clock and security has a guard on the unit during the night."

"What about the outside doors, the ones along the hall? Lottie told me she'd been coming in that way."

"That's been changed, too, after I learned about your ex-wife yesterday. Those doors are locked now."

"I don't know...you don't know her, how vindictive she is." His jaw clenched, he said, "If it was her, I'd kill her!"

"I'm sure the police are on it, Steve," I said quickly. "They'll look into it. What about the restraining order Lottie told me about? If you could get it reactivated maybe I could get another guard for the daytime." Even as I reassured Steve, I doubted that Chief Gerling would agree to it unless he thought he'd be in trouble with the city police.

"We'd have to go to court again," Steve said, "and with Marian like this..." He slumped into the chair, his head down, and his arms dangling between his legs.

Tim came to the door and motioned for Steve.

Before he left, I said, "We'll keep her safe, Steve, I promise."

My computer had shut itself down while I'd been gone so I rebooted and waited for it to complete the opening sequence. Could Nadine Oblansky be Marian's attacker? Surely Harding had investigated her and wasn't just concentrating on Steve as the culprit. If only we could keep Marian alive until the swelling in her brain went down and before the pressure did any more damage, maybe she would wake up and could tell us what had happened, who had attacked her.

"You got your phone off again?" Ruby said through the door.

"Oops."

"Well, get it on. You've got a call."

I let my web search for "Vietnam veterans" run again while I answered the phone.

122

"Have you found out anything?" Agatha asked, breathless. "Sorry, I just ran in the door from the airport and called you immediately. Have you made any progress yet?"

"I went to see that friend of Karl's, Val, the one you told me about."

"And?" Agatha asked.

"She didn't know anything."

"Did you ask her to come in to see him?"

"She didn't want to have anything to do with him, Agatha. I'm sorry."

"I'll do it," she said. "I'll come there."

I was surprised but I acted business-like. "We're on the fourth floor. Ask for me when you get up here. I'll go in with you."

TURNED ON HER side, with her wound undressed, Marian was not looking at all well. Tim had reported Marian's temperature was elevated and that she was sweating. Now I could see the yellow discharge oozing from the incision that sliced the back of her head into a jagged web of black sutures, a drainage tube sewn in place, its collection device carefully hung next to her ear. Another cable emerged from the incision, this one to monitor her intracranial pressure. It looked like a TV cable, albeit narrower. Her hair had begun to grow back, dark stubble scattered over a scalp swollen red and purple from the injury and painted orange with betadine cleanser.

"I got her temp down to 99.0 with rectal Tylenol," Tim said as we studied his patient. The ridge of one bony shoulder showed through her gown, her scapula, too, stood out from her gaunt body. We didn't need a scale to see that her weight had been steadily dropping.

"Just so we can avoid systemic sepsis," Tim said, going back to his work.

Infection unchecked spreads rapidly throughout the body by way of the bloodstream. In Marian's weakened condition, what's commonly called "blood poisoning," would be quickly fatal.

Tim picked up a sterile applicator, drew the end across the wound, placed the specimen in a plastic tube, and added it to several others already labeled as a technician from the lab entered to collect them. By culturing each specimen, the lab would be able to identify which different organism was causing the infection—or infections, if more than one—and, in turn, be able to determine what antibiotics would work best to combat them. But the greatest danger was infection in her bloodstream.

With a sigh, he tore open a package of sterile gauze and dipped it in a solution of antibacterial soap, carefully wiping in one direction with the gauze square.

"How's her pressure?" I asked Tim as I opened another gauze package and handed it to him, keeping my hand in the paper wrapper and the sterile gauze toward Tim.

"We've been maintaining it below 15," he said, referring to the safe level of intracranial pressure.

We continued that way until all the incisions had been cleaned. I was opening more gauze packages for Tim to use to rinse the incisions when Poppi came in to relieve me.

Charlotte was waiting for me. I explained that she'd have to wait to see her sister because the nurses were busy with her at the moment. Accustomed to our work schedule by now, she didn't complain. She told me that she and Steve were trading off visiting times. "So both of us can get some rest."

I cleared off a chair for her in my office and invited her to sit down.

"I wanted to ask you…" She snapped the magnet closure on her tan bag open and shut. She was visibly thinner and paler than she'd been when I'd met her more than a week ago. But that wasn't uncommon for family members of ICU patients.

I shoved papers aside on my desk, bumping against my keyboard. A photo of a GI's helmet, the ace of spades tucked into its band, popped up on the screen. I turned the monitor away from Charlotte and nodded to her to continue.

"If things get bad…will you let me tell Steve? He won't want to hear it. I don't know what he'll do."

"Do?"

"It's that macho stuff. Defeat the enemy at all costs."

"He's in the military?"

"He was a Navy pilot, and even though he's been out of the service for several years he still thinks like a military man."

"Who's the enemy? Her injuries?"

She tucked her finger under the clasp of the bag and pulled it open again, then clicked it shut. She patted the soft leather on her lap. "That's exactly what I mean."

"He doesn't seem like the macho type to me."

"He's not most of the time, but when he gets upset, instead of crying he gets mad. He wouldn't hurt anyone, but he might lash out—verbally—at whoever delivers bad news." She fingered the clasp again but left the bag closed on her lap.

"The police came to the house," she said.

"Oh? I thought they were talking to both of you when you're here instead of home in Illinois."

"They had a warrant to search the place."

"Oh no! Was Steve home?"

"He was here at the time, thank God, I had stopped by to check the mail, see if Marian had any bills to be paid. She handled their money since most of it was hers anyway. But then I had to tell him what happened." She shook her head. "When he realized they'd taken his laptop, he blew up and punched a hole in the kitchen wall. He needs the laptop for his business, which I tried to tell them, but they gave me a receipt and said he could have it back soon. They took a jacket of his, too, a nice black leather one that Marian had given him for his birthday. It was probably my fault."

"Your fault? What did you do?"

"When I talked to the detective, he had wanted to know if they had money problems. I told him not any more. Not since Marian's first husband died. But that was the wrong thing to say. I could tell by the look on his face that he was thinking that her money was a motive for Steve to kill her. But, Monika, he loves her! I know he does! It's so frustrating to talk to the police, though, they get an idea and won't let go. They grilled me about him. Did I think he was having an affair? Was she? Did they argue? Had I ever seen him hit her? When I told him I'd never seen her happier, I don't think he believed me."

"I believe it, Lottie. He seems devoted to her."

"I have to admit, though—and I feel guilty about this every time I think it—that I'm jealous of what they have. I know I shouldn't be bitter, but I never expected to be divorced. You know no man wants to date a divorced woman. They think she's a failure, and I think so, too, sometimes." She fiddled with the clasp on her purse, making it click several times over.

"Lots of people are divorced, Lottie. It's nothing against you when things don't work out."

"I know that in my head, but in my gut I feel like I should have tried harder. Enough of that talk," she said, straightening in her chair. "Marian's the one that matters now. She and Steve. She's been good for him. Especially after 9/11."

"What'd that have to do with him?"

"He's a flight instructor. When he got out of the Navy, he flew corporate planes, mostly, and had just obtained his license to be a flight instructor when they shut down all the airports."

"I thought that was just for a few days."

"Not for the small airports. And they closed all the flight schools. He had investigators all over the place going after his students, too. The FBI was looking at everyone taking flight lessons, you know."

"No, I didn't."

The magnetic catch clicked some more. "He was about to go bankrupt when Marian married him."

"That must have been tough."

"It was a good thing she could help. He'd just bought a plane and would have lost it if not for Marian."

"From her job? She's a school teacher, isn't she?" I asked, thinking of the admission record Steve had filled out.

"Librarian. School librarian. The money came from her first husband's death."

The tone in her voice suggested something I hadn't heard before. "You didn't like him?"

"Let's put it this way. She's better off with Steve."

THE DISTINCTIVE NASAL tone to Cassandra's voice alerted me to her presence on the unit although I couldn't tell where until Poppi shoved a curtain open and Cassandra stepped into the open room, hurrying toward the door when I stopped her.

"You're on the search committee for the new COO," I said. "Any progress?"

Cassandra circled her thumb and forefinger and drew it across her closed lips. "Can't tell," she said, leaving.

"You heard anything about the search, Ruby?"

Ruby mimicked Cassandra zipping her lips.

So she doesn't know.

ONLY A FEW feet away from the man who might possibly be her brother, Agatha waited by the nurses' station desk. Freckles stood out on her pale face but she stood tall, drawn in upon herself.

"Agatha," I said, warming her cold hands into mine.

She pulled away and wrapped her arms around herself. "I'm here," she said as if to assure herself.

"Let me ask you a question before we go in. Was he ever in the military?"

"Hardly. He never answered to authority. He was 'different.' That's what mother always said." Her eyes trailed around the unit and back to me. "Why do you ask?"

"Val said he told her he'd been injured in the Army, but the police took his prints and my police officer friend told me that it's routine to check fingerprints against military records."

"Truth-telling wasn't his strong suit."

"Are you going to be okay?" I asked.

She'd laced her fingers into a prayer-like clasp, her knuckles standing out white. "It's the smell," she said, hunching down inside her coat.

I've heard other people talk about how a hospital smells but I've never noticed it. Not only because I spend every working day here, but because, if I think about it, the smell is pleasant. It reminds me of laundry dried outdoors and heavy with starch. Aunt O told me once that hospitals smelled like that to her, and I've thought the same ever since.

"I can never smell it but remember…" She squared her shoulders. "I can do this," she said.

"I should warn you, though, he looks pretty bad, lots of tubes, equipment." I stopped when I saw her swallow. "Are you sure you want to see him?"

"I need to do it for Mother."

"Okay, let's just peek inside." With one hand firmly under her arm, I pulled the curtain aside with the other.

She looked at the man in the bed for a few moments and turned away. I let the curtain drop back into place.

"It's not him," she said.

Her words implied certainty, but her inflection had made them sound like a question.

"You're not sure?"

She stared at the closed curtain for a moment. "I can't be certain but, no, I don't think the man in there is my brother," she said. "He's way too skinny."

I led her out to my office and when we were seated, she asked, "Can't you do DNA tests to be sure? Compare his blood with Mother's?"

"I haven't heard anyone suggest that, but I'm sure it's expensive, although maybe not more expensive than what his care is costing," I thought out loud. "However, I don't know if that would help. If his DNA didn't match your mother's, we still wouldn't know who he is. I think they'd have to be fairly sure that he was likely to be your brother before they'd risk the expense. And then what would that give us? He can't pay for his care, can he?"

"Mother has some money."

"From the 9/11 settlement?"

"Oh, I see," she said, opening her coat. "If he is Karl, she'd have to return the money his wife gave her from the settlement and, yes, that's about all she has."

"She's not liable for his bill, in any case."

"Roberta probably wouldn't let her use it for him anyway. Have you seen the house? It needs repairs, but Roberta's kept Mother from spending anything on it."

"I did check to see if I could find his wife, but she's not living anywhere in St. Louis, including the east side. At least not that I could find."

"Thanks, Monika, for trying to help." She rebuttoned her coat.

"We still don't know for sure."

"That's okay. You've got enough to do. I appreciate all you've done for us."

"No, wait. Why don't you see if Roberta can find a phone number or an address for Karl's wife?"

"She's probably moved and, anyway, what good will that do?" She pulled beige woolen gloves out of her pocket.

"I could ask her to come in and see him."

"I don't know, Monika. Even if you can find her and she did agree to come in, she'll probably be like the rest of us, not sure."

"Come on, Agatha. We've come this far. I hate to give up when there's still a chance we can identify him or find out for sure that it's not him. Don't you want to know?"

"I do," she admitted. "But you've spent so much time already—"

"Hey, what are friends for?"

"Okay, I'll try. I planned to stop by the house this afternoon. I'll see if I can find anything about Mary Ann. I'll let you know."

After she left, I resumed my search for Rick's name on the DOD website.

"What the?" I said as my monitor blinked and a blank screen popped up. I wiggled the mouse but nothing happened. I checked the plugs and all were connected. As I raised back up, Ruby stuck her head in the door.

"System's down," Ruby said unnecessarily. "Again."

"They say when they'll have it fixed?"

"Don't ask me. It fixed when it fixed."

I stared at the screen, clicking ineffectively. Finally I stretched my arms above my head. Why wasn't Rick's name on the Wall? From his tone, his buddy knew what had happened to Rick, and I'd learn about it soon enough when I met him.

"I THINK HE can," Father Gooden told me in response to my question. I'd caught him coming in the door as I was leaving.

"You mean Hockstetter can just order us to disconnect someone's life support? Just like that?" I said with a snap of my fingers.

He unwrapped the gray and blue scarf from around his neck and loosened the top button of his gray overcoat.

"I'm sorry, Father, I just remembered you've been out of town. You're probably tired."

"Not too tired to talk about this." I followed him back through the lobby and down the hall toward the chapel and to his office next to it. "If no one's paying for a patient's care," he said, unlocking his door, "Hockstetter might be able to order life support shut off."

"But you're not sure."

"I only know what happened in Texas; I don't know if it'll apply here."

"What'd they do in Texas?"

He piled a soft-sided black attaché case on top of his coat that he had laid across the desk. "The governor ordered a man's life support turned off," he said, "even though his family disagreed."

"How in the world could he do that? Didn't the family fight it? Go to court?" I shifted my bag, still stuffed with the mail I had yet to read, up on my shoulder.

"No one could pay his bills was the reason. People in health care ethics still talk about that case even though it's been several years." He plopped down in his chair and leaned forward to turn on a green-shaded lamp on the desk. Light spilled onto the glass-covered top and reflected back up under his chin, leaving his face in shadow.

"What happened?"

"They turned off life support and the man died." He removed his glasses and rubbed his eyes.

"What will you do if Hockstetter tries that here?" I asked as he folded his glasses and put them into a hard-covered case he'd taken from the top drawer. "These are the tough questions, aren't they,

Monika?" He steepled his fingers in front of him and leaned back. "I would, of course, argue strenuously against such action, but I'm a realist. Hockstetter's got to do something to rein in the skyrocketing costs of care. We don't want to have to shut our doors, do we?" Putting his hands down on the desk, he asked, "My question to you is, what would you do? Would you assist in this action? What would you tell your staff? That they should help? Just accept it?" he added, opening his hands, palms up.

"I hadn't thought about it."

"You'd better. Hockstetter's not known for his patience."

Chapter 22

Friday, November 19, 1845 Hours

THIS TIME VAL was alone behind the empty bar and she gave me a half-smile when she saw me.

"Remember me?" I asked. "The nurse from St. T's?"

She flipped a towel over her shoulder. "You're trying to find out if your patient is Karl," she said, retying the knot in the man's white shirt she wore bunched above her waist. She took her time rolling her sleeves, one at a time, up to her elbows. "I remember." She placed a cocktail napkin in front of me.

I took the hint and ordered. "Busch Light." I pulled out a twenty and spread it open beside the napkin.

"You still looking for information?" she asked, eyeing the twenty.

"You remembered something?" I asked while her back was turned, drawing a beer out of the cooler.

She popped the top on the bottle and set it in front of me. "Maybe," she said with another glance toward my money. I put another twenty on top of the first and pushed it toward her. Then I took a swallow of beer.

Two men were playing pool in the back but I couldn't hear what they were saying. The television was on but the sound was turned down. She leaned forward on her elbows and her shirt, unbuttoned to her mid-chest, drooped open. "I got a call," she said, propping her chin in her hands.

"I heard. On 9/11."

"Not that call. Last week sometime. It was from some guy said he was Karl." Her voice shook a little at the last. "I figured it was someone playing a joke on me—a bad joke—someone who knew Karl and called me pretending to be him." She straightened up and wiped her hands on the towel still draped over her shoulder.

"When was this?"

131

"Let's see, today's Friday. I think it was Wednesday a week ago. I got the message when I got home from work."

"What'd he say?"

"Just that he was in Mexico and was coming home to get what was owed him."

"What do you think he meant?"

"Well, first of all, I don't think it was Karl."

"Did you recognize his voice?"

"I don't know. To tell you the truth, I don't think I can remember what he sounds like. I hate thinking that—that I've forgotten so soon but…" She studied the bar in front of her. "Anyway, whoever it was said not to tell anyone he was alive—"

"Doesn't that make you think it was Karl?"

"No, any jerk would say that if he wanted to pull something on me."

"But why? Why would anyone do it? It sounds just too cruel."

"Yeah, well, those guys ain't known for their 'sensitivity.' Anyway the guy says he was coming back for the money and he wanted me to go with him after he got it."

"What money?"

"I suppose the 9/11 money his wife got. But what I couldn't understand was why it took him this long."

"If he was out of the country—"

"The country? He was in Mexico, Missouri," she said, referring a town west of St. Louis.

"How do you know that?"

She flipped the towel off her shoulder and began to wipe the already-clean bar. "I don't know. That's just what I thought."

"There's one way to settle this," I told her. "Come in and see him. See if you recognize him."

She fingered the two twenties and then they disappeared into her cleavage. "I'll think about it."

Driving home I thought about what she'd said about Karl's voice. Would I recognize Rick's if I heard it now? I didn't know if I would. That made me feel sadder than knowing he was dead.

Chapter 23

Friday, November 19, 1925 Hours

"I KNOW MORE than I did before," I told BJ, shoving newspapers off a corner of her couch. Strips of wallpaper still covered the splattered drop cloths on BJ's cluttered the living room floor. The pile had grown since I'd been there on Tuesday.

"Don told me about your idea that the ex of Oblansky's husband may be stalking her," she said, picking up a round blue plastic tool that fit flat into her palm. "Know what she does?" she asked, turning back to me, one foot perched on the ladder in the corner. "She's a parish secretary at St. Augustine's," she said, answering her own question.

"That doesn't make her a saint," I said. "And they did have a restraining order against her. You have to have some proof to get a judge to order one, don't you?"

BJ propped her tool on the ladder's shelf and turned around to sit on the step. "Not much, a simple allegation will do it for the short-term, thirty days. To cover a year, you have to have more indication of a potential threat, like a history of domestic violence or criminal activity. Your parish secretary wouldn't fit into that category, I don't imagine."

"Even so," I said, unwilling to give up on Steve's ex-wife as a suspect, "the sister said Marian was still getting phone calls."

"Was someone threatening her?"

"The sister didn't know. She said whenever she or Steve answered, the person would hang up. They assumed it was his ex."

"Or a wrong number. Monika, you're reading way too much into this."

"That's not all. Steve said Marian was worried about something recently."

"He say what?"

"He didn't know."

She rubbed a spot on her finger and studied the results. "If I tell you something, you're not going to go off half-cocked on this, too, are you?" she asked, pointing at me.

"Just tell me, BJ."

"Harding has found a witness. Someone who saw Mrs. Oblansky talking to a man in the bank parking lot. I think he was pulling into the bank. But it wasn't much help. The guy wore a dark jacket and a black knit ski cap. He thought they might have been arguing but the man wasn't sure. He couldn't identify him in any case. And your Mr. Oblansky doesn't have an alibi, did you know that?"

"He told me he was at home that morning."

"Yeah, and no one to corroborate his alibi, was there? No phone calls, no one stopping by, no nosy neighbors?"

"I don't know about that. I don't have anyone to corroborate my story about where I am when I'm home."

BJ stared at me. "And you're not a suspect either, Monika. What's with you? Why are you so sure this guy didn't do it? Other than he seems concerned about her, which is reasonable because if she dies he could be charged with murder. You know his motive, don't you? She has money, Don told me."

"Well, here's something you don't know," I said as BJ climbed to the top rung of her ladder and studied the wall in front of her. "It's about our John Doe." I told her about Sister Agatha's visit to the hospital and that she didn't think the man was her brother.

"Think? She wasn't sure?"

"It has been several years since she saw him last, and he's all swollen, but she said he was too skinny, and that she didn't think it was him."

"So you know diddly," she said with a smirk, turning back to her wall. She ran the blue plastic tool over an arm's-length section of wallpaper. "Look at this," she said, leaning back. "Ain't it great?"

"What good is that?" I asked, coming closer to see. Pinpricks dotted the swath where she had rolled her tool.

"Here's the best part." She grabbed a sponge out of the bucket balanced on the fold-down tray of the ladder, squeezed it slightly, and smeared liquid over the perforated paper. "Now when I wet it, more solution gets underneath and loosens the paste, making it easier to get the paper off."

A tangy smell permeated the air.

"Ugh, what's that?" I asked, coughing as I backed away.

"Wallpaper stripper," she said. "You need some water?" she asked as I continued to cough.

"Not as long as I stay away from that solution." I waved my hand in front of my face. "What is it anyway?"

"An enzyme powerful enough to cut through years-old gunk. The holes let it get underneath." She tucked her scraper beneath a torn corner of paper and pushed. "Voila!" she said as a strip, several feet long, came loose and fell to the floor. She climbed down and wiped her hands on a rag, taking a seat on a rung of the ladder.

"Doesn't it bother you?" I asked, clearing my throat.

"Apparently not. They told me at the wallpaper store when I went there yesterday to see if they could help me get this paper off any easier that the enzyme stuff might choke some people, but it hasn't bothered me. And they sold me this scoring tool. It's called a paper tiger. See these points around the edge? They puncture the paper as I roll it around on this wheel underneath. Ingenious, eh?"

"How long's it going to take?"

Only a few strips remained on the wall where BJ was working, but she had two more walls to go.

"I'm done for tonight," she said, wiping her tools and placing them on the floor in the corner.

I followed her into the kitchen. "They've tried everything," she said, soaping her hands at the sink, "to try and find out who your John Doe is." She scrubbed at the stains on her fingers. "Directories, databases, every which way to rule him out and he's just not there. Whoever this guy is, he's under the radar."

"Could he be Mexican?" I asked as she dried her hands on paper towels.

"He look Mexican?" She wadded the paper towels and tossed them into an open trash bag.

"Not at all, but his girlfriend told me someone called her, pretending to be him and saying he was in Mexico. She thought Mexico, Missouri. Like most St. Louisans," I added.

"Yeah, they think the world ends at the state line."

"And at the Mississippi."

"She said someone called her? What makes her think it wasn't him? Especially now that there's some guy in the hospital who could possibly be him."

"She seemed fairly certain the call wasn't from Karl."

"Look, Monika, just give it up. You've tried, we've tried."

"I promised Sister. I can't stop now."

"Okay, I get it. You're going to keep playing the religious card so I might as well give up right now. You make a promise to Sister, you made it to God," she said.

I shrugged into my jacket and rummaged in the pockets for my gloves, smiling to myself.

"I do have one thought," she said as she followed me out. "I don't know if anyone checked his taxes. If he filed them. But that's a long shot. He's running from the cops, he's not exactly an upright citizen. But, on second thought, you'd be surprised how dumb some of them are. If he worked for someone who took out taxes, he might think he could get a refund."

"That's an idea, BJ. It's something anyway. But how would I check that. I can't just call up the IRS and ask. But you can."

"Not me, kiddo. You need someone with the authority."

"Don? Would he do it, do you think?"

"Mess with someone else's case? In his own backyard? No way. He didn't get to be detective by coloring outside the lines." She opened the door for me and followed me down the stairs to the front door.

"But I have an idea. You remember Kevin Short? He went to school with your cousin, Roger."

"My cousin's husband," I corrected.

"Whatever. He's a postal inspector now. I ran into him on a case once. I'll bet he'd help you find out if the guy filed taxes."

I pulled on my gloves and dug my keys out of my jeans' pocket.

"Why don't you ask Roger for his friend's number. All the guys from St. Mary's keep in touch. See if Kevin will help you." Outside she turned her eyes straight into me. "But promise me one thing."

"Yeah, what's that?"

"That if you don't find anything after this, you'll let it go."

"No promises," I said, waving her off.

Chapter 24

Saturday, November 20, 1005 Hours

BLACK BEAUTY WAS as reluctant as I was to take this trip; she didn't want to start. Cold weather made her cranky and the dampness of the day didn't help either. At last her engine caught and I made my way through my neighborhood toward the interstate.

While I had resolved to put thoughts of the hospital and our patients aside to concentrate on my trip this morning, I wondered again if I really wanted to know any more about what happened to Rick. He hadn't come home and besides my trip to the Wall I'd tucked my memories away along with his letters in the trunk stored in the basement. Now Rick's friend was making him come alive again.

I felt the way patients tell me they feel when they're facing surgery: they want it over with but they don't want to go through it.

The weather, gray and overcast with intermittent spurts of rain, didn't help my mood. I slid onto the interstate just as the clouds broke and the rain began in earnest.

The traffic slowed and my mind went back to Rick. I had never been able to picture him in Vietnam. When I thought of him he was always at home with his family or mine, celebrating something—a birthday, or Thanksgiving or Easter. He'd always been able to find a reason to get together. Full of fun wherever he went, Rick was the heart of his family—the oldest—and he was adored by his younger siblings. And he in turn adored them.

Darn. I hadn't been paying attention and I'd missed the turnoff. At the next exit I swung off at the ramp, turned left onto the overpass, and made my way down the reverse ramp and back onto the interstate, heading back toward the city.

"Turn right at Richardson Road," he'd said, which would be a left turn now from the direction I was traveling. "Take it for about two miles, then right into the trailer park. I'm the fourth trailer on the left," I read from my note.

Richardson Road turned out to be one long strip mall of used car lots, heavy equipment rentals, storage bins, storefronts offering payday loans, a dollar store, nail salon, salvage company, bridal shop, auto parts store, a thrift shop, and the ubiquitous fast food places that locate themselves along such roads. Finally the retail businesses petered out and I found myself driving through the countryside, stands of trees interspersed with open meadow.

I rounded a curve to face the trailer park on my left. It seemed out of place, as if someone had scraped away the underbrush and dropped a dozen oblong boxes into the clearing. A row of mailboxes perched on a wood shelf near the entrance. A large dog tied to a stake in front of a trailer near the entrance eyed me as I inched Black Beauty towards Mr. Comstock's trailer.

I parked to the side of the trailer and fiddled with my bag, stuffing the directions back inside and taking a drink from the water bottle I'd brought along. I could still back out. He and I had both known Rick but in very different ways, almost as if we'd known two different Ricks. The Rick he knew might not be my Rick. I wanted my memories intact, thank you very much.

And then he was there, in the doorway, waving me in.

Too late to turn back now.

A damp flag drooped near the front corner of his trailer. Dead geraniums languished in stone planter, and a folded aluminum chair leaned against freshly-painted siding.

"Rory Comstock, ma'am" he said, ushering me inside to the one large room that served as both living room and kitchen, the exterior wall punctuated by the front door. The man towered over me, his face roughened by age, his graying hair cut close. He was dressed in a plaid flannel shirt open over a snug Army-green T-shirt, faded jeans, and comfortably-worn sneakers. He took my raincoat, hung it on a hook by the door, and motioned me toward a sofa positioned under the front window in the clean, but sparsely-furnished, room. He offered me coffee. "Freshly-made," he said.

"That'd be good, thanks. And, please, call me Monika," I said, taking a seat and sinking into the soft black leather sofa. A battered cardboard box stood open on the table in front of me.

He brought our cups of coffee to the table in front of me, sat down in the recliner opposite me, leaned forward, and asked, "Now, ma'am, Monika, what can I tell you?" He picked up his coffee and cradled the cup in his hands. "You must be sort of scared to hear this."

I turned my head away as I felt my throat close up. I didn't want sympathy. I just wanted to get this over with. I took my time pouring cream and stirring sugar into my cup, the spoon rattling as I placed it on the table. "Tell me," I said, straightening. "Everything."

Time to head straight into the OR. Without anesthesia.

"Rick was a great guy," he said, "but then you already know that. He was fun, kind of took things as they came. When we needed him, though, he was all business." Rory rubbed his head and went on. "But you want to know what happened. I guess the Army never told you."

"Two of them came to the door one Sunday morning. All they said was he was 'killed defending his country.'"

"I've got a son in the Army now. I can't imagine how terrible that must have been. You have my condolences, ma'am."

Coffee sloshed in my cup so I put it down and clutched my hands together between my knees.

"You sure you want to hear this?"

"I need to know," I said with conviction.

He put his cup down and leaned back, staring out the window for a moment. "I met a kindred spirit in Rick. We had both volunteered for the Army, and we were both gung ho. Not gung slow, like many of the guys. All they could think of was how to get out."

"Did they?"

"Nah, the Army took everyone they could draft and kept them all, screw-up or not. Some guys in trouble were offered a year in jail or join the Army. They joined the Army.

"When they offered special training, we both volunteered. Ranger training, they warned us, would be hard, only for the toughest of the tough. And they were right. But, man, it felt good when other guys flunked out and you were left standing. Weak, but still upright. That's all that counted."

"I remember how proud Rick was when he made it."

"Our Ranger Company was attached to a larger brigade, one made up of regular infantry soldiers. That's when I met Rick—we were in the same platoon—and discovered we were both from Missouri and also that we'd had basic training at Ft. Leonard Wood, 'fort-lost-in-the-woods' we called it." He drank some coffee. "What do you know about what Rangers did?"

"Rick said he'd have to kill me if he told me."

"Ah, we loved bragging about that, and it was a way to keep up morale in the unit, especially before a mission. We were specially trained and never let the other grunts forget it.

"Our history goes back to 1670 when Ranger units helped defeat the Indians, but we officially became organized as Roger's Rangers in the French and Indian War in the 1750s and 60s. Rangers have changed the face of history in conflicts ever since."

"Most people hadn't heard of them when Rick was training."

"That's what we want, to keep a low profile, because Rangers usually go behind enemy lines. Our primary job is recon—reconnaissance—finding out where the enemy is, what strength he has, identifying potential targets, and sometimes handling extraction of one of our own. The Army started training 'LRRPs' early on in Vietnam," he said, pronouncing the acronym as lurps.

"Long-range reconnaissance patrols. In 1969 the brass realized the value of having such assets and LRRP companies became known officially as U. S. Army Rangers.

"By Army standards, we weren't regular soldiers. We dressed differently, used different weapons, including those captured from the enemy, and we weren't too careful to follow regular Army protocol. But we were the best fighting forces the Army had. We could move around in the bush and no one knew we'd been there. We could travel through any kind of terrain without making noise or leaving a trail. Not only did we sterilize the area—"

"Sterilize?"

"Erase every trace of our presence as if we were never there. We would even fluff up the grass behind us to obscure our footprints.

"Mostly we dropped in by helicopter. We could disappear into the jungle before the pilot had time to lift off if he had touched the ground at all. As a diversion, the pilot might do a couple of phony landings before and after our actual drop.

"When we weren't out on recon, we were training. Constantly. Even the experienced guys practiced all the time. It was necessary to keep our edge. To be prepared in case the enemy discovered our platoon we practiced 'break contact drill,' a system of rapid fire in precise order to fool them into thinking they'd been ambushed or confronted by a larger force."

"How many men were in a platoon?"

"Ranger companies were made up of three or four platoons. Typically platoons consisted of three squads of seven or eight rangers in each. Team size varied depending on the METT-T—mission, enemy, terrain, troops, and time—teams might include one squad or several. And teams had differing assignments, again based on the mission. One team might secure the landing zone, another prepare an ambush site, and another establish a security position.

"Rick and I were often on the same team, with one or the other of us the team leader or assistant leader for that mission. Missions could last for days, weeks even.

"You know our motto? 'Rangers lead the way,'" he answered before I could respond."

"Rick was proud of that."

He stopped to take another sip of coffee. "I'll heat that up for you, mine's getting cold." After he'd poured us both more coffee, he said, "But you want to know what happened. Sorry, sometimes I get carried away. Memories," he said. "I have some pictures, too, that I'll show you," he said, motioning toward the box on the table in front of me.

"One night when I was on point—the lead guy—I heard some voices in the grass, right outside a village. We didn't expect any mines that close to the village so I motioned for the guys to follow in right behind me. There was just enough moonlight in the clearing to see, and one of the new guys behind me giggled. The two teenagers who'd been having sex jumped up, the boy obviously not done."

I squirmed in my seat.

"As they grabbed their clothes and ran off, one of the men said something about 'animals' but I realized just the opposite. It was the first time I really thought about the Vietnamese as people like us."

A small, black kitten emerged around the corner of the kitchen, stretched, and yawned. She spied Rory in his chair and bounded up onto his lap. Rory introduced us. "Nightmare," he said, "'cause she keeps me up at night. Or did, till she got used to me."

The kitten clawed himself on Rory's flannel shirt, then turned around several times and curled herself into a ball on his lap and closed her eyes.

"Our platoon leader was Lieutenant Shephorn. He was a good guy, a good leader, not like some. He was willing to go right out there in front to lead. One night we were out on patrol and when we heard enemy soldiers nearby, we set up a hasty ambush and were able to mow a bunch of them down but there were too many, a couple dozen or so.

"Only one man was injured, the lieutenant. We radioed for help but the medevac chopper took more than an hour to get to us. Said they'd been spotted and had to take evasive action before coming back, but finally they got there. Lt. Shephorn was barely breathing by then. He died before they could get him to the hospital.

"After that, morale was in the pits. The platoon felt like no one cared what happened to them. One guy refused to go back out. 'What are they going to do me?' he'd said. 'Send me to 'Nam?' Last I saw of him, the MPs had him in the back of their jeep.

"Rick and I, though, we tried to keep everyone's spirits up, telling them that's what the lieutenant would have wanted us to do. It seemed we were making some progress—a little less grumbling, not so many fights breaking out—when the lieutenant's replacement arrived.

"All full of himself, he was, but really he was just another REMF—rear echelon mother fucker—I beg your pardon, Mrs., uh, Monika. Sometimes I get to talking about it and I forget."

I waved away his concerns and decided against his offer of more coffee. My stomach was in knots already.

"We helicoptered into an area one night with only a five-man team. That happened more and more toward the end. Too many had been killed to make up a full team. A Kit Carson scout—that's a North Vietnam turncoat—had reported this spot where we could find a stash of weapons and explosives. More than anyone had captured yet. There was no stopping Lt. Masters after he heard that.

"Up until this time we'd go over and over our plans, sometimes for a week or two before actually taking action. But as the war wound down a new officer who wanted to earn a promotion might take more chances.

"The usual procedure was to verify a source with a recon plane, but Lt. Masters didn't want to do that—wanted his men to have 'eyes on.' He thought it was better to actually see something than have surveillance photos. So he ordered us to proceed with the mission. As usual, he stayed behind in the rear somewhere.

"But it was a trap. Before we could escape into the jungle, we were hit. Hardcore North Vietnamese. The first man to go down was our radio man—they always try to get him because he's usually close to the officer in charge. I could hear the other radio man frantically calling for help but I was pinned down by fire.

"Combat time is not the same as real time. When you're lying there waiting to be shot, seconds seem like minutes and after only a few minutes you think hours have passed. The other thing about combat time is that when you're the one doing the firing, you can run through a magazine of rounds in a millisecond, even though you know that's not possible.

"When I was sure they were gone, I crawled through the grass to see who was hurt. Rick and I were the only ones not hit. One guy took it in the belly but was still alive; all the others were dead. We got the radios and continued to request extraction.

"Rick and I advanced to the LZ—landing zone—carrying the wounded man who was by then unconscious, and dragging our dead comrades. It was slow going. We had to stop and move a few yards with one man, then go back and get another, and so on.

"Rick went back to get the last body—our most recent replacement—Pfc. Johannsen. Small-arms fire erupted. I didn't know what happened but there was definitely an exchange. I waited after the firing stopped." He looked down at Nightmare on his lap and put his hands protectively over the sleeping kitten. We sat that way until he cleared his throat, swallowed, and went on.

"It was starting to get light and I knew the chopper would be landing soon. Rick still hadn't returned. I started dragging my dead buddies—they were all dead by then—hoping to meet up with Rick at the LZ. I had just reached the clearing when I heard the whop, whop of chopper blades.

"Enemy fire came out from the edge of the LZ, but the door gunner returned it and the pilot was able set down. When the crew and I had all the men on, the pilot started to lift off. I screamed for them to wait, that we had a man left behind..." Rory pulled the recliner upright and Nightmare jumped down from his lap. "I never saw him again."

I felt numb, as if I were listening to a story about a war movie with actors pretending to be heroes.

"I'm sorry," Rory said. "I've always thought I should have gone back and looked for him." Tears gleamed in his eyes and I turned away, determined not to cry. I was afraid if I started I wouldn't be able to stop.

"But...they said he was killed," I said. "Did they find that out later?"

Rory grunted. "That was our Lieutenant. He'd been losing too many men, not knowing what happened to them, so he reported him killed."

"What? What about their bodies? Wouldn't anyone notice?"

"We pledged 'no man left behind' but that wasn't always possible, not without jeopardizing the lives of others. Leaving your buddies behind was awful, but not as bad as when we couldn't find someone."

"Like Rick."

"We assumed he was dead."

"So when they said 'killed in action'—"

"It should have said 'missing in action.'"

"So that's why I couldn't find his name." I told Rory about my search at the Wall.

"No, ma'am, MIAs are on the Wall. KIAs have a diamond shape by their names, MIAs' names have a cross, and then it's changed if they find some...remains," he added, his eyes steady on me.

"I'm okay," I assured him. "But didn't anyone ever tell higher-ups that your lieutenant falsified the report?"

"You don't report your commanding officer, ma'am, not in the Army. Of course, morale was even worse after that. The men thought the lieutenant had been too quick to accept the turncoat's word." Rory grinned. "But he got his."

"Oh?"

"He was transferred to a non-Ranger unit. He was in the latrine when it blew up."

I drew in my breath. "How did that happen?"

"You ever hear of fragging?"

"No."

"It's happened in every war, but no one likes to admit it. It's when an officer's own men booby-trap him, often in the latrine. They do it because they hate him. Because he's put them in unnecessary jeopardy, or they just hate the military."

"That what happened to your lieutenant?"

He didn't answer.

I CRIED ON the drive back to the city, not hard, racking sobs, but gentle tears of regret for what could have been and for the man who seemed so strange now, his picture tucked into my bag. In a jungle clearing, Rick stood smiling, hands on his hips and a bit of swagger in his stance, his dog tags catching the sun filtering through the leaves. Rick had grown up in the time since he'd left me, becoming the man he was intended to be. Now he only seemed like someone I might have known a long time ago.

My tears dried up along with the rain and, as the clouds lifted in the West, the red globe of a fall sun spilled onto my rearview mirror, slanting reflected light in my eyes. All I wanted to do now was to drive home and take a nap.

I turned the corner to my street and saw that wasn't to be.

Chapter 25

Saturday, November 20, 1145 Hours

I PULLED MYSELF out of my car reluctantly, made my way up the steps, passed scattered equipment in my yard, and looked up at the men on the roof. One man, a hooded gray sweatshirt pulled up over his head, raised his hand in salute and then went back to ripping shingles off the roof and tossing them on the ground. I stepped around the broken pieces to get inside.

The roofers had started replacing my roof before my trip to Washington, but hadn't been back since. I knew they wanted to complete the job before weather turned colder and, since I'd had a small leak in my spare bedroom when a heavy snow melted last winter, I wanted them to finish, too.

Since I couldn't take a nap with hammering on my roof, I decided to get the rest of the day's pain over with. Then maybe I could start to heal. At last.

Cat followed me down to the basement and jumped up on the trunk. Stored in the basement of the first flat I'd lived in after finishing college, the trunk hadn't been opened since. I'd thought about going through it when I'd moved to this house a year ago, but then I was busy getting settled and forgot about it. Well, that wasn't exactly true. I always knew it was there, a memory lingering in the back of my mind.

I shooed Cat off, scattering dust across the trunk's scarred and dented top.

Hammering pounded from above, sounding as if it were coming from my kitchen floor.

I sat down on the basement floor and studied the trunk lid where it was bent inward. The latch was gone so I hooked my fingers into the brackets that had once held the clasps, and pulled. The lid didn't budge but the movement dislodged a spider who ran out from underneath. Cat chased it behind the washer and lay down, her chin on her paws, waiting for her prey to return.

I put both hands on the clasp on the unbent side. It released, dragging the dented
side up in a whoosh and sending me sprawling back on the floor. A musty odor escaped as Cat hopped into the trunk and scattered pictures and papers about inside. I tossed her out and rummaged through the archives of my life: grade school report cards, my high school yearbook, pressed flowers, remnants of my corsage from prom night, and the church bulletin announcing our wedding.

Under Rick's basketball letter sweater from St. Mary's, I found the battered stationery box I'd called my treasure box growing up. An angel perched on its embossed top, her white organdy wings missing, the victim of my repeated picking at them when I was young. Inside were Rick's letters, bound in a rubber band, which split when I picked up the stack, spilling the letters that had been ripped open with my fingers in my haste to read them.

I smiled at the eight-cent stamp on the envelope, a reminder of how long ago it had been mailed, and stared at the block letters Rick had used, not trusting his natural scrawl.

My darling,
Remind me never to complain about St Louis in the summer. As we say at home, it's not the heat, it's the humidity and believe me you haven't felt humidity until you've been in the jungle.

Thump, thump, thump sounded above me. I giggled. Here I was in the throes of sadness and the beat goes on. Literally.

More letters spilled out of broken rubber bands, including the ones I'd sent Rick. He'd saved every one and the Army had mailed them back to me in one large package along with his shaving kit and our wedding photo. I'd cried the day that had arrived until Aunt Octavia had called and come over to console me, fixing tomato soup and grilled cheese sandwiches and staying the night, sleeping on the broken-down living room couch I'd had then. After that I'd hauled everything down to the basement and closed the trunk up.

Until now.

Bored, is what Rick had said in most of the letters, every irritant assuming mammoth proportions and tempers flaring at the most minor annoyance in the stifling jungle environment.

He couldn't wait for their next assignment, which he couldn't tell me about or he'd have to kill me, he'd joked in one letter. Then in the next, he assured me he'd never put me in jeopardy. Rick's letters were read before they were sent back to the States so if he had said anything he shouldn't have, they'd have marked it out. Or maybe they returned those to him. I didn't know. Nothing in any of his letters was ever crossed out and he wrote me almost every day.

I'd saved one letter until last.

It had arrived after the officers had knocked on my door that cheery Sunday morning. I'd read and reread the letter so many times that first year, but now I could hardly recall what it said.

I hope you're being true to me.

At the time, the words had brought a smile to my face and triggered a fresh round of tears. When would I have had time to be unfaithful? Between classes, clinicals, and studying, and then working part-time at the hospital and trying to write to Rick every night, I'd barely had time to sleep, much less find a boyfriend even if I'd been looking for one, which I hadn't been. Rick was my only love. To this day.

It was the next sentence that brought tears to my eyes so many times that first year.

Our wedding day was the happiest day of my life. I will always love you and be true to you.

Upstairs, Cat howled at the banging from the roof.

I wondered if Rick's CO ever felt remorse over his falsified report.

I squeezed the letter back into the overly-full box, planning to bring another rubber band down later. As I struggled to close the lid, a small laminated card, about two by three inches, popped out and fell on the floor. I leaned over to grab it but Cat, who'd rejoined me, beat me to it, flipping it with her paw. The card slid under the trunk. I lifted up one end of the trunk up and grabbed the card as Cat pounced toward it.

UNITED STATES ARMED FORCES CODE OF CONDUCT, I read, sitting back down. I remembered that it had come back in the package the Army had returned to me along with the letters I'd sent to Rick.

I. I am an American fighting man. I serve in the forces which guard my country and our way of life. I am prepared to give my life in their defense.

Cat climbed onto my lap and I stroked her for a moment before reading on.

II. I will never surrender of my own free will. If in command I will never surrender my men while they still have the means to resist.
III. If I am captured I will continue to resist by all means available. I will make every effort to escape and aid others to escape. I will accept neither parole nor special favors from the enemy.
IV. If I become a prisoner of war, I will keep faith with my fellow prisoners. I will give no information or take part in any action which might be harmful to my comrades. If I am senior, I will take command. If not, I will obey the lawful orders of those appointed over me and will back them up in every way.
V. When questioned, should I become a prisoner of war, I am bound to give only name, rank, service number and date of birth. I will evade answering further questions to the utmost of my ability. I will make no oral or written statement disloyal to my country and its allies or harmful to their cause.
VI. I will never forget that I am an American fighting man, responsible for my actions, and dedicated to the principles which made my country free. I will trust in my god and in the UNITED STATES OF AMERICA.

I folded my hands over the Code that Rick had fought to support. I hoped it had given him the courage he needed to face… Don't go there! I would remember Rick as I knew him and not conjure up imaginary horrors.

Cat pawed my leg with the cry I recognized as hunger. I closed the lid and followed Cat upstairs to feed us both.

Chapter 26

Sunday, November 21, 1315 Hours

RAIN FROM THE day before had given way to cold sunshine. I'd left the men on my roof again in the morning, bundled up in down jackets, knit caps on top of sweatshirt hoods, and heavy gloves.

"Door's open." Aunt Octavia's voice came through her apartment door. Like other South St. Louisans who greeted every holiday with a plethora of seasonal decorations, Aunt Octavia had hung a bundle of colorful Indian corn on her door and inside a papier maché turkey. A plastic pumpkin still full of Halloween candy graced her living room.

Aunt O stuck her head around the corner of her tiny kitchen and said, "Make yourself at home. I'll be right out."

I followed the scents into the kitchen. "Get out of the way," she said as I bent to sniff the aroma of milk, chocolate, sugar, and cinnamon in the pan on the stove. "I have to keep stirring to keep it from sticking. You don't want burnt hot chocolate, do you?"

I stood aside and told her about meeting Rick's friend and reading his letters. She kept stirring while I went on. "I brought a postcard from the Korean monument."

"Show me," she said without looking up.

I laid the postcard on the counter next to the stove. Larger-than-life, gun-metal gray statues of men, dressed identically in helmets and ponchos, stomped across the open field, their uniforms dull in the sunlight.

"So many lost," she said, turning back to her cooking.

I hugged her shoulder. People said I resembled her, probably because of our diminutive size and our naturally-curly black hair. Over sixty, her curls were more gray than black now and, although I was much younger, my hair had sprouted a few lighter strands.

I leaned against the counter, watching her stir the mixture and savoring the scent of chocolate filling her kitchen alcove. "I remember Uncle Bernie's plane was lost, but not all of the story."

She shut the gas off and tapped the wooden spoon on the edge of the pan. She looked out to window above the sink where a stained-glass cardinal hung from latch, its wings still and silent. She rinsed the spoon and dried it, taking her time. She turned to me, the spoon still in her hand.

"The letter came saying he was on his way home. Everyone was excited. Bernie was the only one in our family in the military and we'd all been afraid for him. But now he'd made it through the fighting and was coming back. We planned a big celebration. Uncle Otto made a big sign for the yard. 'Welcome home Bernie' it said. We'd asked Father Babler to say a special Mass that day and then dinner was to be at Aunt Iris' house. She had the most room and a big yard so the kids could play outside.

"It was June and we'd had beautiful weather all week. Sunny, warm but not too humid. Flowers, trees, and bushes had blossomed out and everywhere you went the most wonderful scents. It was the prettiest June I'd ever seen.

"The Army hadn't said exactly when he'd return, just that it would be by the fifteenth, which was a Sunday. So we'd planned the party for that day. I expected him by the night before. I couldn't sleep. I sat in a chair all night with the lights on. I wanted to be ready to welcome him home.

"Aunt Iris was frying up enough chickens for the whole family and everyone was bringing a dish. I had made German potato salad, using my mother's recipe although I never thought it tasted exactly like hers. Anyway, it was done and left warming on the stove.

"I dozed off sometime the next morning and when they knocked on the door, for a moment I couldn't remember where I was."

Aunt O turned away from me and placed the spoon in the drawer. I knew the rest of her story. The two men at her door, crushing her dreams into dust. His plane had crashed on the way home, ironic that he'd survived the war only to die as he was returning.

I hugged her but she straightened up, sniffed, and waved me into the dining room, following with mugs of hot chocolate for both of us. I gathered up the cornucopia overflowing with seasonal gourds in variegated shades of greens and oranges that decorated the table and arranged them on a side cabinet as she placed our cups and napkins out.

After several false starts, I was afraid Aunt O's patience to teach me to knit might be wearing thin. "Slip the needle behind the loop, then put the yarn over it, and pull it through," she said again. I thought I understood but as soon as I tried it on my own, something went wrong.

"Maybe I'm just not cut out for knitting," I told her, putting aside my work, one row of stitches remaining on the needle.

"Nonsense. Anyone can learn to knit."

"Maybe not today," I said.

"Pshaw! Himmeldonnerwetternochmal!" she said, using the German word I'd heard whenever I did something she didn't approve of, accompanied by an eye roll and up-thrown hands that didn't take a translator to understand. She'd never told me what it meant only that it was the longest word in the German language.

"Just like anything else, Monika," Aunt O said, pointing her knitting needles at me. "If you'll do the work," she said, emphasizing the word work.

I let out a sigh. "The secret to academic success," Aunt O had told me when I'd struggled in nursing school, "is doing the work, whatever it takes. People who fail do so because they didn't put the time and effort into it." I'd taken her advice and studied until I thought my brain would burst, but it had paid off. I had graduated near the top of my class, an accomplishment that astounded the nun who had taught me in grade school when I'd seen her years later at a Lenten fish fry.

"Besides, you're clinically competent. That takes fine motor skills that you've perfected." Aunt O was effortlessly clicking away on the sweater she was making for a cousin's baby, a girl. Pink yarn seemed to fly around her needles.

I studied my book and thought through the actions just as I had when I needed to learn a new clinical skill. In my mind's eye I saw the needles crossed in back, the yarn loop the right needle and slip out to grab the stitch. Okay, now if I can just do it.

"I got it!" I said, holding my work up for Aunt O who nodded knowingly.

She had instructed me to do a sample piece first. For the gauge, she'd said, whatever that was.

I continued to knit back and forth. Some of my stitches were tighter than others but by the time I'd completed several rows, my work had started to even out.

We worked on our knitting for a while, companionably quiet, while a Bach concerto played on the radio.

"See, you're knitting," Aunt O said.

Confident now, I pulled a strand out of the skein and it caught. I tugged harder and a wad of knotted yarn came loose. I squealed and Aunt O came back from the kitchen bringing the pan of hot chocolate.

"How'd you do that?" She poured more chocolate into my cup and, when she returned from the kitchen, took the snarled yarn from me. "You pulled it out in a hurry, didn't you? Knitting is meant to calm you, Monika. Everything you do should be slow, careful, restful. Don't jerk the yarn out like it's a weed you have to eliminate." She went back to the kitchen and I sat staring at the mess. How was I ever going to untangle this?

"It's just like any problem," she said from the kitchen. Running water kept me from hearing what she said next. She came back, drying her hands on a kitchen towel. "When the strands get in a mess, you have to pull each one out, one at a time, and follow it to its source to untangle it, then pull another out the same way. If it's a false lead, leave it, and look for another way through."

Gently I pulled on the most visible strand and stopped when it caught. I fingered the snarl until I could free it, pulling out a length of yarn until I came to two more loops caught together. Carefully I separated those and watched as a length of yarn fell away easily. The rest of the tangle came loose. I wrapped the long strand back around the original skein until only a yard of so remained hooked to my needle.

"That's more like it," Aunt O said, examining my work.

"I remember you teaching me about solving problems the same way," I said, sipping my hot chocolate.

"Knitting teaches you lots of things, Monika. Patience, persistence, and problem solving. There's always a solution. Sometimes you just have to keep looking."

"You're right! That's it!"

"What's it?" Aunt O looked up, her knitting dropped into her lap. "You've thought of something?"

"Too many strands and I've been jerking them out all at once."

"That's just what I told you."

"Exactly." I gathered up my bit of knitting and stuffed it back in the plastic bag. I gave Aunt O a quick kiss and told her I'd call her later. "You helped me more than you know," I said, letting myself out the door.

Chapter 27

Sunday, November 21, 1425 Hours

"ROGER'S NOT HOME," Hannah said when I called. "He's at church helping set up for the kids Thanksgiving program tonight."

Next to Aunt Octavia, Hannah was my closest relative. In the multiple-children families most of our relatives had in the days before Catholics used birth control, she and I were the only children of twin brothers so we'd formed a bond from early days. Her five children—three teenage boys and ten-year-old twin girls—were my "nieces and nephews." I'd had no children of my own.

I had forgotten I'd told the twins I would be at the Thanksgiving program tonight. Too old for the children's parts—after all they were ten now and in the fourth grade—they were in the chorus.

"Roger will be there and I'll tell him you want Kevin's phone number."

We hung up, Hannah agreeing to save me a seat. She had to take the twins early anyway, she'd said.

I wasn't often restless, but this day seemed interminable. I filled the bird feeder, scattering some squawking black birds and squirrels that were munching on spills on the ground, and watered my indoor plants, including an African violet I'd rescued from the trash at the grocery store. Hannah had advised me to buy a special food for it and now the plant looked as if it might come alive. Three new leaves, bright green, sprouted from the center.

I worked some more on my knitting but it took too much concentration for me now. All I could think about was how to uncover the solution to my two problems: Was John Doe Agatha's brother? And who had attacked Marian? Aunt O said to keep trying. If one strand got stuck, it was the wrong one, so you had to try a different strand.

I grabbed a pad of paper and put a line down the middle. I printed "John Doe" at the top on one side and "Marian O" on the other. I sat chewing on the pencil. Cat jumped up on the sofa next to me and nudged her head under the pad. I tossed her off and she stalked away to the kitchen.

Under "John Doe" I listed what I knew. Wilma, whose memory wasn't exactly accurate these days, said he was her son, Karl. Her daughter, Roberta, disagreed. She had said his hands weren't calloused and they should have been since he did construction work. Also Karl was heavier, she'd said, and Wilma's photo confirmed that he was a large man. Nor could his other sister, Agatha, identify him as her brother. However, JD was in such bad shape that it was possible even his relatives, if he'd lost a lot of weight and they hadn't seen him in a while, wouldn't recognize him. If he was Karl Magnason and he didn't have amnesia—an unlikely condition in any case—had he been trying to disguise himself as somebody else, for some reason. To leave his old life behind?

Val had said that someone claiming to be Karl had left her a message on the day JD was admitted to St. T's, but she'd thought it was a macabre joke. If it was Karl, why would he call her if he wanted to stay hidden? Wouldn't he think she might tell someone?

Cat settled down beside me. Her body stretched along the side of my leg but she kept alert. She was always ready for what might be coming by.

If JD was Karl Magnason, where had he been all these years? Why was he back in St. Louis in a stolen car from Texas with the ID of a dead man from New York? I was left with more questions than answers.

Now to Marian Oblansky. The police had made it clear they thought her husband, Steve, had attacked her, money the motive. Charlotte had told me they'd searched his house and that he had punched a hole in the wall when he found out they had taken his laptop. Charlotte did say he might get angry if we gave him bad news. And he didn't have an alibi for that morning. Someone had seen Marian arguing with a man in the bank parking lot. Usually you argue only with someone you know well.

Harding had told me to be sure Steve wasn't left alone with Marian, a request we'd ignored because it was impossible as busy as we were, but I think Tim and Jessie had tried to keep an eye on him if Charlotte wasn't visiting at the time.

I consider myself a reasonably good judge of character and, although I've been fooled before, Steve's concern for his wife was so genuine that I couldn't believe he'd hurt her. Cat pawed my leg, wanting attention. How could you hurt someone you love? I scratched Cat's head absently. Was I really thinking about Steve?

Where had Charlotte been the morning her sister was attacked? As a school teacher, I had assumed she'd been at work. Surely Harding had checked on that. Charlotte wasn't likely to be a suspect in her sister's attack in any case. She'd moved back here after a divorce to be close to her sister who was already widowed. Since then, however, Marian had met and married Steve. Charlotte had admitted she had been jealous of Marian, "all her life," is what she'd said, but I thought jealousy between siblings wasn't unusual for two sisters growing up close in age.

Maybe Charlotte was jealous of Steve, wanting Marian all to herself. If so, she would have wanted to get rid of Steve. I stopped writing. Unless she wanted Steve for herself. Nah. I hadn't seen any indication that those two were involved; only supporting each other through their shared ordeal.

Nadine, Steve's former wife, was angry enough at Marian, whom she blamed for breaking up her marriage, that they'd had to get a restraining order and its thirty days had just run out, according to Charlotte. How much strength would it take to cause as much damage to someone's skull as Marian had suffered? Could a woman do it?

Ruby thought Nadine had called several times to check on Marian's condition and when she couldn't learn anything she'd tried to get into Marian's room. BJ had told me Nadine was the parish secretary at St. Augustine's. She was sure Harding had checked her out. But St. Augustine's was Hannah's parish and I was headed there that very night.

Chapter 28

Sunday, November 21, 1850 Hours

"I'VE SEEN HER around," Hannah told me when I asked her about Steve's ex. We were seated on the bleachers in the gym, waiting for the program to begin. "I think she's fairly new. Someone said she had been a parish secretary somewhere else so I guess she came with experience."

I knew St. Augustine's well. All five of Hannah's children had been baptized there, beginning eighteen years ago with Richard, named for my husband. The first twins, Robby and Tommy, who now at age fifteen preferred to be called Rob and Tom, came next. Tina and Gena were born on my birthday, the fourth of July. They were now ten or, as Tina was fond of reminding us, ten and four months, the latter number changing every fourth of the month.

"You know anything more about her?" I asked Hannah.

"She coughs a lot. Kind of a hacking high in her throat." Hannah demonstrated.

"Is she sick?"

"I don't think so. She's had it every time I've seen her. I can always tell where she's sitting at mass. I think it's just one of those nervous habits some people have."

Roger squeezed by the family next to us and wedged himself down into a spot beside Hannah. "Here's Kevin's number," he said, passing me a note. "He has a new baby so they'll likely be up if you want to call tonight." He took Hannah's hand in his. Hannah had miscarried early in the spring but they both seemed to have recovered, Hannah from feeling guilty that she hadn't wanted another child and Roger because he had wanted baby number six.

Confusion quieted as a teacher came to the microphone and announced the evening's program. First the primary grades played out the story of the first Thanksgiving. Then, when the pilgrims and Indians had exited, older boys brought in benches to make two tiers amidst a background murmur as families of the younger children made their way out.

I fingered the note Roger had given me. Would Kevin be willing to help me? My experience, albeit limited, with law enforcement types had taught me that they didn't tend to be very forthcoming.

Two men pushed an upright piano into place to the side of the benches. A woman followed and took her seat at the piano, opened her music, and adjusted her seat. The chorus entered, with some students looking straight ahead as they marched in, a few whispering to friends, and others scanning the audience for their families. The students took their places, those on the top tier climbing awkwardly into place. The twins were in front. Gena gave a flip of a hand up in response to Hannah's wave, but Tina looked away, old enough to be embarrassed by her mother's attention in public.

The director tapped her baton on the music stand, nodded to the pianist, and the first piece began. The children's voices sometimes blended and sometimes wobbled away toward different notes. But their sweet faces, intent on following the director's signals more than made up for the lack of musical cohesion. Hannah snapped pictures and Roger focused a video camera on the action. While they sang, I looked around for Nadine, listening for her characteristic cough in the quiet between numbers, but only the rustling of an audience released from its hush and a baby's cry interrupted the break.

As we made our way out, Hannah reminded me about Thanksgiving dinner at her house. Roger's family were all coming so there would be about twenty, she told me. She planned to make the turkey and trimmings and I offered to bring one of the salads.

"You don't have to work, do you?" she asked while we waited for the girls to join us and Roger to return with the car. I shivered in the unlined jacket I'd grabbed, fooled by the day's sunshine. Now a mist had begun to fall again, reflected in the overhead lights in the parking lot.

I told her about John Doe, who Agatha's mother thought was her son.

"The mother would know."

"She's a little confused."

"Mothers know these things," she said. "Just like I can tell the twins apart. A mother knows her own child."

"I CAN'T JUST call up the IRS," Roger's friend Kevin said after I'd told him who I was. "I'd have to have a court order and a reason for it. And a judge has to order tax records released."

A baby wailed in the background.

"Should we talk later?" I asked him.

"The baby's hungry and my wife just got home. If you're looking for someone, there's lots of websites to try. I could send you some that anyone can use if you'll give me your email address. Others are just for law enforcement."

"I'd appreciate that," I said as the crying stopped. "I just wanted to know if the person had filed taxes. I'm not looking for any financial information."

"Why do you need this?" He sounded all business, reminding me of Detective Harding. Or BJ when she had on her cop voice.

"Sister Agatha's a friend of mine and her mother thinks this man might be her son. He's a patient of mine, unconscious, and without identification. I'm trying to help them."

"Your name sounds familiar. You any relation to the Everhardts on Pernod?"

"They're my late husband's parents." I hadn't told them yet about what I'd learned about Rick's disappearance and I wasn't sure I would. They had grieved enough.

"Oh, you're Rick's wife. Rick went to St. Mary's, too, didn't he? He was ahead of Roger and me in school though."

Someone interrupted him, and he said he'd be just a minute more. "I knew Rick got married before he left, but I lost track of him. I was transferred around a bit before I got assigned back here in St. Louis. Tell you what. I can call and ask informally if a person's filed. What's the name?"

"Karl Magnason."

"I'll see what I can do and let you know," he said as the baby began to cry again.

COMING BACK FROM the convenience store, I noticed a dark, old-model sedan that had made the last two turns I had and stayed close behind me. Could it be those teenagers from a week ago? No, they hadn't followed me then and they wouldn't know where I lived anyway. Maybe it was just some turkey out joy riding and I wasn't going fast enough to suit him.

I made a quick turn into the park, which I realized belatedly wasn't such a good idea because the road led me deeper into the park where street lights were too few and too far apart on this dark Sunday night.

Headlights caught in my rearview mirror, momentarily blinding me. I moved my head to the side and realized I'd slowed down. The car was on my tail. Any moment now I'd feel the bump. I stomped on the accelerator, jerking forward. I held onto the steering wheel, squealing around a curve, and looked behind me. My pursuer had dropped back but I had missed the easy exit out of the park.

I took the next turn, coming to a stop at a red light at the Morganford exit. Unfortunately it was the street on the opposite side of the park from my house. At least I was facing a main thoroughfare.

I had spied the winning lottery ticket where I'd left it by the phone while I was talking to Kevin and, after we hung up, had decided not to wait any longer to cash it in.

I kept my eyes on my rearview mirror but I didn't see the dark-colored sedan I thought had been behind me. I was being paranoid, doing too much thinking about people hit over the head, and crashing into trees. And feeling guilty about gambling. At least that would be what BJ would say if she were here.

I made the right-hand turns necessary to reach my street and pulled up in front of my house. A car passed me and parked several doors down. I jumped out and skirted the boxes of shingles the roofers had left scattered on the walk, wishing I'd replaced my burned-out porch light before I'd left.

I had my key almost in the door when the man pushed up against me. "Just the money, lady," he said, his knees pressed into my thighs. His clothes had the lingering odor of motor oil and grease. "Hand it over," he said, letting up so I could turn slightly. He held a baseball bat in his right hand, and was clenching and unclenching his left hand.

I could taste bile as it rose in my throat, regretting the piece of the German chocolate cake I'd eaten at Hannah's after the girls' church program. Suddenly I thought I might laugh, picturing vomitus spewing on my attacker, but an image of Marian's head made me swallow it back down. If I were bent over to vomit, he could smash my head, take my money, and leave me until morning, or until I died, whichever came first.

"I saw you get it back there, now give it to me!" he demanded with a quick glance around. He bounced up and down on his feet.

Voices from a television and a lone dog barking somewhere on the next street were the only sounds. Surely a car would come by soon, but what would they see? If they could see anything at all they'd only be able to make out two figures on a dark porch. No one would know what was happening.

My mouth was too dry to trust my voice and, besides, I thought I might cry if I tried to talk so I just nodded, trying to look resigned to losing my winnings.

The gallon jug of milk was in my left hand and, keeping my keys firmly clutched in my right hand, I leaned forward as if to pull my money out.

It's now or never.

As I raised back up, I swung the milk jug toward his arm holding the bat, throwing the force of my body behind it. Even in the dark I could see his look of surprise as the jug hit the bat, sending it flying into the bushes below to the porch. He staggered back against the handrail and I stabbed his neck with my key, pushing him over the railing and into the shrubbery as the sound of a siren screamed down the street. The man was struggling to extract himself from the bushes as a cop car screeched to a halt and BJ jumped out, her gun drawn. Two other cop cars squealed up behind hers, angling into place, and spilling St. Louis city cops onto the street.

I slumped to the porch and started to cry, watching milk dribble down onto my jacket and jeans. My right hand held the bloodied key to my front door. Cat was wailing as several cops dragged my assailant away and BJ joined me on the porch. She holstered her gun and stood looking at me. She wasn't smiling.

"How'd you know to come here?" I asked her, my voice wobbly.

"Some woman walking her dog saw the guy get out of his car and sneak up behind you. She called it in."

"I still have my hundred." I pulled out the wadded bill I'd refused to give up.

"Never fight them. I've told you that a million times. If that guy had been doped up, he'd have been unpredictable, doubly dangerous."

"I took a self-defense class, remember? You told me to," I said in a voice that sounded like that of a child justifying her actions to her mother.

She sat down beside me on the step. "Not so you could take on the bad guys. All you had to do was give him the money and, most likely, would have left. Fighting is stupid. No amount of money is worth your life," she said, giving me a rough hug.

She followed me into the house, checked it out, including the basement, and gave Cat her due—a head scratch. She turned at the door. "I thought you told me you weren't going to gamble."

I DREAMT ABOUT Rick that night. It wasn't the first time he had shown up in my dreams, but it had been a while. I never quite remembered what happened; just that he was there, hovering around the edges of my awareness.

This time the dream was different. He was in my house as if he belonged there, in a house he'd never lived in. Events seemed to be happening, but I couldn't remember what they were. The dream played out like a movie. I'd wake up, realize I was dreaming, and go back to sleep. The movie would start up from where I left it as if it had been turned off when I woke up and restarted as soon as I fell asleep again. This seemed to happen over and over during the night. As in the past, I couldn't remember what had actually happened in my stop-and-start movie dream, just benign events, comforting in an obscure sort of way.

At the end, Rick turned to go down the basement stairs, not looking back. Then
he was gone.

Chapter 29

Monday, November 22, 0815 Hours

GALA PROMOTION WAS in full swing the next morning. Cassandra held court at a makeshift stand in the lobby directly in front of the life-size poster advertising the event.

Why hadn't I taken the underground tunnel that bypassed the lobby and led directly to the elevators?

"Have you bought your tickets to the gala?" Cassandra asked the three nurses ahead of me. They stopped to dig money out of their bags and I tried to slip around them.

"Monika! You said your family's coming? How many tickets do you need? I have plenty." She lifted a roll of orange and blue tickets and waved them at me, an insincere smile pasted on her face. "Twenty, thirty?" she asked, depositing the money the nurses had given her in the cash drawer open on the table in front of her and handing them stickers, "I support St. T's gala" emblazoned across the front.

"Not now, Cassandra, I'll catch you later." Several weeks ago I had promised to pick up tickets for Hannah and Aunt Octavia, but we hadn't discussed how many tickets they'd need.

KEVIN WAS AS good as his word, leaving a long e-mail message for me the next morning. I'd dashed in and bent over to click on my computer and moaned. Last night I'd told BJ I wasn't hurt, but when I'd crawled out of bed this morning I'd felt the effects of last night's attack. The muscles in my arm, shoulder, and upper back ached, and when I had lifted my arm to turn on the shower pain had stabbed through my shoulder as bone rubbed against bone in the joint socket. Who knew that smashing a plastic jug of milk into a bat would hurt so much?

Holding my left arm as still as I could, I extricated my right arm from my jacket and then used my right hand to pull the sleeve out on my left arm. I tossed the jacket on the floor and switched on my computer. It went through its opening sequence and Kevin's message popped up.

There are several ways to look up a person, his message began, *if you have some information more than just a name, such as an address, phone number, or social security number. Most of these directories are online these days, but access to many of them are limited to various officials. Law enforcement has the greatest access. Credit bureaus have more access than the public but less than law enforcement. Some directories are available to anyone.*

I rummaged in my desk, looking for aspirin or acetaminophen or ibuprophin. Old mail was jammed inside the drawer but surely I had something in there I could take to reduce the inflammation in my arm and shoulder. I shifted in my chair, sitting up straight to keep my shoulder in alignment, and let my sore arm sit on the armrest. I went back to Kevin's message.

Here are several websites you might try: www.Infospace.com, www.haines.com, www.SmartSearch.com. We use a system called Autotrack almost exclusively. Your access to it would be limited.

You can find databases of property owners, both real estate and personal property, such as automobiles and boats, drivers licenses in Missouri and other states, and professional licenses. I can look you up and find out if you are a licensed nurse.

Most of the information is not in real time. If you were to buy a property or get a new car or driver's license, etc...today or last week, it may take a few months, sometimes longer, to be available through these products.

Finally I found a battered bottle of aspirin and shook out the last two. Where was a bottle of water? I thought I'd left one in my office the other day after I'd returned from that disastrous meeting with the step-down staff. Shifting flyers, mail, and nursing journals to the side, I spied it on the floor. Only a scant amount remained, but it was enough to swallow the tablets. I returned to Kevin's message.

Cell phones have added another wrinkle to finding people. When cell phone numbers stayed with a specific company, we would see a telephone number prefix and be able to identify the company that controlled the phone. It still took a court order to find out who owned the phone unless we could talk someone into disclosing the subscriber's name. Now people keep their numbers when they change companies so it becomes a bigger job for us, which involves getting individual court orders. Plus there are throw-away cell phones. You could easily get a phone and give false information. You pay up front and if you pay in cash, no one checks. Drug dealers especially like those.

He closed by saying he'd let me know what he found out from the IRS about whether or not Karl had filed taxes any time in the past few years.

I needed to check in with the unit before I started on the budgets. Reaching for my lab coat behind the door, once again I forgot that I'd been injured until my shoulder screamed in complaint. One arm at a time, I reminded myself.

I opened the door to face Poppi.

"Okay, Monika, what gives?" Poppi said, her arms crossed in front of her, wrinkling her pressed navy scrub suit.

"What? What are you talking about?"

She leaned back against the door frame and squinted through stylish, rimless glasses. "What is it about me you dislike?" She raised her hand to stop me from interrupting. "I don't give a hoot if you don't like me. That's not the point. What does bother me, though, is how it affects patients."

I bristled. "I wouldn't do anything to hurt my patients!"

"There," she said, placing her hands on her hips. "That's what I mean. 'Your patients?' Aren't we all responsible for 'our' patients?" Not waiting for an answer, she went on. "I'm one of the most skilled nurses you have. I have years of experience. I learned my way around here in the first week and now it's been a month and still I don't get the complicated cases. Bottom line: you don't assign me to the sickest patients and I want to know why."

I turned away to give myself time to think. She was correct, and I had no excuse. At least not one I intended to tell her.

"You're right," I said at last, my sense of fair play overcoming my envy. She held eye contact until I said, "I've been unfair to you."

"That's more like it. So what are you going to do about it? Tim's wife's about to go into labor. I want Marian Oblansky when he's off. Agreed?"

"Agreed."

Before she left, she asked me, "You hear about Missy? What she did yesterday?"

"What?"

"Ask somebody else. It makes me too mad to talk about it."

"Tell me," I demanded. "Did anyone get hurt?"

"The patient's fine," she said, her hand on the door frame. "This time," she added over her shoulder.

I watched her march back into the unit, the doors swinging wide as she pushed through them. What business did I have taking out my petty jealousy on a fine nurse? My chair rattled as I plopped back down on it. What if something had happened to a patient because I hadn't assigned the best nurse to care for him or her?

I knew what Aunt Octavia would say about what I'd been doing: Mistakes are learning opportunities. Today I'd had the chance to discover that it's better to be confronted by an angry, mistreated employee than risk a patient's safety. At least my closed-mindedness had caused no more than hurt feelings. This time.

"THOSE NURSES OVER in step-down been pestering me all morning," Ruby said. "You go over there and settle them down. I got too much work to do to fool with them."

"They were here this morning?"

"I stopped by, that's all, just to see what their new clerk's like."

"I'm glad to hear they found someone."

"She don't know nothing. I'm going to have to be there telling her stuff. And me working overload already."

"You are not, Ruby, you don't have any more work than usual. What are you complaining about?"

"I do too. You don't know about all the new forms and stuff we have to fill out with that HIPPA thing."

"You're full of it. You have less to do. We don't put patient names up anywhere and you used to do that—"

"I can't tell anyone anything on the phone, then they come in here and I gotta watch they don't get in. I'll tell you, it's too much. I might just take early retirement..." She peeked up at me from her lowered head.

"Oh, no you don't. Threats don't work with me. Haven't you learned that by now? You quit and we'll hire someone else."

"I'll bet she wouldn't know what's going on around here, stuff you like to know."

She had me there. "I'm overworked too, Ruby, for godsakes. I had my workload doubled when Hockstetter gave me the second unit to manage."

"And you best be managing."

Ruby's complaint reminded me of what I wanted to do. Whether I could change anything, I didn't know but, as Aunt O says, 'The answer is no if you don't ask.'"

HALLWAYS THROUGHOUT THE hospital were festooned with bright orange and blue posters announcing the gala. Auxiliary members were stationed at corners, passing out matching flyers. One woman, whose doctor husband had been one of Aunt O's favorites before his death, sat with orange and blue balloons tied to her wheelchair, greeting people who stopped to talk to her.

I passed a number of staff sporting the colorful gala stickers I'd seen Cassandra handing out in the lobby. One nurse's scrub top was covered with a cluster of them. If I had time later today, I'd call Hannah, Aunt O, and BJ, if I could reach her, and find out how many tickets we'd need. We usually had a full table, which made me popular with administration and the envy of my peers.

"Yes, yes," Mr. Hockstetter said, looking up from the papers on his desk. "Is it important? I have a lot to do as you can see. New Medicare rules, employer contracts, a gala to plan if we want to have enough money. Heh, is this about your John Doe, paying for him?" He rubbed his head, leaving several gray strands standing, and squinted at me. "Did he die?"

"Our patient is still alive." For how long, I couldn't predict.

"What about the mother? Think she'll pay for his care?"

"Are you convinced she is his mother?"

"Why would she say she was if she wasn't?"

"She's never accepted his death, her daughters both told me. What about DNA testing with the mother? Wouldn't that confirm that he's Karl Magnason or not?"

"Humph! Where would I get the money for that?" he asked. "Way too expensive. Maybe he has insurance. Has she said? Why don't you call and ask her?"

"Mr. Hockstetter," I said, my patience wearing thin, "if he was declared dead, he wouldn't have health insurance."

"You don't know that. Maybe he got it through another employer. I doubt the insurance companies comb the death records in every state just to see if someone who's applying might be dead!" He straightened up. "If she says he's her son, that's good enough for me."

"That wasn't why I came here. I want to talk to you about the reorganization."

"I know. You have too much to do. Well, don't we all?" He waved me away. "I can't do anything about it. No money, you know."

"What I know is I can't keep this up. I'm behind on everything—"

"So just keep at it. That's what I do."

"You'll give me some leeway on reports and such?"

"I didn't say that. You don't have a family. Stay late and get caught up."

"Oh, so if I did have children, you'd let me off? Isn't that discriminatory?"

"Only if you're the one with kids. Single people don't have any legal protection from discrimination unless you're a minority and, last time I looked, you weren't." He chuckled at his own joke.

"Or older," I said, regretting it when I saw the red flush spread up his face. I was over forty, quite a bit over, but I didn't want to get into an argument about that.

"I'm busy, Monika. Unless you have something else to say, don't you have work to do?" He waved across the papers on his desk. "I sure do," he said, dismissing me.

I had come here to ask him to relieve me of managing the step-down unit, but somehow I'd been sucked into an argument I didn't want. Not seeing a way out of the conversation, I told him, "I'll get to it when I can," and made my way out. I should have thought through the best way to approach him. The management council would be meeting again on Thursday; maybe someone there would have some ideas about what to do.

I knew I couldn't continue as I was, especially since I wasn't attending at all to the step-down unit. Although their patients weren't as critically ill, they often relapsed or the staff might not be as observant as they should be and the patients would be sent back to ICU. At least so far no one had died because of the staff's or my neglect. Not yet, anyway.

"I THOUGHT WE were doing okay with her pressure," Tim said to Dr. Lord as I joined them beside Marian's bed.

"This kind of damage evolves over time," Lord explained, studying the ICP—intracranial pressure—record on Marian's chart. "It's a cascade effect." He handed the chart off to me and waved circles in the air with his hand. "The initial injury causes ischemia and the swelling injures other parts of the brain. And so on."

"She's been on midazolam hydrocholide and propofol," I noted on the chart. A sedative and an anesthetic, respectively. Drugs that should have kept her in a continuous sedated state.

"But she's not responding to them. The slightest movement makes the swelling in her brain worse," Tim said. "What do you think?" he asked Lord as we walked out together.

"Honestly?" Lord answered.

I bumped into the doorway and grabbed my arm as pieces of loosened paint fluttered to the floor.

"You okay?" Lord asked as Tim picked up the scraps and tossed them in the trash.

"I had an altercation with a bat Sunday night. My arm's still sore and I keep forgetting to be careful."

"A bat? Did you he bite you? Did they catch it? You might need a rabies shot."

"A baseball bat," I corrected.

"That's worse! Have you had an X-ray?" He frowned with clinical concern.

"I'm okay, nothing serious, I'm just still sore."

Tim turned to Lord with a nod toward Marian's room. "We get the seizures under control, and the antibiotics you ordered appear to be helping, and then this."

Lord rubbed his head. "I think the brainstem's been damaged, which is not that uncommon with the damage she's sustained."

Located at the base of the brain, the brainstem connects the brain to the spinal cord and controls breathing and blood pressure, among other essential processes.

"Is there anything else we can do?" I asked Lord.

"Nothing you want to hear about."

"Why?"

He fingered the stethoscope peeking out of his lab coat pocket. "Only one more thing we could possibly try."

"And that is?"

"A frontal lobotomy."

"My god."

"That's only as a last ditch effort."

Her quality of life would be so diminished that it brought to mind how difficult these decisions were. Do you save someone to have them barely functional? Do you even try when the procedure itself might cause death?

"Would her husband allow it?" Tim asked. "She didn't have a living will or durable power of attorney for health care."

"Let's wait and see what happens," Lord answered. "It's too soon to even consider such a radical move."

"DID YOU HEAR what Poppi did?" Serena asked me. "You know Mr. Samuelson?"

Mr. Samuelson's blood pressure had been dangerously high during most of his stay, and he had been on numerous drips, including nipride, a vasodilator to reduce his blood pressure.

"Missy mixed up his IV tubing," Serena said. "She put the nipride tubing in the wrong pump, and he got a huge dose of nipride."

"Oh, my God!"

"Right into cardiac arrest he went."

"Is he all right?" I glanced toward his room, number six.

"Thanks to Poppi, he is. She heard the alarm, ran in, saw what happened, turned off the nipride, grabbed the code cart, and had resuscitated him before the rest of the code team even got there!"

"I'll tell you what," Ruby said, "that girl's got balls."

Serena giggled.

"Ruby, watch your language," I told her.

"I don't care what anyone says, what she did took balls, and that's that!"

"Is she a great nurse or what?" Serena asked rhetorically.

I TRACKED DOWN Missy in the med room and sent her packing back to the step-down unit. When I finally had some time to spend on the unit, I'd see how she was doing in her job there. Maybe coaching would help. Supervising good-performing nurses is easy and, thankfully, most of our nurses were above average on their skills. It is the twenty percent who don't perform well that managers spend eighty percent of their time on.

"SHE'S HAD SO much. It doesn't seem fair," Charlotte said later when I went in to check on Marian. Charlotte blew her nose and looked up, her eyes still damp. "Here I am crying when she's the one who's..."

"She doesn't know what's happening, Charlotte. You're the one here, having to go through the pain of watching her."

I checked Marian's ICP monitor. Her pressure had gone down slightly I was glad to see.

"We had so much we wanted to do together after we'd lived so far apart for so long. I just want to be with her as long as possible."

"You need to take care of yourself, too." Too often family members wear themselves out, exhausted when death finally comes.

"Steve needs to do the same. He doesn't want to stay away like we planned, taking turns. He's so crazy about her. I'm worried...what's going to happen to him?"

WHEN I FINALLY got back to my office, the step-down unit's budget on the top of my desk stared me in the face. I turned it over and went online. I tried the directories Kevin had suggested and came up with nothing. I only knew the name, Karl Magnason, not his address or social security number or place of employment, queries the sites requested. No site had any record of him. I even tried Karl Niedringhaus in case he'd used his mother's first married name. Still nothing.

After a few unsuccessful tries, I hooked into the Missouri State Board of Nursing website and found my own name listed as a registered nurse. Remembering a problem a few months ago with another nurse, I typed in names of a few nurse friends. They were all appropriately licensed.

Kevin hadn't said, but school teachers must be licensed, too, and according to Agatha, Karl's wife was a teacher. Finding a licensed teacher, though, proved to be more complicated than locating a licensed nurse.

I Googled Illinois teachers and a link led me to the Illinois Board of Education. "Now we're getting somewhere," I said but, as it turned out, I spoke too soon. Probably written by an educator, the site listed, in painful detail, the requirements to become a teacher in Illinois, including the nature of the work, working conditions, job prospects, and earnings potential. Links led to a list of teachers' associations but not to a roster of teachers licensed in Illinois.

Nurses in Missouri are often licensed by reciprocity in Illinois to enable them to work on the east side or attend school over there. Maybe teachers had similar arrangements and, possibly, the Missouri Board of Education might list teachers online, but that was not the case. Even if public records were available on site either in Chicago, where the Illinois Board of Education was located, or in Jefferson City, home of Missouri's, I didn't intend to travel that far to find out something that was a long shot at best.

Several frustrating tries later, I gave up. The system was either too complicated for me or the state of Illinois didn't reveal teacher licensees' names as easily as it did nurse licenses.

What if she'd remarried? I logged on and linked through to Illinois marriage certificates, but I couldn't find a list for the people who had been issued marriage licenses. When the web doesn't work, use the old standby. I dialed information. A woman answered at the St. Clair County Courthouse and sounded as if she'd answered my question many times.

"But I thought public records were all online these days," I insisted.

"Not ours," she said, hanging up.

Was it worth a trip to the east side? Maybe I should just tell Agatha and let her go over there to see if her sister-in-law had remarried if she really wanted to know. What if Karl's widow remarried somewhere else? Or never remarried? She could be dead for all I knew.

I'd been putting off what I didn't want to check: the list of names on the Vietnam Wall. Rory Comstock was certain Rick's name was there and that I'd just missed it before. I logged onto the site. The names were listed in alpha order, not separated by years. I braced myself, my fingers on the keys.

Yelling in the corridor interrupted me. I swung around and opened my door to see Steve struggling to free himself from Detective Harding and his partner, but the two detectives gripped Steve's arms at the elbow. Caught in their grasp, Steve's hands flapped uselessly.

I hurried to join them but Harding saw me coming. "You stay out of this, Mrs. Everhardt."

"I didn't do it!" Steve said. "I couldn't hurt her. You don't know—" He wiggled, trying to pull away from his captors.

The elevator doors slid open and the detectives stepped back to let the two nurses, who worked in the step-down unit, to pass. The detectives hustled Steve onto the empty elevator.

As the doors swished shut, Steve pulled himself upright between the detectives and said, "I want a lawyer."

"They're only taking him in for questioning," I said to Tim and Ruby when I reached them in the unit. "They're not arresting him."

"Same difference," Ruby said, heading for the door.

"Oh no," Charlotte said a few minutes later when I told her the police had left with Steve. At least she hadn't seen them take him away. She'd arrived early for her turn to sit with Marian and, at Tim's insistence she'd gone down to get a bite to eat even though she'd told him she wasn't hungry. "They can't think he had anything to do with the attack on Marian, they can't! It had to be someone else!"

Chapter 30

Monday, November 22, 1715 Hours

"They say he's worse than Judyth," Wanda told me as we walked through the tunnel to the parking garage.

"Who?" I asked, fumbling in my bag for my keys and trying not to move my left arm any more than necessary.

"What's wrong with you?" Wanda asked.

"It's a long story."

"I love long stories."

"Later." I didn't intend to have the story of my attempted mugging become a tale in tomorrow's lunch room, especially the part about collecting my lottery winnings. There's nothing wrong with playing the lottery. So why did I feel so guilty about it?

"He's from New York and they hired him to 'clean up the place.'"

"Who?" Had I left my keys upstairs? In my office? No, I'd locked the door behind me so they must be in here.

"The guy they're thinking about hiring for our COO," Wanda said with steadied patience.

"And you know this how?"

"Well, I don't for sure. That's what they're saying."

"Aren't there other candidates?"

"That's all I know about so far, but if we get him—" She made a cutting motion across her throat. "Don't worry, I'll keep you apprised."

"I'm counting on it," I said, discovering my keys in my pocket.

Wanda clicked the latch on a dust-covered SUV parked at the end of a row. "You see my plate?" She pointed to her rear license plate. "SO4RIL," it read. "So far Illinois," she said, chuckling. "It's a joke, Monika. Illinois is just a couple of miles, if that, down the highway from here."

"I wish I could go there right now." When she asked why, I told her about my search for Karl's wife.

"The county courthouse is in Belleville. I could go there for you if I can get out of here some day before they close."

"Thanks anyway, Wanda. If I decide to follow up on this, which I doubt, I'll go myself. It's such a long shot. It's my friend who wants to know if he's her brother. It's not your job."

"Suit yourself, but I'll go if you want me to."

"You're a friend, Wanda, a good friend."

"Hey, what are friends for?"

AT HOME I went straight to the blinking light on my answering machine in spite of Cat's howls. Two messages awaited me.

Kevin's voice told me that there hadn't been any taxes filed for Karl Magnason since 2001, when his widow filed for them both and none for her since. He also checked out some online sources that law enforcement can access, but he'd found no record of Karl Magnason or his wife.

Had she remarried? Or was she hiding out somewhere with him?

"By the way," he said at the end, "I'm glad to see you've been filing your taxes the past thirty or so years." He hung up with a chuckle.

Agatha's message was next. "I found where Karl and Mary Ann used to live," she said, giving me an address in my old neighborhood.

NO ONE ANSWERED the bell at the flat where Agatha had said her brother and his wife had lived. Built in pre-World War II years, the four-family structure had been well cared for, its brick siding newly tuck pointed and its window and door trim recently painted. Unlike many other buildings on the street where smashed windows had been boarded up, broken furniture sagged on porches, and trash lay strewn around in yards.

I drew my jacket closer as the wind whistled through the porch, rattling the windows and toppling an empty flower pot on the step. A woman hurried by, her shoulders hunched against the cold.

A car passed slowly and I shivered from more than the cold. After last night's attack I was anxious to find out if Mary Ann Magnason still lived here and get on my way. I pounded on another door and checked the street. The car had moved on.

The door next to the one where I'd knocked opened. The woman who opened it was too old to be Karl's widow and, although no one had said, I didn't suspect that Mary Ann was black. Her face was friendly enough, though.

"I'm looking for some people I think used to live here," I told her. "The Magnason's."

Her face fell. "Oh, he was the man killed in 9/11, wasn't he? Are you a relative?"

"No, I'm trying to find his wife, Mary Ann. Widow, that is."

"She moved out, poor thing, right after. I own this building," she said, straightening the fronts of her cardigan sweater over her slender body.

"It looks wonderful. I can tell you care for it."

"It's not easy around here but I worked a lot of years at Famous Barr to save for the down payment. But you don't want to hear about my house. You're looking for Mary Ann?"

"Do you know where she went?"

"I keep wondering what happened to her, but she didn't tell me. Say, wouldn't you like to come in? You must be cold standing there." With that, she ushered me inside and closed the door behind me.

"I won't take but a minute," I said, staying by the door. "You said she didn't tell you where she was going?"

"She just said she was moving back home to Illinois. I don't know where. I'm so sorry. I've worried about her, being alone. Not that he was any great shakes, no sirree. Guys like him's the reason I never got married."

She offered me a seat and joined me on the sofa. "He had a temper, that one did. I could hear him and so could everyone else. 'Course in this neighborhood..."

I unbuttoned my jacket in the warmth of the room and asked, "Did he ever hurt her?"

"That I couldn't say." She leaned back and squinted at me. "Why are you so interested? What's she to you?"

I explained about the man we had in the hospital, that I was trying to find his wife to help identify him, and about Wilma Magnason's claim that he was her son.

"Poor woman. I never had any kids but I have nieces and nephews and if one of them had been there that day...well, I'd help you if I could."

"What about a lease agreement? Wouldn't there be a contact on that?"

"Where you been, girl? Around here they don't know what the word 'lease' means. All they understand is pay up or you're out. Sorry, I wouldn't ever keep these flats rented if I asked for a lease."

She chuckled. "And it wouldn't be worth the paper it's written on anyway. They'd probably put down fake names or people who wouldn't help anyway, not if they ran out owing me. I do make sure they got a job, though, and she was a school teacher, she paid every month right on time. Another reason I liked having her here. I could count on the money."

"What about her mail? Did you have it forwarded?"

"She must have. Only junk mail came for her here and I threw that out. Maybe you could ask at the post office."

"I doubt they'd have anything after this long and probably they can't tell me anyway."

"Um. I hadn't thought of that."

I stood, stifling a groan as I forgot how sore I was from last night. Carefully I slid my bag strap over my shoulder. "I appreciate your talking to me," I told her as we walked toward the door.

"Not that I could help, though."

As she let me out, she said, "Listen, if you find her, tell her hello for me. And if she's ever in the neighborhood..." At that, she glanced up and down the street, wrinkling her nose. "Tell her to come by. I'd like to know how she's doing."

I assured her I would.

I decided to stop by Hauptmann's Tavern, a place I knew well, although 'tavern' was too fancy a word for the bar in our old neighborhood that BJ and I frequented still. The bartenders changed periodically but the clientele remained working men and, more recently, women. Loyal to their patrons, many of whom still worked at the Anheiser Busch Brewery nearby, Hauptmann's only carried Busch and Budweiser brands of beer.

Someone there should know where Mary Ann Magnason went after Karl's death, if he was dead.

I was wrong. Only Walter, a fixture in his spot at the end of the bar next to the wall, offered information. The others said they didn't know Karl or his wife.

"I knowed 'em," Walter said in a whisky-garbled voice.

I took a seat at right angles to him and motioned for the bartender to bring him another shot.

"Beer back, too," Walter added and I nodded okay to the bartender. He stared into his empty shot glass and toyed with the beer can in front of him.

"You knew Karl?" I asked, putting a five on the bar.

"Huh?"

The bartender placed the shot of whisky and beer in front of him, cleared away the empties, and took the five.

I put my hand upright in front of Walter's drink and pushed it gently away from him.

"Hey!" he said, turning bleary eyes on me.

"After you tell me about Karl Magnason."

He eyed his drink, shrugged his shoulders, and turned on the stool toward me. "He could sure put them away, drink anyone under the table, he could. In fact, one time—"

"I want to know about after 9/11. Have you seen him since then?"

"'A course not! He were killed, weren't he? What, you think I can see a ghost? Hee, hee," he said and turned to the few people scattered along the bar. "She's a joker, she is, or she's seeing things." His voice cackled with the telling.

He got a few smiles and the others went back to their drinks and conversations.

"His mother thinks he didn't die," I explained. "And I'm trying to find his wife."

"Lived in the neighborhood, they did. Right down the street. Some nights he had to drive home, he was too drunk to walk." He hooted at his own joke.

When I pulled my hand away, Walter grabbed the shot and downed it. He had the beer in hand when I left him.

Chapter 31

Tuesday, November 23, 0842 Hours

STOPPED ON THE entrance ramp that led onto the bridge spanning the river, I watched the muddy Mississippi churn beneath me and slammed my hand on the steering wheel, jarring my shoulder. At least I'd remembered to take aspirin when I first got up. Then I'd stood under the shower, letting hot needles of water pound my arm and back so by the time I was dressed, had fed Cat, loaded my go-cup with coffee, cream, and sugar, and grabbed a bagel to take with me, the pain was tolerable. Until now.

Besides, what was I doing taking more time off trying to find out if Karl Magnason's wife had remarried? It had been a spur-of-the-moment decision. Wanda had convinced me that Belleville wasn't that far from my home, and I'd called Ruby on my cell as I'd pulled out onto the highway. When I found out I could see the marriage records at the courthouse, I decided to follow up this one last lead and untangle the only strand I could pull on.

The traffic ahead began to move, then stopped again. Most vehicles were heading in the opposite direction, into St. Louis to work, so the delay in this direction must be due to an accident or stalled car. Ahead of me sat an eighteen-wheel semi-tractor trailer, smoke spewing from the upright exhaust pipe hugging the cab, its fumes carried away on the wind. A gust of wind sent debris bouncing across the highway and rocked a small, tan sedan to my right, but Black Beauty's weight held her steady, retaining a solid grip on the pavement.

Finally we started up, passed the obstruction—a tractor-trailer jack-knifed over the concrete median—and soon we were speeding along on the multiple lanes that criss-crossed the river. I watched for signs to Belleville and soon saw my exit.

Already decorated for Christmas, Belleville had a small-town feel. Local shops lined the narrow street leading into town, and green pine roping dangled from lamp posts tied with red ribbons. In the misnamed town square, which was round, stood a giant Christmas tree behind a Santa display on one side, and a nativity scene opposite it. An oversized Christmas stocking, a candy cane stuck inside, dangled from a pole.

The courthouse faced the round square and I made several circles around it until I figured out where to turn off. In a parking garage I pulled into a spot I thought would be closest to the courthouse entrance. It turned out I was on the opposite side. Clutching my jacket around my thin cotton scrub suit, I faced into the biting wind that whistled between the buildings as I climbed the steep hill, once again regretting my decision to make this trip.

The county clerk's office on the second floor housed vital records, a man waiting by the elevator told me.

"The fee for a marriage license is $27.00," a young woman told me when I'd finally reached the front of the line. Annie, according to her name tag, flipped her hair back behind her ear and yawned widely without covering her mouth.

"I don't want a license. I want to see if someone else got a license here."

"The first certified copy is $11.85," she told me. "Additional copies two dollars each. No personal checks, no cash." She spoke words she'd repeated numerous times.

"No cash? That's all I have. I thought everyone took cash."

"Money orders or cashier's checks only." She started to turn away.

"Wait, wait. What if I don't find what I'm looking for? Do you charge just to check to see if a name's here?"

"We have back to 1763," she said. "What year are you wanting?"

"I don't know. Sometime since 2001."

"Wait here," she said and disappeared into a row of cubicles while I tapped my toe in frustration. If I could just see if Karl's wife had remarried, and if the record included an address, then maybe I could track her down and try to get her to come in to see our John Doe. A wife would be able to recognize her own husband, surely.

"Follow me," the woman said, waving me around the corner. She unlocked the door and led me into a small room cluttered with machines and supplies. A microfiche machine the size of a large computer monitor stood on a table.

Annie explained how to use it. When I looked confused she sat down and asked me for the years, then pulled out a four-by-five inch piece of plastic film. Each sheet held one year, she explained. She began with 2001.

"Husband's name?"

"I don't know that. Magnason is the wife's name."

Nothing in 2001.

Annie checked each subsequent year up to the present, including licenses issued within the last month. It took a few weeks for the application to be entered, she told me. No one named Magnason, male or female, had applied for a marriage license, according to their records.

"What do you need for a license?" I asked Annie as we walked back through the doors to the hall.

"You have to be eighteen, unless you have parental consent—that's if you're at least sixteen—and two forms of identification. One must be a photo ID. If you've been divorced within the past year you need to bring a copy of your divorce decree."

"That's it? That's all you need?"

She let me out into the hall and added, "And $27.00, of course."

"What if the first spouse died? Don't you need a death certificate?"

"Not in Illinois," she added, disappearing back into the maze of bureaucratic offices.

"No prisoners allowed on public elevators," a child read out loud from the sign by the elevator. "Where do they go?" he asked his mother.

"Maybe they walk down," she answered.

Unwilling to wait any longer for the elevator, I headed for the stairway and hurried down. The wind caught the door as I pushed it open, flinging it back against the outside of the building. I struggled to push it back closed and thought. Why had I come here at all? If I had found that Mary Ann Magnason had remarried and if our patient was Karl, her current marriage wouldn't be legal. How would I be able to convince her to come to St. T's to try to identify him, even if I found her? As BJ often reminded me, I wasn't a trained detective. Nonetheless, I doubted if Detective McNamara had come over here to see if he could find a record of her remarriage. At least I'd done more than the police.

"You in trouble," Ruby said, smacking her lips. "Again."

"What now, Ruby? Spill it." My jacket unzipped, I'd stopped by the unit before heading to my office.

"Red's been here and he's mad as heck. First, 'cause of your budget. You stealing our money, girl? And then 'cause you weren't here. He left this." She tossed my budget pages, marked up with red slashes, circles, and heavy underlining. "He said you used the wrong budget so you gotta redo it and," Ruby said, dragging out the last of Hockstetter's message. "He wants to know where is the step-down budget. You better get yourself in your office, stat."

I waved her off and said, "That's just where I'm going."

The budget for the step-down unit lay face up on my desk. Reconciling it would not be difficult. It only required that I match categories of expenses with their corresponding amounts allocated in the budget. What I didn't know was if the budget accurately reflected projected costs. That's what a manager learns by dealing every day with staff, supplies, and incidental expenses. Were the overtime expenditures for the past quarter out of line with projections? Did the unit have a higher acuity level in the aggregate than expected?

Ruby's call interrupted me. "You'll want to see this," she said, hanging up.

Val waited by the desk, drumming red-lacquered nails on the counter, a black coat over one arm. A faded pumpkin-colored sweater stretched tight across her braless chest. An orderly delivering linens stopped to stare, sheets piled in his arms.

"She wouldn't talk to anyone but you," Ruby complained. "I don't even know what she wants." She gave the orderly a stare and he went back to storing sheets in the linen closet.

"You came in to see him?" I asked her.

"I figured it was the least I could do for the guy. After all, I gave him three years, waiting for the big score he kept promising me."

As I had with Agatha, I tried to prepare her for how he looked, but she waved me off. "I've seen sick people, my dad, grandmother, were all in intensive care. Nothing will shock me."

Nonetheless, I tried to keep close, scurrying behind her march into the room.

At his bed, she flung back the sheet and raised his gown. "Yep, it's him, the bastard."

"Are you sure? His sisters didn't think it was him. They said he was heavier, that his hands were too smooth, not rough from his work. And his hair, they said, that he loved his curly hair and, as you can see, he's kept his head shaved." A stubble of hair covered JD's head, grown out during his stay. Because the damage had been inflicted on his face, not the back of his head like our other head trauma patient, we hadn't had to shave his head.

Val pointed to his naked genitals. "I'd know that dick anywhere. See there's this little—"

"Never mind," I interrupted, covering him back up.

Chapter 32

Tuesday, November 23, 1125 Hours

"I'LL BET WE get reporters in here when they hear about a 9/11 victim coming back to life," Serena said to the group of staff who had gathered around the nurses' station. Her voice held the excitement that critical care nurses crave.

"Media attention is seldom good for hospitals, Serena," Tim told her. "At the least, a notable person has died, and at the worst, the hospital is accused of contributing to a death. That's happened before, in case you don't remember."

Jessie spoke up. "No matter what the reason they're here, it detracts us from our work."

Poppi slammed a chart down on the desk and stalked away.

"What's wrong with her?" one of the new nurses asked.

"She was there in New York City," Serena said. When the nurse still looked blank Serena added, "On 9/11! She saw the whole thing, worked in a firehouse and on the street taking care of people."

"I'm sure it's hard for her to be reminded of it," Jessie offered.

"What was he doing in St. Louis, do you think, Monika?" asked Serena.

"Going after the money his wife got, according to the woman who was in here."

Ruby had disappeared as soon as she'd heard Val say she didn't want anything to do with Karl or his family. At this moment, Ruby was probably spreading the news throughout the house.

"At least that wife of his, she'll have to give back the money. Ha!" Val had said. And she'd admonished me not to report to the authorities that she'd identified Karl. "I don't want nothing to do with cops," she'd said, leaving behind the smell of cigarettes, beer, and body odor.

First, Agatha needed to know. She was the one who had started me looking for her brother, and she deserved to hear from me, but the line was busy. BJ's voice mail was on when I tried her next.

"I hear you know who our John Doe is," Hockstetter said. He'd come in while I was leaving a message for BJ.

"A friend of his identified him as Karl Magnason," I told him as Ruby returned.

"Well, that and the mother's good enough for me. Call her up, will you? Tell his mother I want to see her."

"I'll bet he does," Ruby said after he'd gone. "Wants her to pay his bill, that's what he wants."

"I'm sure he does, but she's not responsible."

"Why not? She's his mother, ain't she? I have to pay for my kids."

"Not when they're adults, Ruby."

"I bet she would, though, she's that kind of person."

"How did Hockstetter find out so quickly that someone had identified JD? I asked, squinting at Ruby."

"Hey, I don't tell Red nothing. It was that Cassandra," Ruby's lip curled with the name. "She was standing here at the desk when you were in with the girlfriend. She hurried right out."

"The people who need to know are the police."

"I ain't calling them. That's your business."

The phone line to the convent was still busy. That didn't make sense. I'd seen the receptionist's phone; it had several lines so one of them should have been free by now. A call to the operator gave me the answer: the phone lines in that part of town were down. The wind had knocked a tree over on a transformer. She expected repairs to be completed by tomorrow morning, she told me.

BJ called as soon as I hung up. I told her about Val identifying Karl.

"I don't know, Monika. How reliable is this woman? Also it's been several years, and you said yourself both sisters said it wasn't him. Did you get a hold of Roger's friend I told you about? The postal inspector?"

"I did."

"And?"

"He couldn't find any record of taxes filed for Karl Magnason. Even so," I said, "don't you think I should call McNamara?"

"Too late. He retired Saturday."

"What about Harding?"

185

"He already thinks you're a meddler."

"What? After I found the killer before?"

"You think cops like to have civilians solve crimes? Hey, where's our job security in that?"

"What about Marian Oblansky? Harding picked up the husband yesterday. Aren't they looking at his ex for this? Are they only concentrating on him?"

"Monika, this is police business and none of yours. Tell you what, I'll tell Don when I see him in a while about the girlfriend identifying your patient and let him decide what to do. If the family wants to call them, or the girlfriend does, let them. You stay out of it."

HOCKSTETTER APPARENTLY DIDN'T trust me to call Wilma Magnason. Correctly as it turned out. She and Roberta showed up right after lunch.

"See, his hair's coming in. Now I can tell, it's his." Today Wilma seemed lucid. "And," she added, "he's always trying to get in shape, that's why his body's thinner, although he could use some of my cooking." She peeked up at Roberta. "I'll fix spaghetti when he comes home." To me she said, "It's his favorite."

"Somebody needs to pay his bill," Hockstetter said behind us.

"Oh, I can," Wilma said. "I have lots of money. Don't you worry. I can take care of my baby."

Roberta grunted. "You do not. Your puny social security check barely covers anything."

"I do too." Wilma's chin rose. "I have that money she gave me."

"Who?" Hockstetter asked.

"His wife," she answered, glancing toward her son. "I'll think of her name in a minute."

"If this really is Karl, you'll have to give the 9/11 money back. So would she." Roberta turned to Hockstetter. "His widow gave Mom part of the money she received from the fund for family members of those killed in New York on 9/11."

"Someone's got to pay," Hockstetter said. "His care isn't free, you know. Somebody in the family, I don't care who," were his final words.

"You need to call the police if you're sure," I told both of them.

"We aren't telling anyone and you don't either," Roberta said. "Besides," she added out the side of her mouth so her mother couldn't hear, "it's not him anyway."

186

Wilma didn't answer, her eyes had faded to the blank look I'd seen before.

"OF COURSE NOT, Monika," Lord said later. "He's a grown man, responsible for his bills. Hockstetter's just blowing smoke, trying to scare them into thinking they're responsible. That's his job."

"So it won't work."

"Not if they talk to a lawyer. But people are so distraught, sometimes they feel guilty and pay anyway. It's a way to care for their loved one."

"Hockstetter takes advantage of that, doesn't he?"

"He sure does. He preys on their vulnerability."

"It doesn't seem fair."

"Fair has nothing to do with it. To Hockstetter, fair is what helps St. T's survive. That's all that matters to him."

"I THINK IT was hyperthermia that increased her pressure," Tim said, joining me at the coffee pot in the conference room. "At morning report the night nurse told me about Marian's fever. We've got ice blankets packed around her body, cooled IV fluids are hanging, but so far it hasn't helped."

"What's her temp now?"

"According to the rectal probe, 104 degrees when I checked a few moments ago."

I stirred my coffee absently.

"Have you heard anything about her husband, Steve, since the police picked him up yesterday?"

"He was in earlier today. He didn't say anything about the police, but obviously they let him go."

"For now," I said.

"He said he had a student pilot and had to leave." Tim returned to his patient as Serena came in and grabbed the last donut from a box of Krispy Kremes the night staff had left on the counter.

She pulled a piece of gooey dough off the donut and asked me about Marian.

"With central hyperthermia, the hypothalamus is damaged; her brain's not regulating her body temperature anymore. That's why we have to try and do it for her."

She waved the donut at me. "She doesn't feel hot to the touch and she's not sweating."

"That's why it's hard to even notice, sometimes for days. And the symptoms can mimic infection. That's why it takes a while to recognize."

"What if we can't get her temp down?" Serena stuffed the piece of donut in her mouth.

"It's too soon to know if the ice bags and cool fluids will work. It could stay high—104 to 104.5—for several days. We've been trying meds, even increasing her morphine. To dangerous levels."

"And?" Serena said, swallowing.

"It could go higher...105, possibly."

"Any higher than that, she's—"

"Yes. Above that, death occurs."

"There's not much hope, is there?" Serena wiped her hands on a napkin. "She's not going to make it."

"It's a long shot, Serena. Sometimes...I've seen them recover. But no, not very often."

"ARE YOU GOING to talk to the family?" I asked Lord, as he wrote in Marian's chart when I returned after lunch.

"Better do it sooner rather than later," he said. "It's so much harder if they're not prepared."

"You'd think with all the complications that she's had they'd realize how sick she is. But that's not how it works, is it?"

He nodded agreement. "We usually have to spell it out for them."

"No one wants to hear that their loved one is dying."

"No doubt they're in denial," he said.

"Sometimes denial helps them get through it until they're ready."

"Death comes when the patient's ready, not the family. So do you want me to talk to them?"

"I'll try to find the right time."

As it turned out, the opportunity came almost immediately.

"We're doing all we can," Lord began when Steve and Charlotte were seated in a corner of the family waiting room which, fortunately, was empty at this early hour. When I'd found them together in Marian's room, I'd asked them to wait, paged Dr. Lord, and we met a few minutes later.

I pulled my chair closer to the settee where Steve and Charlotte sat side by side. Lord sat opposite me, also at right angles to the couple.

"I think I know what you're going to say," Charlotte said, her hands cradled around a lidded cup of coffee. "It's bad news, isn't it?"

"Her injuries are substantial," Lord said.

Charlotte nodded. The cheek bones on Steve's face stood out in silent relief, the pulse on his neck visible.

"As you know," Lord said, "she's had some seizures but those are under control. Then she developed an infection in the wound and we treated that. The swelling in her brain has caused the pressure to increase in the part of her brain that regulates body temperature, which has gone up. We haven't been able to get it down."

"If you keep putting ice around her, will that help?" Charlotte asked.

"Unlikely, I'm sorry to say," Lord said.

Charlotte looked at Steve and then back at Lord. "And then what?"

"Her heart's struggling now." He left the words hanging.

Steve interjected. "Maybe she'll get better."

"From my experience, Mr. Oblansky, when there's this much brain damage—"

"So even if she lives," Charlotte said, "she might stay like she is."

"She may never wake up," Lord confirmed.

There, he'd said it. The words no family wants to hear.

Charlotte teared up and her cup wobbled in her hand. I took it and placed it on the table to the side and covered her clutched hands with mine.

Steve closed his eyes for a moment and when he opened them, he said, "She wouldn't want to live like that."

"Did she put that in writing?" Lord asked but Steve shook his head.

"She told me, too," Charlotte said, struggling to keep control of her emotions. "Many times."

Lord continued. "If you're both in agreement that she wouldn't want extraordinary means taken when she has little hope of recovery, we'd like to know how much you want done if she arrests."

"If her heart stops," I translated. "Do you want us to try to revive her?"

"If you did, what then?" Steve wanted to know.

"It's unlikely her condition would change," Lord said. "We'd just be prolonging the inevitable."

"You only have to decide for the next twenty-four hours," I told them. "If you change your mind or her status changes, we have to write a new order tomorrow anyway."

"She's dying, Steve," Charlotte said, turning to her brother-in-law. "It's time to give up."

"Give up hope? How can I do that to her?" He leaned forward and dropped his head forward into his palms. His shoulders shook as he gave in to quiet tears.

Charlotte patted his back as Lord shifted uncomfortably in his seat.

Finally Steve raised a tear-stained face to look at Charlotte. "What do you think we should do?"

"If her heart stops, I think we should let her go. I don't think they should resuscitate. Let's not put her through any more."

"Yes..." He couldn't go on.

Lord stood and squeezed Steve's shoulder. "You've made the right decision," he said.

I handed Steve the clipboard with the forms and showed him where to sign. He took the pen, scribbled his name, and Charlotte and I witnessed his signature.

I stayed with Charlotte after Steve had gone back to Marian's bedside.

"How long do you think?" she asked me.

"I couldn't say. It depends on how long her heart can keep going. It could be a day or a few days. Not longer than that, I wouldn't think."

"I understand. It's just...it's so hard to accept. This is so sudden, and now when she's happy for the first time in a long while, this happens. It isn't right."

I WAS SITTING at the nurses' station desk processing the DNR order when I realized that Steve hadn't become angry like Charlotte had worried that he might when we'd given him the news that his wife was unlikely to survive. In fact, he'd remained calm except when he appropriately gave in to his tears. His grief was sincere, that was obvious no matter what Detective Harding thought.

I entered the "do not resuscitate" order on the chart, noting the date and time when Steve had signed it. I grabbed a green wristband and collected a sheet of round green stickers from the shelf under the counter. I slapped one on the front of the chart, and stuck two more on my fingers before heading for Marian's room. One of the green stickers went on the information panel beside her door and the other I took into her room for the board above her bed.

The young woman in the bed hadn't moved. Only the rise and fall of her frail chest, the vent artificially forcing air into her lungs, told me that Marian Oblansky was still alive. I touched her arm, feeling the bones through translucent skin. "Marian, can you hear me?" I asked, not expecting an answer. I lifted her left arm and wrapped the wristband around it, pulling the end through the plastic guard to its tightest notch, and snapping the clasp. No one on the staff could miss the order that the green labels signified: this patient was not to be resuscitated. For the next twenty-four hours anyway.

"I saw the DNR order. Isn't there anything else we can do?" Poppi asked me. "Has he tried everything? She's so young. Why are they giving up so soon?"

Critical care nurses come in two versions. One type recognizes that death is inevitable in spite of all possible medical efforts. The other type never gives up, thinking that there must be one last intervention to try. Poppi was the latter.

I sighed. Type twos rarely can be convinced to become a type one, but I had to try. "Her brain damage was just too severe from the beginning. The initial injury has caused one complication on top of another." This information wasn't news to Poppi. "Anything we did now would just be prolonging a life that's essentially gone."

"Are you Catholic?"

"Uh, yes."

"Then don't you believe in the sanctity of life?"

"Of course I do. But she doesn't have any life right now, not one that we can sustain indefinitely. Sure, we could bring her back if she arrests but to what? The same unconscious state she's in now? What kind of life is that?"

"I don't believe in giving up. Life is God's to take, not ours."

"We don't want to give up, Poppi, but there comes a time to let the natural process occur even if it means death. You know, she's only alive now because of medical advances. Fifty, even twenty, years ago people didn't live after this much trauma."

"So you're saying we shouldn't use life-saving means because keeping them alive wasn't allowing God to take them?"

"No. It's just that the technology has made it harder to know when it's time to discontinue them."

"I still don't understand," Poppi said, heading back to her patient.

Chapter 33

Tuesday, November 23, 1620 Hours

"So it is true," Agatha said, leaning back in her chair. "I never would have believed it." She folded her hands in front of her. "I'll pray for him," she said, her head lowered.

I'd stopped by the motherhouse on my way home to tell Agatha about her brother's girlfriend identifying Karl.

Straightening, Agatha asked, "What happens now?"

"I guess it's up to the police. Right now they have conflicting opinions about whether the man is your brother. If they decide he is your brother and if he lives, I assume he'll face charges of some kind. At the very least, he was driving a stolen car."

"But Val was sure."

"She recognized his body." I didn't intend to tell Agatha what part she'd recognized.

"How about the police? What will it take to convince them that he's Karl?"

"I imagine they could run DNA, but that's expensive." I told her about checking the courthouse records for marriages and searching online and at the library.

"Thank you, Monika. You've gone to a lot of time and trouble. I appreciate all you've done."

"I'm just glad the girlfriend finally came forward."

"I'm sorry I couldn't identify him. Maybe it was my anxiety about being there or—"

"He didn't look the same, Agatha. He'd changed his appearance a lot, slimmed down, shaved his head."

"I should have come in sooner in any case. I'll tell you why."

I tried to interrupt, to tell her she didn't need to explain herself to me, but she stopped me. "You deserve to know the reason, Monika." She took off her glasses and wiped them on a corner of her cardigan sweater, thin with age.

"When my grandfather was in the hospital," she began. "I was just four or five when Mother took me to see him. Apparently I wiggled away from her, I think because he smelled so bad, and I tripped over a cord on the floor. All I remember is the noise, alarms shrieking. I think I started screaming, too. Mother grabbed my hand and pulled me out as a throng of people crowded into the room. They came out a few minutes later saying Grandfather had died.

"I knew I'd killed him. The cord I'd unplugged led to his ventilator and he had stopped breathing. Mother reminded me over the years that he had been dying anyway and that unplugging the machine for that short a time hadn't made any difference.

"The first time Mother was hospitalized I had such an anxiety attack that I had to leave. I thought by the time I graduated from high school that surely I was over my fear of hospitals. But then during that first week in clinical I knew that I might someday be able to conquer my fear, but I could never be a nurse. I'd be too afraid that my anxiety would reoccur at a time when a patient needed me, and I couldn't risk that."

"You came to the hospital this time, though."

"I did, didn't I? I'm glad. I imagine Mother will be in the hospital and I'd hate to think I'd be so anxious I couldn't be with her if she needed me."

"You'll be all right, Agatha, and I'm sure you'll be able to be with your mother or anyone in your community if you need to visit the hospital."

"If the man is my brother, where's he been all this time?"

"Do you think his wife might have been with him?"

"You mean did they conspire to deceive the government and collect the money?"

"No, I don't. His widow—wife—gave your mother some of her award when she didn't have to."

"Maybe Karl had her do that to help out Mother. No," she said after a moment, "that doesn't sound like Karl. He wouldn't be that thoughtful. Mother gave some of it to my community, too, did I tell you? Not that Roberta was happy about it."

"So you'll have to give that back."

"That's all right. We can't keep money that's not ours."

"Roberta still insists he's not Karl. Do you know why she'd do that?"

"No, I wouldn't. She's spent more time with him than I have."

"Maybe—" I began.

"She doesn't want to give the money back either. Isn't that what you were about to say?"

"It's possible. So why'd he come back to St. Louis, do you think? To see your mother? He might have been going there when the cops chased him into the park. And how does Val fit in? She said he called her and told her he was coming home to get the money. I'm assuming he meant the money his wife had collected."

"Just because you didn't find her doesn't mean she's not living right here in St. Louis and we'd have no way to know. But wouldn't that be risky if she didn't know he was alive? She might report him."

"Then she'd have to give up the money, too, in that case. He didn't have that much on him when he came in. I forget what they said but it wasn't any large amount."

"So he hadn't found her yet."

"Or she'd turned him down. Let's leave it to the authorities to figure it out. At least now they've got something to go on. Hopefully they'll pursue it. I've done all I can."

"And believe me, Monika, I appreciate it," she said, standing.

"I was glad to help," I said as she shut the door behind us. "Can you do me a favor before I go?"

"Of course. What do you want?" she asked as we made our way down the hall.

Rumor had it that the motherhouse held the largest collection of relics in the United States. I'd taken a neighborhood tour once but the tour guide had said seeing them was impossible because you had to be invited to go inside.

"I'd like to see the relics."

"We call them Saints," said a woman who had come up behind us so silently I hadn't known she was there until she spoke.

"Sister Martha, this is my friend, Monika."

Sister nodded in my direction. "The phones are fixed," she said to Agatha. "You have some calls waiting," she added.

"Maybe I'd better go." I started to zip my jacket as Sister Martha walked away.

"Not before I show you the relics. It's the least you can do for all the help you've given me."

Inside the chapel entrance she turned left and led me to an alcove at the side of the altar. We stood silently in front of the display. On each side was an oblong glass case housing a young child. The girl to the right wore a deep-red velvet dress. Graying lace edged her sleeves and neck and the alabaster that covered her skull and hands shown translucent through the glass.

"She was a young girl, martyred in the early years of the Church," Agatha said. "So was he," she added, with a nod toward the opposite side where a boy lay encased in glass, his body small yet somehow looking strong.

"Why were they martyred? I've never quite understood that. Why do people care about what anyone else believes?"

"It's about power, power over people, land, money. Remember, at that time the government and religion were inextricably bound together."

Agatha stepped up on a platform in front of a display of glass cases where skulls gleamed inside separate glass enclosures on either side of central case, which held a jumble of leg and arm bones. "We have many more." Agatha reached behind the display and jiggled a pulley. Bones rattled, toppling one on top of each other, and shuffled to a stop. "See," she said. "A whole other group of relics is revealed. There's plenty more stored away and we rotate them every so often." She started to step down but a cough from the opposite side of the display stopped her.

Steve's ex-wife, Nadine, stood there, her eyes wide, looking like an animal caught in a gun sight.

Agatha recovered first. "Nadine, how'd you get in there?" she asked.

"You know each other?" I asked as Nadine clutched her mud-splattered coat around her, her spiky hair contributing to her startled look. "And what have you been doing at St. Teresa's trying to get into ICU?"

A grimace crossed her face.

"Monika's a nurse there," Agatha explained.

"Why do you want to see Marian Oblansky?" I repeated.

"Nadine comes here sometimes to pray," Agatha said as the doors swished open and Sister Martha spied us.

"There you are, Nadine. I've been looking for you." Martha's stern voice was in character as I remembered nuns from my past.

"And here I am," Nadine said, rushing down the steps. She grabbed Sister Martha's arm and tugged her toward the door.

"We've got lots of donation letters to get out today." Sister Martha said to Nadine. On the way out, she gave us a frowned warning. "Better get those calls made, Sister."

After the doors had closed behind them, I asked Agatha how she knew Nadine.   "What's she doing here?"

"She haunts the convent."

"Haunts?"

"There are lay people who haunt the convents and novice houses. Men and women who wanted to join a religious community but, for some reason, they don't or can't. They hang around, offering to help, run errands, they do help out but it can be too much. Sometimes it feels like they're haunting the place. Nadine spends lots of time in the chapel."

"She wanted to be a nun? In your order?"

Agatha nodded.

"What happened?"

Agatha led me to a row of chairs along the wall where we'd sat when I'd been here the week before. "Not everyone is admitted, Monika. We have to be certain they've received the call."

"How do you know?"

"Knowing if you have the call is called discernment. You turn to God, read, pray, and talk to a trusted religious."

"Is that what you did?"

"Not exactly. At about the time of my first communion I knew that I wanted the religious life." She motioned toward the altar and the tabernacle lit within.

"But you started nursing school with me."

"That was my father's idea. He thought I should have a year of college before I made a final decision."

"And you chose nursing."

"I wanted to be a historian but mother said I should study nursing. It was something to fall back on if I had to support myself."

"How many times have I heard that? At least, today women have more choices. But, back to Nadine. So you thought she didn't have the call?"

"She didn't get that far."

"Why not?"

"She got pregnant."

"Oops."

Agatha frowned.

"I guess it's not that uncommon."

"Sadly, no. She did get married, as you know. And divorced."

"What about the baby?" I asked.

"She miscarried. She couldn't get pregnant after that."

"Oh, my."

"So now she hangs around here."

"Trying to atone for her sins?"

"I wouldn't know about that, Monika, and I only told you this because you're worried about your patient's safety. But, no matter how mad she might have been at her husband"—she held up her hand to keep me from interrupting—"and even if she followed his new wife around, I'm sure she wouldn't have harmed her."

"How did she get behind the relics?"

"Apparently she found the trap door. Maybe she found this way in because we've sent her away too often. I'll have to admit, she gets on my nerves."

"Trap door?"

Agatha led me back to the front and behind the relics' display. She pointed to the floor. "See here where the floor's been cut into a square?"

"It's not very big. About three by three feet?"

"About that." Agatha grabbed a metal loop attached to one side and pulled the trap door up.

I peered down onto the dirt below. "This goes outside? Where does it lead?" I asked as she let the lid back down and dusted her hands. "What's it for?"

"We're one of the orders that helped with the Underground Railroad. Down the hill is the Mississippi River. The early nuns put the trap door here so they could escape if the convent was attacked."

"Attacked? By whom?"

"You don't remember how the early religious were persecuted? In the east, especially, they were burning convents with the nuns still in them. The trap door offered an escape route and access to the river. Later the convent served as a stop on the Underground Railroad. So they'd send slaves down here to hide and then they wouldn't have to lie when they said there weren't any slaves in the building. Also the nuns figured if they searched the building they still wouldn't want to get very near the relics."

"I never heard about the trap door. Or any of this history for that matter."

"Most of my community hasn't either. But I'll have to report this. We can't have the trap door unlocked even if very few know about it. It's not in any official records. In fact, it's not even in our archives. Our first archivist made sure of that in case the records were confiscated. Sister Agnes—she was archivist before me—says I'm not supposed to tell anyone."

"Why not? It's not like there's any runaway slaves coming through now."

Agatha brought herself up straight, looked down her nose, and mimicked Sister Martha, "It's not in our official records, so it doesn't exist."

"That sounds rather silly. What is that, some rule or other?"

"You've never been a nun," she said. "If you had, you'd know about rules."

Chapter 34

Tuesday, November 23, 1735 Hours

DRIVING OUT OF the convent's parking lot I thought about what Agatha had said about official records. If the trap door wasn't in the archives, it didn't exist. Although we assume such documents are accurate, they may not be. So which record about Rick was correct? According to his buddy, Rick was still missing in action. But the official letter stated he'd been killed in action. What was the truth?

I swung onto Minnesota, waited at the stoplight, and thought about JD. After all my efforts to find some trace of Karl Magnason's widow, I'd failed miserably. I'd followed every strand but no matter what I did, they remained tangled. No one knew where Mary Ann had gone, and I couldn't locate, not easily anyway, licenses for school teachers, which might not have helped since her address probably wouldn't have been available to the public. Nor had I found any record of a marriage license in Illinois where possibly she had moved after her husband's death. As BJ has said, I wasn't a trained detective. The light changed and I turned onto Grand.

And I was no closer to helping exonerate Steve Oblansky from his wife's attack than I had been when I'd started worrying about Detective Harding's suspicion of Steve to the exclusion of everyone else including Nadine. Now there was a strange one. Stalking Marian, harassing her with phone calls that apparently didn't stop even after they'd secured a restraining order, and more recently trying to get to her in the hospital. But what puzzled me was finding her at the convent's motherhouse and learning that she spent time there, helping the staff, and praying in the chapel. Was her image as a deeply-religious person contrived? It didn't fit with her attempts to harass Marian.

I slid into a parking place in front of my house and took a quick look around. Seeing no one on the street, I clamored out and noted the abbreviated stack of shingles that remained by the sidewalk, much diminished from the mounds the roofers had had when they'd started the job. I unlocked the front door and slid inside as quickly as my sore body would let me. Shaking off my fear from Sunday night's attack, I focused on finding out more about Nadine Oblansky. I had to hurry, though, before Marian died and Steve was charged with her murder.

Chapter 35

Wednesday, November 24, 0825 Hours

EVEN THOUGH I had talked with Father Rollings on numerous occasions, I hesitated at the door to his office. How could I ask what I wanted to know without offending him or his staff? Before I could answer myself, Father Rollings opened the door.

His startled look became recognition. "You're Hannah Schumann's sister, aren't you?" he asked, motioning me inside.

"Cousin. I'm her cousin, Monika Everhardt. Do you have a few minutes?"

He offered me coffee, saying he'd been on his way out to get some when I'd arrived.

While he was gone, I looked around his office, expecting it to be surrounded by religious imagery but his office appeared to be no different from that of any other busy administrator. His desktop and the credenza behind it were littered with files and papers. At right angles to the desk stood a filing cabinet of indeterminate color and showing its age, and a dusty-colored sofa and chairs were along the wall. It was into one of those chairs that Father Rollings had directed me.

Would he be willing, or able, to help me learn more about Nadine Oblansky? Now that I knew she'd given up her goal of the religious life to marry the father of her unborn child and then he'd left her, I realized she had a more compelling motive to attack Marian. With Marian's death imminent, Steve could be charged with her murder and, regardless of what BJ said, I didn't believe he would hurt her. Nadine was a much more likely suspect in spite of her apparent religious life.

"I was just working on next Sunday's homily," Father Rollings said, taking the seat opposite me. "What can I do for you? There isn't anything wrong with the Schumanns, is there?"

"No, no. It's about something else."

"If this is a spiritual matter, you really should see your own priest. We try to not overstep into each others' parishes."

"This isn't about me.

He leaned back in his chair and his white collar cut into a fleshy neck, spilling a fold of skin over the top. He balanced his coffee cup on his paunch and studied me through bifocals.

I sipped my coffee, put it on the table to the side and asked, "You have a secretary, Nadine Oblansky?"

"Yes," he said. "I'm lucky to have her. She's worked in a parish office before, which is always a help. What about her?"

"Has she been here long?"

"About six months. Do you want to see her?"

"No, no. I want to ask you some questions about her."

"Really? What? And why?"

"I'm a nurse at St. T's and—"

"What does that have to do with Nadine?"

"It's about her ex-husband's wife. She's my patient."

"Are you supposed to be telling me this? I thought patient confidentiality was as sacrosanct as the confessional."

"I trust you to keep this confidential."

"We're not in the confessional, Mrs. Everhardt."

I took a breath. "But you can keep a confidence."

"Of course." His tone changed, suspicion tingling his voice. "That's why I can't say anything about her, either."

"I just have one question: was she here two Wednesdays ago at about nine in the morning?"

He pushed forward, coffee drops splashing onto his black jacket. "Why would you want to know that?"

"That's when her ex's wife was attacked."

"And you think she did it?" he asked. "I think you'd better go, Mrs. Everhardt. If you have any suspicions about my secretary, you can talk to the police." He shoved his chair back and stood. "If you want to talk to her about this, you can. I'm not at liberty to say anything."

I tripped over the chair legs trying to get out of there, embarrassment warming my face, as I stumbled out the door.

Angering a priest. Add that to my list of sins.

I had the car door unlocked when an older-model black sedan pulled in beside me. I followed the driver as she started toward the rectory door. "Mrs. Oblansky."

She turned, saw me, and started to walk away.

"Wait up. I want to talk to you," I said, reaching her at the door.

She dipped her head and let her bag slip off her shoulder into her hand where it hung there.

"Why do you keep coming to St. T's? You're not a family member—"

"I know that, they told me I couldn't see her." She looked up and tears pooled in her eyes. "You wouldn't understand," she added, looking away.

"Try me."

She shifted her bag back up on her shoulder and pulled her gray weathered coat closer around her. She clutched her bag straps with gloveless hands, her knuckles white with cold.

"Look," I went on. "Someone attacked her. If you haven't had the police to see you, you will because you'd harassed her. Tell me and maybe I can help you."

"I guess," she said finally. She blinked and the tears disappeared. "At first I did want to see her just to know she was suffering. But then...when I couldn't get in I realized what I was doing. For so long, I hated her. She took the only thing I had left after...and I blamed him, too, for leaving. When they got that restraining order, I stopped. I realized I was treading on dangerous ground, that it really was serious if you follow somebody and call them up and, well, I don't want to go over all that.

"I prayed about it, how I felt, and finally I prayed for them. Talking to Father has helped, too, and the nuns. Finally, I just wanted to tell her how sorry I was, that I wouldn't have hurt her or Steve.

"When the cops came and asked Father if I'd been here that morning, thank goodness I was. I wanted her forgiveness, but that was selfish of me. I would never have hurt her. I was just so angry. But I finally realized that making them miserable and afraid really didn't help me feel better. If I could just tell her how sorry I am..."

"I'm afraid she won't be able to talk to you. She's dying."

Nadine slumped against the railing and tugged her coat closer. "You can never undo the past, can you?" she asked rhetorically. "They were sweethearts in school, did you know that? If it hadn't been my husband, I might have thought that was romantic, meeting your high school sweetheart years later."

She rubbed her hands together. "I better go, Father's waiting."

"Thank you, Mrs. Oblansky—"

"I went back to my maiden name, it's Macalvie."

Driving away I thought about Rick again. He'd been my high school sweetheart, too. What I wouldn't give to see him again.

Chapter 36

Wednesday, November 24, 0955 Hours

"THERE YOU ARE," Ruby said, grabbing my arm as I came through the door. "What's the matter with you, girl, being late every day? You want to get fired? Leaving me here to handle old Red's hissy fit."

I slipped out of my jacket and laid it across the corner of the counter.

"Jessie called in sick, Poppi refused to take JD as her patient, so Tim's trying to take care of both Marian and him. He's running back and forth between their rooms like his shoes are on fire, he's about to have his baby. He says he needs to talk to you ASAP and—"

"Okay, okay, I've got the picture. Go on wherever you were going. I'm here now and I'll handle things." When she didn't move, I told her, "Go, get out of here. Everything's under control."

"The painters are on their way up," was her parting shot.

I dealt with Poppi first, catching her in the med room. "What's this Ruby tells me? You don't want JD—I mean Karl Magnason—today? Isn't this what you wanted, to get the more complex cases? Isn't that your criteria? God knows he needs a skilled nurse."

"After what I saw on 9/11? And heard about what families went through? Do you know some of them had only a bone fragment to bury? Can you imagine anything worse?"

I could. Not having a body at all to bury.

"Every day the New York Times had stories about those who died," she said, waving her hands for emphasis. "It went on for months until they had profiled all of them. Reading and reading about these people, they came alive in their stories. They weren't just numbers anymore. No one can relate to numbers but when you read about their lives, what they did for a living, their families, they become real."

"I understand what you're saying, Poppi, but you're a professional. You must put your personal feelings aside to take care of a patient. This is just like if you were in the military. Those nurses took care of enemy soldiers as well ours. And you took care of him before."

"That was before I knew who he was. Pretending to die when all those others really did. I saw them, Monika, bodies and body parts and the rescue workers..." She looked up, her eyes full. "I'm sorry. Please don't ask me to care for him today, please." She turned away, her hands stilled on the tray of syringes and medicine cups in front of her.

"Okay," I said. "I'll pull someone from the step-down unit who can help Tim with both of them and you can go there for a day. Tomorrow I'll figure out what to do about him."

"Don't send Missy back here, she isn't worth squat."

"I'll find someone else. By the way," I said before she left, "what is it you and Cassandra have been in conference about lately? I've seen you talking with her a couple of times."

"You don't want to know."

"If I didn't, I wouldn't be asking you."

"She wanted to know about a COO candidate, he worked at my hospital in New York."

"And?"

"I told her he was ruthless, that she wouldn't want him at St. T's."

"That's it? That's all?"

"No. The more I told her about him, the more she thought he was, what did she say? Oh, yes, 'just what we need around here.' Now can I get back to work?"

Chapter 37

Wednesday, November 24, 1037 Hours

"SHE REFUSED OUTRIGHT?" Tim asked when I returned with a nurse from the step-down unit and explained that Poppi would work over there for the remainder of the day. "Doesn't she know she can't abandon a patient? Not if she wants to keep her license."

"She took another assignment. You wanted to see me?" I asked to change the subject.

"It's Magnason. We'd better get the family in. When I got here, the night nurse said his pupils had become irregularly shaped and fixed at about five a.m. this morning. They haven't changed."

"What does Lord say?"

"Central herniation of the brain. The vascular system's compressed, destroyed, or lacerated, and ischemia's set in."

"Brain death," I added.

Although we now assumed that he was Karl Magnason, I couldn't stop thinking of him as JD, and I didn't share Poppi's aversion to him. He was our patient. We'd done all we could for him over the past two weeks, accepting each complication as one more challenge we expected to overcome. But now it sounded like our efforts were coming to an end.

The cell phone clipped to Tim's pocket ran. "Oh, my God, it's the baby," he said, noting the number. "Susie's in labor, I've got to go, oh what will you do? Maybe I should call, see how far along she is, maybe I can stay awhile—"

"Go! Go! We'll manage here. You take care of your family. That's what matters now."

"Okay, okay," he said. "Where's my coat?" He patted his lab coat pockets. "My keys? Where'd I leave them? Maybe they're in my coat." He ran into the conference room and I followed.

"Sit down, call your wife, but first give me your locker combination. I'll get your things together for you."

He plopped into a chair. "Fifteen, eighty, ten. I think that's it." He pushed a button on speed dial. "Yes, yes, I'm on my way," he said a few seconds later. "Really? Okay. Okay." He clicked off. "They're coming about two minutes apart. Her mother's on her way to stay with the girls."

I handed him his coat and the keys that were lying on the top shelf. "Go. Get out of here. And let us know," I said to his back.

Chapter 38

Wednesday, November 24, 1115 Hours

AFTER TIM LEFT I let myself into my office and checked my e-mail to find two messages from Hockstetter. "Where are your budgets?" they both asked. I deleted them and sat there thinking. Some strand was still skirting around in my head. What was it? Something about Karl Magnason, but what? Had I tried everything I could to find his wife? Why did the police still think our John Doe might not be Magnason?

A death certificate! That's it. That's what's been bothering me. Even though the clerk at the courthouse had said Mary Ann Magnason wouldn't have needed a death certificate to apply for a marriage license, she must have had one to receive the money from the WTC fund.

Maybe death certificates are online. I clicked through to the New York City Department of Health and Mental Hygiene. The site told me how to apply for a death certificate but not how to see if someone had died there.

I called Agatha and she answered immediately.

"They issued many death certificates without a body," she said. "As I recall, Mary Ann didn't have any problems getting one. More than a thousand people were never identified," she added with a sigh.

We hung up and I went back online to find the application for a death certificate. That wouldn't work either, I discovered, because only those with a "documented lawful right or claim" were eligible to receive a certificate of death.

At last I could think of nothing more to do to help Agatha be certain JD was her brother. It was up to the family, law enforcement, and the hospital to decide what to do next although I doubted it would matter much. The man's death seemed imminent. I clicked off and went out to our other patients. They needed me more.

Chapter 39

Wednesday, November 24, 1345 Hours

CHARLOTTE SAT BY her sister's bed, her hands clasped in her lap, her eyes closed while I checked the monitor connected to the rectal probe. Marian's temperature had risen to a dangerous 105.2, up three-tenths since the last reading ten minutes ago when Tim had placed fresh ice blankets around her body.

Charlotte stirred when I came around to her side of the bed to check Marian's drips. Cooled fluids were still running, but there wasn't much urine draining from her bladder into the bag that dangled below the bedrail, one more sign that her body systems were shutting down.

Charlotte's bony wrists dangled over the bedrail, her hands tracing thread on the light-weight blanket covering her sister. "We've always been so close," she whispered, turning her gaunt face to me. "My poor sister, first a 9/11 widow, now this."

"Her husband died on 9/11?"

"In New York City."

"I didn't know that was how he died."

"I told one of the nurses, I thought everyone knew. That's where her money came from. The World Trade Center Fund. That's how she could help Steve with his business."

I placed my hand on Charlotte's shoulder. There was little we could do for Marian now.

"I can feel her slipping away from me," Charlotte said, stroking her sister's hand.

"It could still be awhile."

We stayed like we were, Charlotte watching her sister's face, the ventilator still forcing air through her mouth into her lungs, while I watched the squiggly line running across the cardiac monitor, indicating she was in ventricular tachycardia, her heart vibrating more than 150 beats a minute, a rate that her body couldn't continue for long.

"Do you think she's in pain?" Charlotte asked into the quiet.

"She's not aware of anything now, Lottie."

"Steve's on his way," she said. "At least I'm glad he signed for her not to be resuscitated. I don't want to put her through any more trauma. That's the right thing to do, isn't it? He talked to the doctor again and he told Steve that if her fever didn't go down, there wasn't anything else they could do. I'm not so sure he wants to be here, at least not in the room when..."

I nodded, not trusting myself to speak. Watching a patient's life come to an end is one of the most difficult parts of being a nurse. No matter who the patient is or how old or sick, it still brings a lump to my throat.

I had heard staff wandering in and out as Charlotte and I waited at Marian's bedside. I told Charlotte I'd be right back and went out to speak to them.

"You can go in and talk to her," I told one new nurse standing with Serena.

"I don't know what to say," she said.

"Just tell her you were glad to take care of her sister or ask her if you can get her anything—coffee, water—whatever she might need to make her comfortable."

"Charlotte's our patient, now," Serena told her. "There's nothing more we can do for Marian."

"You've come a long way, Serena," I said when the nurse had gone into Charlotte. "I remember when you'd had a tough time with every patient's death."

"I've seen a lot since then and, besides, I'm taking a class on death and dying this semester. I've been keeping a journal about her and John Doe. I'm going to use it for my paper. That's helped me see how we're not failing them when they're dying and that we care for everyone, family and patient, as we'd like our family treated."

When I returned to Marian's bedside, I found two other nurses standing to the side, silently supporting Charlotte.

"I can't imagine why Steve's not here by now," Charlotte said. "Except..."

Marian's heart fluttered, then hesitated. Charlotte shifted on her seat. Weak beeps on the monitor began again and then stopped for good. The monitor wailed a straight line.

"Mary Ann, my dear," Charlotte said, clinging to her sister's hand through the bedrail.

"Mary Ann? I thought your sister's name was Marian."

"It is. Or was," she said, choking a sob. "But when I was little, I couldn't say Marian all in one word so mother taught me to say Mari...An. The family always called her that."

"His name! Her first husband's name?"

"Karl."

"His last name?"

"Magnason."

I left Charlotte still holding her dead sister's hand and went out into the unit. Could it be that Marian Oblansky was the same person that the Magnason's called "Mary Ann?" It all fit. Marian's husband died on 9/11 and she married Steve Oblansky. The Magnason family had lost contact with Karl's widow, Mary Ann.

An alarm screamed from Karl Magnason's room. I turned toward it and ran into Dr. Lord. We weaved back and forth trying to pass each other until finally I tugged at his sleeve and pulled myself by him. A floral delivery man waited at the counter, and Ruby was talking to a middle-aged couple. The painters had arrived, a ladder straddled the entry to room five, its legs spread open in front of me. I ducked underneath it, narrowly missing the shelf that held a can of paint. I shoved a wheelchair to the side and flung back the curtain to see Roberta standing by the wall, the cord to Karl's ventilator in her hand, her face registering surprise.

Someone had followed me into the room as the operator announced the code for "Room one, ICU" over the loud speaker.

I grabbed at the cord but Roberta pulled it out of my reach, the alarm still shrieking. I lunged for the cord again, this time catching my hand on it. "Give me that!" Her hand slid down the cord and caught at the plug.

I jerked the cord and Roberta fell backward, hitting her head on the wall. I sat back on my haunches. She lay still as I pulled myself up on my knees and wiggled the plug back into the wall, my hands shaking. The pump reengaged and air swished through the ventilator tube.

I looked around to see Poppi leaning over Karl's body.

"Stop!" I screamed, struggling to get to my feet.

"Shhh," she said. "I'm listening for heart sounds." It was then I noticed the stethoscope positioned on his chest. His trach tube had been reconnected, its alarm silenced.

"What are you doing here?" I asked, my breath coming in spurts.

"I heard Tim was having a baby so I traded back," she said, raising up.

The code team was jockeying into place as Lord entered.

A straight line showed on the monitor.

Lord ordered epinephrine, which Poppi drew up and inserted into the IV port.

"No change," she said and squirted gel on the orange pads as he raised them to her. "He's already in asytole," she added.

He nodded and slapped one large rectangle over the sternum and one on the left lower chest. "Charge 360."

Nothing.

"Charge, clear."

"More epi?"

He shook his head and bent over, checking for a pulse in Karl's neck. He looked at the clock. "Patient pronounced, 14:53," he said.

Poppi repeated the announcement and, as the team turned away, Poppi and Lord noticed me and Roberta on the floor.

Lord helped me to my feet while Poppi checked Roberta who had begun to moan.

A gasp from the doorway revealed Wilma leaning heavily over her cane and her eyes darting from the bed to Roberta and, finally, coming to rest on me. I took her arm and led her to the chair as Poppi helped Roberta to her feet.

"I have bad news," I said to Wilma whose eyes had begun to cloud.

"Do you understand what I said?" I asked again.

Wilma looked around as if she didn't know where she was as Roberta shook off Poppi, gave her mother a glance, and ran out the door.

"Stop her!" I shouted at Poppi and Lord. "Stop her, she tried to kill him!"

I struggled to free myself from Wilma who clawed at my lab coat whether she realized what was happening or not.

Poppi ran out and Lord started for the door, clicking a number on his cell phone.

I coaxed Wilma out of her son's room and sat her at the desk next to Ruby while I called Agatha, only telling her that she needed to come to St. T's immediately. She didn't ask any questions, just told me she'd be there within fifteen minutes.

Ruby told me Lord had called security and gone out while I'd been on the phone with Agatha. "You look like you been battling a ghost," she said.

"I have," I told her, plunking down into the chair Ruby wheeled around from behind the desk before she answered the phone.

"They got her," Ruby said a few moments later. "The Magnason woman. She was just out the door. Wanna know who caught her? Poppi did. I told you that girl had balls. Slammed her down on the pavement, smashed her face in, they said."

Chapter 40

Wednesday, November 24, 1925 Hours

I BATTLED THROUGH the crowd to my seat in the Savvis Center downtown. That night was the annual night-before-Thanksgiving Guns 'N Hoses boxing match, when local cops fight their counterparts from the fire departments in the metropolitan St. Louis area. Proceeds go to Backstoppers, the organization that provides financial assistance to families who have lost a police officer or firefighter in the line of duty.

I scrambled over three guys making side bets on the matches to my seat next to BJ just as the announcer stepped to the center of the ring. BJ gave me a "where have you been" look but I shook my head as the crowd quieted for an announcement that the ten-bell count, commemorating our city's fallen police and firefighters, was about to commence. At the sound of the first mournful bell, more than twenty thousand people fell silent.

After the bells ended two fighters entered the ring as their names were announced. Sitting in the section of police supporters, BJ and I rose to cheer the boxer wearing blue trunks and sat down when the firefighter in red was introduced. Both boxers sported head gear in flag-designed red, white, and blue.

"The cops will win, we've got the best trainers, our own gym," BJ bragged as the boxers touched gloves, and a bell signaled the beginning of round one.

"Your guy did it," BJ said. "Your Karl Magnason is the one who bashed in his wife's head," BJ said. "We found the gloves, his wife's blood still on them. They were in his car where it had been towed. Blood all over the car was Magnason's. Also on his leather jacket so McNamara assumed—wrongly—that the blood on the gloves was Karl's, but he didn't stop to think why they were on the front seat instead of on his hands, which they would have been if he'd been wearing them when he crashed. Of course McNamara didn't connect it with the attack on Marian because Harding was on that case. And then McNamara retired."

"So it's a good thing I kept after this, wasn't it?"

"Aw, we would have gotten around to it eventually."

The referee separated the boxers locked in a clutch and began a standing hand count of the boxer who had stumbled away.

"If he'd lived, he'd have been charged with murder then," I said, watching the referee give thumbs up to continuing the fight. "What about his sister, Roberta?"

"She admitted she'd unplugged his ventilator."

"But why? Val had already identified him. What would Roberta have to gain? Her mother would still have to return the 9/11 money."

"Not if John Doe wasn't ever proved to be Karl Magnason."

"So Roberta thought that if her brother died before anyone knew for sure who is was, her mother could keep the money," I said. "So she knew all along Karl was her brother."

"Apparently. But she didn't know the cops were in the process of finding Karl's dental records. So even if he died, they would've been able to discover whether he was Magnason or not."

"She and her brother were alike that way—both wanted money that wasn't theirs. The same money, as it turns out that the mother will have to give back now since he wasn't killed on 9/11."

"Keep your head up," BJ shouted to the cop-turned-boxer. "What you doing, looking for your car keys?"

Laughter broke out around us and a man behind punched BJ good naturedly on the shoulder.

"Roberta didn't kill him," I told BJ when the laughter had died down. "Dr. Lord said he wouldn't have survived much longer."

"We'll see what the medical examiner has to say. Maybe attempted murder, though."

The bell rang, indicating the end of round one.

"Here come the round girls," said a man in our row. "The best part of the show."

Two young women in skimpy black dresses entered the ring and paraded around it, holding up signs labeled "Round Two."

The bell rang and the next round began. A punch to the face knocked the fireman-cum-boxer to the canvas. The referee called the match.

"He just slipped!" screamed a woman in a fiery-red shirt. "What, are you blind?" she added to scattered applause.

The cop winner strutted to the sideline where an official raised the man's arm in triumph, an oversized championship belt grasped in the winner's hand.

"Had she lived, Marian Oblansky would have had to return the 9/11 money also. She didn't have a will, her sister told me, so anything she had would have gone to her husband. But since she'd still been married to Karl when she'd married Steve, I guess that second marriage wasn't legal. That's funny. They lived in Illinois, but I couldn't find any record of Marian Magnason requesting a marriage license."

"You went there?"

"The courthouse in St. Clair County, yeah."

"When are you going to learn to stay out of things that aren't your business? To show you how little you know, they lived in Collinsville, the part that's in Madison County, north of St. Clair County. They probably got their license there. But what I can't understand was why the families didn't run into each other at St. T's. They must have known each other."

"I wondered that, too, until I realized that Karl was in room one, which is at the opposite end of ICU from room ten where Marian was, and the nurses' station obscured the view of one from the other. Plus, the Magnason family wasn't there all that often."

"Why were you so sure Oblansky had nothing to do with the attack on his wife?"

"It was just that, that...he reminded me of Rick."

"He looked like him?"

"From the back. Sort of."

The crowd jumped to their feet, booing. The cop boxer had taken a punch to the groin and was doubled over against the ropes. The referee stopped the fight, the cop winning by default.

"How did Karl find Marian?" I asked as we waited for the next bout to start. "McNamara couldn't, neither could I."

"Her school. She'd been at the same school in Belleville for fifteen years."

"He probably made some of the phone calls she'd received. Steve said she'd been worried about something lately. He was coming back for the money, the girlfriend said, so he must have been trying to get some from his wife. Agatha said he always had one scam or another going."

"Yeah, he was a 'person of interest' in a fraud case the cops had been investigating before 9/11. Can you imagine how shocked she must have been when she thought he'd been dead for several years?"

I could.

As the next bout began BJ asked me again if she could fix me up with her partner. "He's a super nice guy. Except to the bad guys, of course."

"I'm sure he is."

"You've had years. It's time to put the past behind you."

Two women boxers entered the ring, touched gloves, and went at it, throwing punches back and forth.

"Hey, Denny, that your wife out there?" asked a man nearby.

"Nah, that'd be her, the other gal'd be on the mat by now," he shot back to guffaws around him.

After the women left the ring, the female firefighter winning in a decision, BJ poked me in the arm. "Watch this, next up is my partner."

"You wanna put your money on that?" asked a man seated next to me who leaned across to challenge BJ.

She gave me a glance. "Nah, not this time."

"That any way to treat a partner? You gotta support him better than that."

With another look my way, she agreed. They shook hands in front of me as the bell rang to start the round.

"All right, Danny, hit him." BJ jumped to her feet. "You can do it!" she screamed.

Clad in opposing shiny blue and red trunks and perspiration shining on their muscular torsos, the men looked evenly matched, both medium height and weight, which BJ had explained was standard procedure. They bounced around, taking measure of each other, throwing an occasional punch, a few connecting. Then, in a flurry of punches, Danny pushed the fireman to the ropes and the referee intervened. They backed up to neutral corners and, at the signal, came out punching again.

"Maybe we could double-date for St. T's gala. How about it?"

"He's cute, I'll give you that."

"See that?" BJ asked to no one in particular. "A great left, right combination!" she said as her partner knocked his opponent backward. The man staggered and the referee stopped the fight for a standing eight count.

As we waited for the count to end, BJ said, "If I was still single—"

"But you're not."

"You, on the other hand..."

"I'm not sure, BJ."

"You know that Rick's dead, don't you?"

Danny pummeled his opponent some more.

"I do now," I said, holding myself steady. At her questioning look, I said, "I had a letter today from that nurse I met in DC."

The men returned to circling around each other, throwing the occasional punch.

"She included a photo of Rick's name on the wall, and a rubbing of it."

BJ wrapped an arm around my shoulder and hugged me.

"So I decided to go back to the hospital after that, and I found Rick's name online on the list for the Wall. 'Killed in action,' it said."

"Oh, honey, I'm so sorry. But it's not a surprise, is it?"

"When I went to Washington, I expected to find his name. It was just when I didn't I started imagining all sorts of things, like maybe he'd been hiding all these years. Maybe had a new family in Vietnam."

"But he's not alive, is he? Even without his body you know that, don't you?"

"He's assumed dead."

"And you feel like you're betraying Rick if you go out with someone else?"

The bout ended in a decision, BJ's partner, Danny, the winner. The man beside me handed over the five dollars he'd lost in the bet with BJ.

"I don't mind losing," he said, "I'm a cop, too. I just wanted some action."

"I learned something else at the hospital," I told BJ as we walked out. "St T's has been sold to a for-profit chain."

"What's wrong with that?"

"They answer to stockholders, not to the community, not to a local board. All they'll care about is making money."

Outside, big, wet flakes of snow had begun to fall, glimmering under the overhead street lights and shining through the headlamps of cars.

"One good thing, though."

"Yeah?" BJ asked, keeping her cop eyes scanning the crowd for anything untoward.

"I've been relieved of the step-down unit. They put Rosemary back in charge over there."

A woman bundled up with a heavy scarf wound around her head paid up on a side bet. "Even the losers win tonight," she said, referring to the families that would benefit from the proceeds.

"You didn't buy any lottery tickets today, did you?" BJ asked me.

A snowflake landed on my cheek and I left it there. "Powerball's up to $200 million but, no, I didn't buy even one."

"Then you can pay for an extra ticket to the gala for your date with that hundred you collected from your winnings."

"I don't have it any more."

"What? Not on some other bet?"

"I gave it to the shelter for the homeless. For their Thanksgiving meal. You satisfied?"

"Yeah." She left me at my car. "I was right. You are too good."

Inspired by the nurses who cared for her dying husband, Eleanor Sullivan began college to study nursing after his death. Although she had five young children (the oldest was 12, the youngest 6 weeks) and little money, it never occurred to her that going to college might be impossible. Overcoming the odds, Eleanor graduated at the top of her class and was elected class president. Thus began her amazing career, first in nursing and now as a mystery author.

After earning a doctorate from St. Louis University she went on to become a leader in the nursing profession. Dean of the University of Kansas School of Nursing, president of an international nursing organization, editor of the Journal of Professional Nursing, and author of award-winning books in nursing are just some of her remarkable accomplishments. She has testified before U. S. Senate committees, served on a National Institutes of Health council, presented papers in the U. S., Finland, the Netherlands, Germany, Australia, been quoted in the Chicago Tribune, Kansas City Star, St. Louis Post-Dispatch, Rolling Stone, and named "Who's Who in Health Care" by the Kansas City Business Journal.

To her career as a mystery author, Eleanor brings the same commitment and dedication to learning her craft that helped her overcome a devastating personal tragedy to become successful in nursing. Her mystery series, featuring nurse-sleuth Monika Everhardt, captures the reality of nursing in a fast-paced hospital environment. The series debuted in 2002 with TWICE DEAD, continued with DEADLY DIVERSION (2004) and ASSUMED DEAD (2006). Eleanor currently serves on the national Board of Directors for Sisters in Crime.

In addition to her literary career, Eleanor is a sought-after speaker about issues in the nursing profession today, including both problems and prospects. In gratitude for the opportunities she has had in nursing, Eleanor contributes a portion of her book sales for nursing scholarships.

Her five children grown, Eleanor, an Indianapolis native, lives in St. Louis with her cat, Theodore Baer (aka Teddy Bear) where she is writing the next mystery in the Monika Everhardt series, PLAY DEAD.

Visit Eleanor at www.EleanorSullivan.com

Printed in the United States
60039LVS00003B/73-90